World on Fire

World on Fire

Geonn Cannon

P.D. Publishing, Inc.
Clayton, North Carolina

ISBN-13: 978-1-933720-64-7
ISBN-10: 1-933720-64-6

9 8 7 6 5 4 3 2 1

Cover art by Stephanie Solomon-Lopez
Edited by: Day Petersen / Verda Foster

Published by:

P.D. Publishing, Inc.
P.O. Box 70
Clayton, NC 27528

http://www.pdpublishing.com

Alexandra Crawford's first thought was that this was, at long last, the boogeyman from her closet finally come to get her. Great waves of smoke rose behind him, and he wasn't shaped like any other man she'd ever seen.

Usually, whenever she woke up during the night, she would soothe herself by looking up at the glow-in-the-dark stars and planets her daddy had stuck to the ceiling over her bed. Now the pale green constellations all seemed very distant, fuzzy, like the real stars that she could see outside. Sometimes clouds got in the way and the stars looked like they were about to burn out; that's what her personal solar system looked like now. But how could clouds have gotten into her room? Did the boogeyman bring them?

Alex blinked her eyes, which were watering, and started to sit up. The man put a thick, gloved hand on her shoulder and held her down, but somehow it wasn't scary. She stayed where she was and he said, "Hold tight, honey, we'll get you out of here. But we have to stay low, okay?"

She nodded, eyes locked on the big black number 26 that was on the front of his helmet. His voice was nice and his hand wasn't hurting her, even though it was holding her against the mattress. With his helmet and the heavy coat he was wearing, he looked like a miner. But why would a miner be in her bedroom? And why was he wearing a coat when it was so hot? It was too warm for her to stay under her princess-adorned quilt. He pulled the quilt down and drew her to the side of the bed, then set her gently on the floor. "You okay?" he said.

She nodded as she watched him fumble with something by his side. Alex was scared again, but only for a moment. He put the thing over her mouth and nose and told her to hold it there. She did as she was told, never taking her eyes from where his face was supposed to be.

"We're going to get out of here as quick as a flash, okay? But we're going to have to crawl first, because there's a lot of really hot air over our heads."

"Will it make us cough?" she managed in her small, scared voice.

"Yeah," he said. "I don't know about you, but I hate to cough. So we'll just stay low, okay?"

She nodded again and he bundled her to his chest, holding her with one arm and making a tent over her body with his own. He crawled on his knees and his one free hand, moving through the small bedroom with a speed that almost made Alex feel like she was on some kind of weird amusement park ride. She wrapped her arms around the monster-man's neck and held on as tight as she could. The thing he'd fastened on her face was slipping and she tried to rearrange it.

"No, honey, you have to keep that on," he said as he covered her hand with his thick glove. "I know it's uncomfortable, but it's better than what's out here."

As he crawled out of her room, she could see the living room and kitchen of their little apartment. That was where Daddy sat by the window and smoked his cigars, watching traffic go by. That over there was where Mommy did her crossword puzzles and looked in the dictionary because that was learning, not cheating. Something smelled bad, like when Mommy "flubbed one" in the kitchen and they ordered pizza for dinner.

Now they were in the hallway and she could see Jessica Harvell's apartment door across the stairway. It had been broken. Maybe by the monster-man. Maybe they were taking all the little girls. She felt scared, remembering the scary stories her daddy sometimes told her. She didn't want to be holding on to the monster-man anymore, she didn't want to be in this gross hallway; she wanted to be in her bed looking up at the stars like—

"You like stars?" the monster-man asked.

Alex jumped. Afraid that he could read her mind, she shuddered.

"I saw the posters in your bedroom when I was coming to get you. You like stars?"

"D-Daddy put up a solar system in my bedroom."

"Did he? I missed that. Will you show me when we get your home all fixed up?"

Fixed up? What did that mean? She nodded even though she wasn't sure and then pushed her face against his neck despite how scared she was. The thing on her mouth and nose pressed into her skin and she wanted to yank it off but was scared of what the monster-man might do if she did. Now that they were on the stairs, he wasn't crawling anymore.

Over his shoulder, it looked like the upstairs of their apartment was disappearing in fog.

Like Alice, she thought. *She followed someone away from home, too, only I don't think the white rabbit was quite as scary as the monster-man.*

"My sister bought me a telescope one year for Christmas. Just sits in the corner of my living room collecting dust."

"Daddy gave me a telescope."

"Really? What kind is it?"

She rattled off the details her daddy taught her. She didn't know what they meant, but he'd seemed so proud when he presented it to her. She knew the gift had probably cost more than they could afford, so she had jumped up and down and kissed him on the cheek and said he was the best daddy in the whole world. And he was, because he didn't get another new fishing pole for almost two whole years after that. Mommy told her that. Alex still wasn't sure what it meant, but the way Mommy said it...

They were outside and it was so cold now. She clung to the monster-man while he carried her across the parking lot, mostly because he was still warm. There were so many cars, so much noise, and flashing lights all around, she was starting to get scared again when she heard her daddy's voice from across the parking lot.

"Alex? Alex!"

Twisting in the man's arms, she looked frantically for her daddy. He was in his pajamas, naked-chested, and running barefoot toward her. The monster-man released her and her daddy wrapped his arms around her at the same instant. She hugged him, smelling his smell instead of the stinky smoke smell of the monster-man.

"They wouldn't let me go back in," her daddy was saying over and over again.

Her mommy was stroking her hair, crying really loud, and Alex wondered if the monster-man had broken something in the apartment. The street was so loud and so bright. Why was everything so bright when it was the middle of the night? Why was everyone being so loud? Didn't they know people were trying to sleep?

Holding her tight, her daddy sat on the back of a truck that was red on the outside and very, very white on the inside. He placed her on his knee and she leaned against him because he didn't seem to want to let her go. That was okay, though. Daddy was much better than the monster-man, even if he'd had a nice voice. She spotted the monster-man a few feet away, recognizing him because of his gloves — the little finger was torn and ragged. She remembered seeing that finger in her bedroom.

As she watched, the man took off his helmet and put it down on the back of the big red truck with a ladder on top. He yanked off something that was on his head — it looked like a stretchy sock — and a wave of black hair appeared. Someone walked past him and he turned, smiling at the other man's comment. Alex frowned, leaning to one side to look at the man's face.

"What is it, hon?" her daddy said quietly, rubbing between her shoulders. "What are you looking at?"

"That man."

"What about him?" her mommy asked.

"He's..." Alex screwed her face up and tilted her head, trying to find the right word. "He's just...an ordinary man."

"Yeah, honey." Her father smiled, cradling her head to his chest. "Sure he is."

Chapter One
Ordinary Woman

It had taken the better part of a year, but Alex had finally mapped out the perfect jogging route. She'd tried using the track at the nearby high school, but the simple oval track was too monotonous for her tastes. She tried to find an acceptable route through her neighborhood, but too many single — and even not so single — men had taken an interest in her for that to last. Finally, she discovered a footpath through Woodbine Park that suited her needs perfectly: nice location with plenty of gorgeous scenery, quiet but not abandoned, the perfect length.

The path wound through the park, following a man-made canal shored up with bricks for a few hundred yards until the two parted ways. They eventually crossed each other again at a small footbridge. Half the trail was in a sparsely wooded area, providing shade when the sun was too strong, and a windbreak when it was too cold. The first and last portion of the path was flanked on either side by large, bench-shaped blocks of concrete where very serious senior citizens pondered their next chess move. A few of the regular players sometimes waved at Alex and she always responded with a cheerful greeting of her own.

The main draw of the path, however, was not the scenery or the company. As Alex neared the front gate of the park, her pace began to slow almost entirely on its own. She stepped onto the sidewalk and turned to the right, ducking across the street and into the small café that she'd happened upon while scouting running locations. She checked her watch as she stepped through the front door and made a mental note about her time. She hadn't beaten her personal best, but she wasn't slacking off, either.

Most of the café's patrons were businessmen and women on their way to work, the men in power suits and the women in pantsuits and high heels. Alex had long ago stopped being embarrassed about being among them in her SFD sweatshirt and sweatpants, but she was still self-conscious about her smell after a jog. She moved to one side of the counter to check her pulse so she wouldn't offend the white-collars.

By the time she'd counted off a minute, the first customer was gone and the proprietor was smiling at her from behind the cash register. He was tall and just heavy enough that he couldn't be called gangly, with a wave of black hair falling over his right eye.

"Peter," she said, pulling the iPod plugs from her ears. He extended a tall, cardboard cup of cappuccino over the counter and she took it greedily. "Ah, Saint Peter," she amended.

"Light of my life," Peter said. "Give me two reasons why we don't run off and get married somewhere. I'm thinking Vegas or Atlantic City."

"Two reasons." Alex paused to take that nearly religious first sip of her coffee as she pondered the question. She leaned against the counter and ticked off the reasons on her fingers. "Okay, how about the fact that your father would kill you if you abandoned his café?" Peter rolled his eyes and shrugged.

When his father, Jacob, decided to retire and move to South Carolina, Peter wanted to take it over, but Jacob was reluctant. He was torn between selling his café and keeping it in the family. He only handed over the reins after he'd tasted Peter's cappuccinos and personally tested half of Michael's menu. Jacob had made the right choice, in Alex's opinion.

"My father would un-retire. Fishing and sitting on the porch doing nothing? He's just waiting for me to call him up so he can take the place back. Next excuse?"

"Are we ignoring the gay thing?" she asked.

"Yes, the gay thing doesn't count as a reason."

She pretended to think a moment before she rapped the counter with one knuckle. "I've got it. Michael!"

Peter's eyes grew wide and he made a "cut-it-out" gesture, slashing a finger across his throat. The kitchen door swung open and a muscular man in a blue t-shirt peered out. Peter looked nervously at him and waved nonchalantly. "Hey, Mike. Alex here was just gonna tell you how she wanted to start paying for her coffees."

Alex smirked. "Sorry, Mike. Never mind."

Michael rolled his eyes and made a chatter-box motion with his fingers before he disappeared again. Peter glared at her. "Never nice to play like that, young lady."

"You started it." She stepped to the side to allow his next customer to step up to the counter. The woman ordered and Peter moved to the cappuccino machine.

"You got a shift today?" he asked, looking at Alex over the counter display.

She nodded as she sipped her coffee. "Yeah. Noon to noon."

Peter gave her a stricken look. "So I won't be seeing your gorgeous face tomorrow morning? How will I cope?"

"I'm sure you'll survive. If not, I'll make sure Michael throws you a very melodramatic funeral. Besides, I may not be running much longer if the temperature keeps dropping." It was still warm for mid-September, but before long, spending an extended amount of time outside would qualify as cruel and unusual punishment. "And hey, you never know, I may have a chance to stop in tomorrow despite the shift. They're jerking me around again, so I may be out and about."

"Another inspection?"

"Mm hmm." Alex took another drink.

"You work for swine. Big, fat, rutting pigs is all they are," Peter scoffed as he handed the next customer her drink. "Thank you, come again," he said. "So these inspections, anything special?"

She ignored the insult about her bosses; it was nothing worse than what she'd thought herself at times. "Nah, they're not too bad. Just some regular, lame old fire inspections. Go look at a new building; make sure it conforms to the fire code, counting sprinklers, checking all of the fire exits, that sort of thing."

"Pays your dues, I guess," he said.

"I guess. You'd think my dues would be paid off by now."

"The interest on dues, sweetheart," he exhaled, "it's the worst in the business."

Alex laughed and raised her cup to him. "Thanks for the lifeblood," she said as she headed for the door. "Apologize to Michael for the teasing."

Peter laughed, waving her off. "Oh, he knows."

She winked at him as she backed out of the café and turned down the street. She found her Jeep right where she'd parked it — a minor miracle in this part of town — and climbed inside, seeing that she had a whole hour to make the fifteen minute trip to the firehouse.

Turning the key, she revved the engine and decided to try to beat a different personal best.

The tires of her Jeep squealed in protest as it lurched into her regular space, next to Murray's SUV and a few spaces down from the chief's truck. As she climbed out, she saw that she'd managed to make the trip in just under seven minutes. She smiled, made a mental note that she'd lowered her personal best by one full minute, and headed for the main doors.

The station house was a squat, two-story brick building with a small hill between it and the main road. This gave the impression that the second story was the ground floor and that the trucks emerged from some secret exit like the Batmobile.

A six-foot wall extended from the edge of the building and curled around the parking lot like a bony finger, separating it from the driveway. As she rounded the wall, she spotted Chief Leary sitting in a white lawn chair just outside the apparatus bay. He was with Wayne Murray and Alfred Jones, the probie, and the chief was the only one seated. The other two firefighters flanked him like guards in an Arthurian legend.

"You always drive like that?" Leary asked, not taking his eyes off the road that went past the firehouse.

"Only when I'm trying to beat a record, Chief."

He smirked and nodded without either chastising or praising her for her reckless behavior. She nodded to Murray and Jones, both of whom tendered a wave as she headed inside. "You guys been here long?" she asked. They were on-shift with her and weren't acting as if they had just arrived.

Murray smirked at her. "You may have beaten your personal best, Crawford—"

"But the boys still hold the title," Jones finished.

Alex laughed, still amazed at how quickly Probie had started finishing Murray's sentences. Pretty soon, the two would become inseparable. Thoughts of possible nicknames for the two were already the impetus of several contests throughout the house. The most popular at the moment seemed to be Frick and Frack, while Alex was a proponent of the Muppets characters Statler and Waldorf.

The fact that Jones was a lanky white guy and Murray was a muscular black man also provided a bevy of suggested nicknames, most of them racial in nature. The chief was lobbying hard for Riggs and Murtaugh, the characters from the *Lethal Weapon* movies. Nothing had been decided upon yet, and Murray was adamant they wait to see that Jones didn't go running home to Mama before they started assigning nicknames, so they were still just Murray and The Probie.

The storage cubbies were located along the western wall of the apparatus bay in a foxhole-like depression that was covered by a wooden awning. Each firefighter got a tall, narrow cubby of their own; a curtain on a rod served as a door. Lockers were unnecessary. A firefighter who didn't trust their belongings in their own house didn't belong in the house to begin with. Alex skipped down the three steps, passing Eric Wizell on her way to her nook. She tossed her bag into the cubby hole and turned back to the lieutenant. He was hunched over on the bench, reaching down to lace up a pair of boots.

"Planning on a hike?" she asked as she pushed back the curtain on her cubby. She peeled off her exercise shirt without hesitation; Wizell had seen her in her underwear too many times for her to worry about being seen in a sports bra. She yanked a t-shirt over her head and squirmed into a pair of trousers as Wizell tightened the laces on his boots.

"Like 'em?" He sat up, angling his foot this way and that so she could see the bright new leather. His face was shaped like a heart, wide at the top and pointed at the chin. He kept his thinning hair cut short, forming an M on top of his head. The goatee framed his sly grin perfectly, earning him the nickname Weasel. He stood and worked his right foot back and forth. "Just got 'em. Thought I'd test 'em out tonight, see how they stand up to a little action."

"Here's hoping." Alex pulled the curtain shut. "Has the chief said anything about the inspections?"

"Yup. He told me who it was that called."

Alex closed her eyes. "Oh, no. Please, tell me it's not..."

"Sorry, Alex. It was the revered Mister Lancaster," Wizell said in a tone that most people reserved for Hitler and their mothers-in-law.

Alex shuddered. "How many damn buildings can one man design?"

"Hey, the man is an entrepreneur. Took his daddy's company and sank his teeth in. Daddy was responsible for half of the town; I think Junior wants to put his mark on the other half." He picked up his thermos and hoisted it to her in salute. "And guess who he requested do the inspection?"

"Murray? Please, tell me he requested Murray."

Wizell held his hands out in a "what-can-I-say" gesture and shrugged. "Sorry, kid."

Alex sighed and shook her head as Wizell beat a hasty retreat. Having to do inspections was bad enough. Doing inspections for Martin Lancaster were as close to torture as she'd ever experienced. She'd met him when she was assigned to inspect one of his buildings. It was sheer luck of the draw but, ever since that first meet, the designer had apparently harbored a crush on her.

She had tried being subtle, she'd tried being harsh. She was thinking it was time to just slap the guy across the face and tell him flat out that she wasn't interested. It was bothersome enough pulling inspection duty without worrying about some fawning admirer. If she had her way, she'd just pawn the inspections off on

Probie and be done with it. But, as Peter said, it paid her dues. As a female firefighter, she had a lot of dues to pay. She'd just have to grin and bear whatever they threw her way.

She left her grumblings behind in the cubby area and headed to the chief's office to sign in. She was halfway across the apparatus bay when the alarm bell clanged to life.

She moved without thinking, already standing over her turnout gear before she consciously realized she was going to work. Wizell fell in right next to her. He yanked his turnout pants up in one smooth motion and climbed into the truck without waiting to pull his jacket or helmet on. Chief Leary's position was that if you could do it while standing around, you could do it in the truck. Alex followed Wizell into the cab and slipped her arms through the loops of her pack just as Murray climbed into the truck.

Alex looked over her shoulder at the driver, an Irish former boxer named Chuck Flannigan. He smiled over his shoulder, flashing a gold tooth and said, "You fellas ready to fly?"

Alex, not knowing whether he'd forgotten she was there or just lumping her in with the boys, said, "What're you waiting for, a green light?"

"Not on your life, Al," Flannigan said.

Jones just barely made it into the cab before Flannigan launched the truck forward. Alex smiled as she braced herself against the wall of the cab with one hand. Murray whooped and banged the roof with his fist. "Fly, Flanny, fly!"

Flannigan looked in the mirrors for signs of the ladder and laughed when he finally spotted it. "Come on, Grandma, give that thing some gas."

William Sawyer, the driver of the ladder, came back with, "Hey, I'm-a leave you in the dust when some LEO pulls you over for speeding."

"Where's the fire, m' man? Just tell me where to aim this thing," Flannigan said and hung up, drumming his hands on the wheel.

Alex was seated with her back to the driver, unable to see into the cab without turning around. She was glad for that; this way, she couldn't possibly see the speedometer and she would never know just how fast they were going. She looked over her shoulder and asked Wizell, "Where's the fire?"

"344 Texala Road," the lieutenant said, referring to the map he had folded in his lap. "Warehouse district. Possibility of squatters, but otherwise clear of tenants."

Alex nodded and tightened her air pack. They would still have to go in and check, a cursory look if nothing else. Next to her, Jones had his eyes closed, and he bobbed from side to side with the sway of the truck. The last time they'd gone out, she'd punched him playfully and told him to wake up before he missed the fire, only to find out he'd been praying. In retrospect, she realized that the cross drawn in black Magic Marker on the back of his yellow helmet should have clued her in. She turned away and let him finish his prayer in peace.

"Damn it, Flannigan," Wizell said. "Do you even see these damn people on the road in front of you?"

"We saves they lives when they in a fire," Murray said, "but if they in front of us, they just collateral damage, right, Flanny?"

Alex shook her head, marveling at how Murray's language suffered when he became excited. The eloquent man who had, in a calmer moment, recited Puck's monologue from the end of *A Midsummer Night's Dream* was reduced to a whooping, hollering escapee from a mental institution. Alex leaned forward and looked through the window at the pedestrians standing on the sidewalks with dazed looks on their faces. Probably counting their blessings that they'd just avoided being crushed by several tons of screaming fire truck.

"Has he ever been in an accident?" Jones said, eyes still tightly closed, although Alex assumed he had finished praying. He had been in the station long enough to become friends with Murray, but until a day or two ago he'd been assigned to the ladder. He'd spent four months there, would spend another four months on the engine, and then make a decision as to where he wanted to be permanently assigned. Given Flannigan's driving, Alex figured it was a safe bet which he would choose.

"Ol' Flanny has been in lots of accidents," Murray said, "but none that were his fault."

Jones looked skeptically at Alex, who nodded and confirmed, "It's true. Every accident he's been in, he was the victim."

"Unbelievable," Jones muttered as he closed his eyes again.

His lips started to move and she knew he'd found something else to pray about. Alex figured this new prayer was something along the lines of, *By the way, God, about the guy driving this truck...* She chuckled and turned back to the window.

Wizell was on the radio, informing nearby companies that they were responding. Jones exhaled sharply and Alex reached over to pat him on the back. She was worried that most of his probationary period would be preoccupied with getting accustomed to the way Flannigan drove.

The warehouse district flanked the west side of Shepherd, Washington like a barnacle, clinging to the more successful suburbs of the town. Evergreens loomed on three sides of the district, giving the entire area the feeling of a severely underdeveloped neighborhood. It was only when you looked closer that you saw the cracks. Dozens of the sprawling brick and concrete buildings were abandoned. Their parking lots were locked behind chain-link fences, littered with garbage, and festooned with sprigs of sickly yellow grass rising from cracked slabs of pavement.

Fortunately, the fence around the building of interest to them was standing wide open. Alex had once seen Flannigan ram through a chained gate with the truck and, while it had been amusing, she didn't want to witness another subsequent reaming by Chief Leary.

She watched through the window as the burning building came closer. Flannigan slowed to a stop as they rolled across the parking lot, the tires of their truck rocking over the broken and uneven pavement. He drove past the front face in order to get a look at the third side of their target. It was a two-story warehouse, surrounded on all sides by a parking lot, overgrown with weeds. Half the windows on the upper level were shattered, although it was unlikely they had been broken by any explosion. The building had been a derelict for a long, long time.

Wizell jumped from the truck and followed Alex and Jones toward the gear box as the ladder pulled into the lot. "Get up the ladder, Jones, Murray; I want a hole in that roof." Lieutenant Thomas Franklin, the other truck's officer, hurried over as the ladder began rising. "I'm the Incident Commander until Leary gets here," Wizell added for Franklin's benefit.

Franklin nodded as he looked up at the building. "Squatters?" he asked.

"Don't know. I'm sending Murray and The Probie up to the roof to vent."

"We're not doing a steam attack?" Franklin asked.

"You worried about water damage in this heap?" Wizell scoffed. He motioned to Alex. "Crawford, you're coming in with me to search."

"Yes, sir," Alex said. She took off her helmet and fitted an SCBA mask over her face in one quick motion. She made sure the strap was tight before she replaced her helmet.

Wizell did the same, turning as the chief's bright red Suburban pulled into the lot. When Wizell spoke, his voice was heavily filtered through the SCBA facepiece. "Lieu, fill the chief in on the plan. We'll keep in contact."

Franklin nodded and went to rendezvous with the chief while Alex followed Wizell toward the front door of the warehouse. They walked along the side of the building, looking into each window they passed to gauge the extent of the fire.

"Some bastard set this," Wizell muttered. "Fire don't spread that way naturally." He stopped a few feet shy of the door and held up a hand to let Alex know they weren't going in that entrance. He leaned against a broken window and peered inside.

Alex looked past him and saw that the fire had spread across the concrete floor, without a doubt following the trail of some accelerant. Wizell was right; no way this fire started accidentally. The blaze reached right up to the front door; they would walk into an inferno if they went that route.

"The front door's a no-go," Wizell said. "We're going in here after all."

Alex thumbed her radio as Wizell threw a leg over the sill. "Crawford to Chief Leary: Wizell and I are entering the building through a broken window on the main level."

"I see you, Crawford," Leary's said. "Jones has the roof ventilated and we're going to be setting up the fans on the ground for you."

"Much obliged, Chief," Wizell said.

Wizell went in first. He threw his leg over the windowsill, putting his hands against the rotting frame to keep his balance. The interior of the building was darkened by smoke, forcing them to try and see by the scant light from their flashlights and the flickering tongues of flame at the far end. He slipped into the building and turned to help Alex through. When she hit the floor, she took a quick scan of the room to get her bearings.

The main floor of the warehouse was basically one huge room; a block of offices on the opposite side of the building were the only interior walls she could see. An exposed steel staircase hugging another wall led up to the second level.

"We have about a half dozen offices over here," Wizell reported to his radio. He moved to his left and motioned for Alex to take the opposite end. "You go there, I'm this way," he said.

She nodded and headed in the direction he'd indicated. She was thankful the smoke was still thin enough that she could see him through it. She'd been in several fires where it was impossible to see two feet in front of her face. She got to the first office and tried the knob; it was locked. Thinking a squatter might be inside and using the lock to protect what few possessions he had, she banged her palm against the wall and called, "Fire Department! Anyone in there?"

There was no reply. She reached for her belt, groaning when she realized that one loop was unoccupied. The memory was very clear — she had used the tool to open a door at their last fire and took it from her gear to wash the soot off the blade. Apparently she failed to put it back. "Yo, Weasel. I need the hooligan."

Wizell unhooked a long bar from his belt and tossed it across the distance between them. She snatched the halligan, or hooligan to most of the people in the company, beneath its two-pronged head. The tool had two blades on the business end, one curved and sharp, the other straight and sharp like a spike. The bottom of the tool was curved like the claw of a hammer. Throwing such an object was probably not exactly advised, but truth be told, she shouldn't even have asked. Giving up equipment in a fire was a no-no. Now he was unprepared. She was lucky he hadn't just pretended not to hear her.

She was grateful that he hadn't offered to pop the door himself, but she wasn't about to make a big deal about it. She hefted the halligan and said, "Jesus. Next time just launch it at the facemask, Weasel."

"Next time you come into a fire unprepared, I'm leaving your ass behind, Crawfish."

With the mask, his face was an expressionless mirror, but she knew he was grinning at her as she turned the tool over in her hands. She slipped the claw between the door and its frame and shoved the bar with both hands. The door cracked and swung open to reveal nothing but some scattered papers and a few cardboard boxes marked LBD.

"Nothing here," she reported.

"Ditto," Wizell said. He moved to one of the inner offices and pushed the door open. He was greeted by a wave of fire, blowing out like the exhalation of a dragon. Alex took a step back, staring wide-eyed as Wizell dropped. The door he'd opened was now awash with flame, the backdraft reaching out to lick his uniform.

Alex's stupor lasted all of two seconds before she was on top of Wizell. She smothered the flames licking his jacket with her own turnout coat as Wizell screamed and slapped at his uniform. As she slapped his shoulder, the flame spread down her own glove.

Wizell tried to push her off and screamed something through his fogged mask, but she wouldn't leave. When she'd tamped down the flames on his turnouts, she rolled to the side to avoid the flames licking at her back and pressed herself against the concrete floor. The entire bank of offices was awash in flame, a wall of fire that looked impossibly high.

She grabbed the nape of Wizell's collar and began scrambling backwards like a crab, dragging him along with her. Wizell was squirming, still slapping himself and trying to extinguish any fire that might have gotten into the lining of his uniform. Either that or he was panicking, which frightened Alex.

"Wizell's hurt! We're coming out!" she called through her radio. She rolled Wizell and got her arms under him to load him back out through the window first.

As she stood, powerful arms gripped her shoulders and hoisted her the rest of the way out, practically carrying her a few feet before dropping her roughly on the ground. "You all right?" Franklin asked, screaming to be heard through both of their masks.

She motioned behind her. "Weasel's burnt."

"The medics got him. Are you all right?"

"I'm..." She looked down and saw her right glove was completely blackened. Cinders had poured from the cuff and down her sleeve and she was only just now feeling the burn as they skittered across her forearm. She stretched out her arm and shook it wildly as Franklin tugged her glove off.

"Medic!" he shouted over his shoulder. As they ran over, Franklin patted her on the shoulder. "You'll be good, Crawford," he said. "Good work getting Weasel out of there."

"Murray and The Probie?" she asked, ignoring his praise and looking toward the roof.

"Both fine. They cut the hole and got the hell out of there."

She nodded and collapsed on the ground, arms spread out to either side. She took a moment, breathing hard and staring at the bright afternoon sky. When she got her breath back, she rolled onto her side and pushed herself up. She made sure she could trust her knees and then made her way over to the ladder where she had spotted Murray and Jones.

"How badly was Wizell burnt?" she asked.

Murray motioned at the medic truck. "Looked okay to me, but they're making a pretty big fuss about him. We'll never hear the end of it."

Chief Leary, positioned by the medic truck, had taken off his helmet and his short silver hair was standing up in spikes. His black coat flapped around his white uniform shirt as he approached Alex and Murray. "Weasel will be fine," he said, his casual use of the man's nickname indicating that the crisis was over. He nodded at Alex and jerked a thumb over his shoulder. "Crawford. Go to the hospital with him."

"I'm fine," Alex said.

Murray and Jones were looking Alex over. "Did you get hurt?" Jones asked.

"Franklin saw your glove," Leary said. "Probably a few embers down in your suit." He put his hand on Alex's shoulder and gently guided her in the direction of the medic truck. "Just go, get yourself checked out, and keep Weasel from accosting the EMT."

Alex turned reluctantly and headed for the medics. She was halfway there when one of the reporters on the other side of the barricade thrust a microphone toward her. The woman's body was pressed tightly against the sawhorse that was keeping the press away from the action, and her arm was outstretched as if she might actually reach across the thirty yards between them. "Excuse me!" the woman called. "Are you the firefighter who made the rescue?"

Alex motioned over her shoulder. "Not me. You're looking for Lieutenant Snipe. I saw him back that way."

She walked on and climbed into the back of the medic truck. She sat on the runner next to the gurney and scanned Wizell's body. He'd been burnt on the neck and face, his ears a bright red with black flakes on the lobes. It hurt to look at, but Alex kept her eyes on his and managed a smile. She sat and clapped him on his uninjured arm. "How you doing, Weasel?"

He grinned at her. "You see the EMT I got?" He gave a wolf whistle and then quickly added, "I got dibs on her."

Alex held her hands up as if to say "no contest", and Wizell's eyes moved to her hand. "Jesus, Crawford..."

She looked at her hand in the harsh light of the truck. There were a few burns on the heel of her hand, tracing a shaky line down toward her wrist. She dropped the hand back to her lap and tried to hide it under the hem of her coat. "It's nothing, Wizell. Don't worry about it."

He nodded, but kept his slate gray eyes locked on her hand. "The reporters didn't get ya, did they?"

"I told them Lieutenant Snipe made the rescue," she said with a smile.

"Sent 'em on a snipe hunt." Wizell laughed. "Beautiful. Ooh, and speaking of beautiful..."

He thrust his chin toward the back door of the truck. Alex turned and saw a blond paramedic climbing into the back, skirting the edge of the gurney to sit opposite Alex.

"How bad?" the new arrival asked, her eyes assessing Alex's wrist.

"Nothing to worry about. Couple of bandages, I'll be fine."

"We'll let the doctor be the judge of that," the EMT said. "You two fancy a ride to the hospital?"

"I'm fine," Alex said again. "Just slap a little Neosporin on there, maybe a gauze pad or two..."

Wizell muttered, "Leary said something about drills tonight."

Alex immediately shifted gears. "But you're the expert, and if you think we need a trip to the hospital..."

Wizell, despite his burns and obvious discomfort, managed a grin that, to Alex, looked more than a little like a grimace. "I call shotgun."

Upon arrival at the hospital, Wizell was immediately taken to a burn unit, wheeled into the elevator by his newest crush. As the blond EMT pushed him toward the elevator, Wizell winked at Alex, who stayed behind in the emergency room. "Don't be offended, 'Lex. She just wants to get me all to herself."

Alex flipped him off with her uninjured hand and sat on the bed the EMT had pointed her to. She didn't have to wait long. A few minutes after Wizell's grinning mug disappeared behind the elevator doors, a woman behind her said, "Alexandra Crawford?" She turned toward the voice and saw a petite doctor stepping up to the bed, her face buried in a chart. She flipped the top page of the chart down and looked up to meet Alex's eyes.

Alex was stunned. The doctor put Weasel's EMT to shame. Her eyes were so dark brown they were practically black, and her long black hair was pulled back into a ponytail that was in danger of coming loose at any moment. Her skin still appeared slightly tanned, despite the fact that the calendar was inching toward October. Alex blinked and uttered a brief, "Hi."

"Hello." The doctor unleashed a grin that knocked Alex for another loop. "I'm Dr. Tom. You're the one with the," she looked down at the notes, "burnt wrist?"

Alex looked down at her arm and eyed the burns. "Um, lower arm, really."

"Oh," the doctor said. "Must be another burned firefighter named Alex Crawford. I'm sorry for the confusion." She slipped back around the curtain.

Panicked, Alex jumped from the bed to catch up with the doctor, and came up short when she found Dr. Tom standing just on the other side of the curtain. Alex blushed beneath the soot on her face and tried to look casual as the doctor tried valiantly to refrain from laughing in her face.

After a moment, Alex said, "I was just thinking. I mean, I guess you could say this is my wrist."

"Excellent," Dr. Tom said as she preceded Alex back around the curtain. "In that case, I think we may have something to work with."

The digital age was the impatient arsonist's dream. No need to wait until the pictures were developed to see how they turned out. Plus, there were more options on how to develop them. No longer did he have to worry about a nosy photo assistant at the Walgreen's getting suspicious of him. Nor did he have to splurge on a dark room to develop them himself. Just plug the photo card into the computer, fiddle with some settings, and presto! Better than the ones that Mom used to take.

He sat in the dirt at the foot of a recessed stairway with his legs crossed Indian style, thumbing the Next Picture button beside the display screen.

It was still the middle of the afternoon, but he was good at keeping out of sight. He was on the property adjacent to the burnt husk of the warehouse, trying to keep from giggling as he looked at his latest creations.

He'd been surprised when the heroic firefighter removed her helmet and revealed herself to be a woman. And not any woman firefighter, oh no. It was Alexandra Crawford. Oh, little Alex, making the save. It was heartening to see she had what it took to play with the boys. He had feared the department had lowered their standards to get their quota of girls, and he harbored a sinking worry that Alex would be a disappointment when push came to shove.

It was nigh impossible to tell when they were all geared up in their turnouts...gender and race free, like a group of robots programmed to jump into action whenever their smoke detectors went off. Little bugs. Little meaningless things that would be replaced in an instant if one fell.

He felt no remorse for the trap he'd set, wouldn't admit to any remorse if confronted with photos of the injured fireman's wife, two kids, and his Dalmatian dog. Firemen were cockroaches. Kill one, two more crawled out of the woodwork.

They were the perfect sacrifices for his fires.

No one died in this blaze, but that was okay, he supposed. It was his first. Mistakes might have been made.

He would correct them next time.

Tucking his camera into his knapsack, he lifted himself onto his toes and peered over the lip of the underground staircase. Firefighters were still swarming the site, even though the blaze was long extinguished. He understood. They were getting all the junk out, hoping to prevent a re-ignition. They were probably also trying to figure out why their unlucky friend had almost been flame-broiled.

He settled back down and pressed himself into a corner, tucking both hands into his armpits. He couldn't leave until the firefighters left without risking being spotted. That was okay. He'd planned for a long night. He closed his eyes and nearly fell asleep, jerking when he realized he couldn't be found this close to the site of a fire. If he slept, they could sneak up on him.

Slapping his face a few times, blinking his eyes wide, he wrapped his arms around himself and rocked slowly as he waited for the crowd to disperse so he could slip away unseen. Patience was a virtue, but he needed to go.

He had fires to plan.

Chapter Two
Finding a Round Tuit

A blue and white name tag swung precariously from the flap of the doctor's lab jacket. It read "R. Tom, MD". As Dr. Tom treated and bandaged her arm, Alex played a little game with herself trying to determine what the initial stood for. The doctor didn't look like a Roberta. Rhonda didn't seem right, either. They chatted about inane things, the conversation mostly veering toward the heroic Lieutenant Snipe the news channels were all clamoring to interview.

When the bandage was set, Dr. Tom looked at her handiwork and then at Alex. "I saw the fire on the news this evening. These burns, did you receive them while helping Lieutenant Snipe?"

Alex smirked. "Actually, I feel kind of bad breaking this to you, but—"

"Snipe doesn't exist?" Tom raised her eyebrows and her lips curled in a knowing smile.

Alex laughed. "How did you know?"

"I was sent on a snipe hunt once. Medical school. They sent me off in search of a box of round tuits."

Alex frowned. "I don't get it."

"T-U-I-T," she spelled. "A round tuit. As in 'I'll get around to it.'" When she said it like that, Alex laughed out loud. Dr. Tom grinned. "I figured it out after, oh, forty-five minutes. I grabbed a coaster in the cafeteria, wrote 'TUIT' on it and brought it back to the nurses' station. After that, I swore I'd never again fall for a snipe hunt." She glanced conspiratorially over her shoulder and stepped closer to the bed. "Were you the one who saved Wizell?"

"I went in with Lieutenant Wizell. I saw the fire and did what I was supposed to. It was my job."

"Modest much?" the doctor asked.

Alex shrugged. "It's not modesty so much as...I don't want the recognition. There was a guy in the academy who told us that we weren't training to be heroes, we were training to be firefighters. He wanted to make sure we got that through our heads right off. A few years ago, Chief Leary was involved in a rescue. He told a reporter that Lieutenant Snipe had done it. The whole snipe thing kind of steamrolled from there."

"No one's figured out this guy doesn't exist?"

"As far as the media knows, he's just a very secretive guy. His phone number is unlisted; he likes his privacy and his friends respect that. And just to cover our asses, every local firehouse lists a Joe Snipe on the duty roster every couple of months. If anyone asks, we say he's a floater. 'Oh, you know, you just missed him. He moved to Ladder 14' or something similar."

The doctor laughed. "Brilliant strategy. By heaping the glory on the fictional firefighter, you get privacy for yourselves."

Alex rocked slightly on the edge of the bed before sliding to the floor. "You know, I really am fine. I shouldn't keep you. There are probably other patients..."

"Yeah, a few." Tom grinned. "If you're sure you're okay."

"Well, I'm not exactly thrilled to leave," Alex said. "But I really shouldn't monopolize your time."

"Okay, then." The doctor nodded at the elevator. "By the way, if you wanted to go say hi to your friend, I'm sure they wouldn't gripe too much. Just so long as you keep it short."

"Okay, yeah. Thank you."

"No problem, Ms. Crawford."

"Call me Alex," she said, unsure of what prompted her to say it.

"Okay. Alex. In that case, I'm Rachel."

Rachel, Alex thought, watching the other woman walk away. *I have a new favorite name.*

Wizell was in the burn unit, his neck and ears wrapped by thick bandages. He glanced toward the door when Alex walked in, his lips pulling back in a fierce grimace. He jabbed a finger in her direction and sneered. "You! I've been looking for you!"

"What did I do?" Alex asked, shocked.

"My boots! My brand new boots! Ruined!" He slapped the bed. "Ruined, I say!"

Alex laughed. "Okay, I apologize for not dragging you from the fire feet first. I'll know better next time." She approached the bed and rested her uninjured hand on the railing while keeping the other behind her back. "Beyond that, how are you doing?"

"My ears, neck, bah...just skin. But those boots. Man, I searched weeks for those boots." He feigned sobbing. "Those were the perfect boots. And now? Gone. Gone, gone, gone!"

Alex brought her bandaged hand out from behind her back and placed a teddy bear on the bedside table. The bear's tiny plush paws were wrapped around an ice cream shake she'd smuggled into the ward. Wizell's eyes widened and he said, "But boots come and go. Friends, friends are forever." He licked his lips and asked hopefully, "Are you gonna spoon feed your poor, disabled friend?"

"Not a chance," Alex said. "That's non-negotiable."

"I'm injured."

"Which is precisely the reason I asked a certified medical professional to assist you." She stepped to one side and said, "Brandi?"

The EMT from earlier came into the room and smiled warily down at the injured man. "She swears to me you're a good guy."

Wizell beamed.

"Get well soon, Weasel."

"Yeah," Wizell scoffed, eyeing Brandi. "Like I have an incentive to leave this place..."

It was late afternoon by the time Alex managed to get out of the hospital. Chief Leary was upstairs talking to Wizell and had offered to give her a ride back to the station when he finished up. The sun was setting, casting red and orange light over the parking lot. She stood in the shadow of the chief's truck and watched a group of orderlies smoking in a designated area next to the building.

Her turnouts were folded neatly in the back of Leary's truck, her equipment weighing the clothes down so they wouldn't fly away. She was wearing the trousers and t-shirt she'd been wearing when the call came in.

"Hi," said a voice from beside her. "It's Crawford, right?"

She straightened up and turned around before her brain registered the voice. She smiled. "Hello, Dr. Tom. You keep sneaking up on me."

"I'll start wearing a bell around my neck."

"Don't. You're a nice surprise." She kicked herself at how corny that sounded, but the doctor smiled.

"All right, then. And it's Rachel," the doctor reminded her with a shy smile.

"Then I have to be Alex," she said. She felt somehow strange talking to this woman. It was nice, but uncomfortable at the same time.

Rachel nodded. "Okay, Alex. I was on my way out, saw you standing over here by yourself..." She shrugged and looked across the parking lot. Her hair was getting in her eyes and it took every ounce of restraint in Alex's body not to reach out and brush it aside. "I don't know, I saw you over here and I was just wondering if you wanted to maybe grab a drink or, or something. There's a bar not far from here or a restaurant—"

"I'm truly sorry. I'd love to take you up on that, I would, but I'm...I'm still on duty."

"Oh." Rachel turned away, touching her forehead absently. "I should have realized. I-I just, I didn't think that—"

"It's okay," Alex said. "I get off tomorrow at noon. Maybe we could meet for some lunch, maybe?"

"I'm working tomorrow at noon," Rachel said. She scratched her eyebrow. "But I get off at five."

Alex calculated that would give her time to get a nap, shower, and change into something that didn't smell like smoke. "An early dinner? Say, six?"

"Make it seven and you've got a date," Rachel said. Her smile returned and Alex was thrilled to see it. "There's a really good restaurant downtown. The Lumber Bar & Grill? It's not very fancy, but I think it'll do."

"I've been there. It's good," Alex said and smiled. "So, tomorrow. I can't wait."

Rachel hesitated and then nervously added, "So, do you have a cell phone or..."

"Oh. Right, I'll give you that number." Without thinking, she plucked a pen from the breast pocket of Rachel's blouse. Alex blushed slightly when she realized what she'd done, but recovered quickly and took the small notepad the doctor offered. "This is for my cell. You can reach me any time, but if it goes to voice mail..."

"Okay, no problem. And I'll call you if anything comes up to keep me from meeting you."

Unable to think of anything coherent to say, Alex just nodded.

Rachel took her pen back and glanced at the number before she folded the notebook paper and slipped it into the pocket of her slacks. "So, I'll give you a call if anything comes up, but I should be free. I look forward to it."

"Yeah," Alex said, still a bit dumbfounded by what was happening. She nervously scratched below the collar of her t-shirt, unsure of a subtle way to ask what she was thinking. Finally, she simply said, "It's a date, right?"

Rachel laughed. "Yes, Miss Crawford, it's a date." Her eyes widened and she hurriedly added, "If you're free, that is. I didn't mean to—"

"I'm single," Alex assured her. "But I just...I'm not the smoothest person in the world. I just wanted to be sure it was a date, like—"

Rachel stopped Alex with a wave of her hand. She stepped forward and stretched onto her toes, put one hand on Alex's shoulder to balance herself, and pecked Alex on the cheek. When they parted, Alex was blushing and Rachel was smiling. "It's a date," Rachel said.

"Okay."

"I'll see you tomorrow, Lieutenant Snipe."

Rachel turned and walked across the parking lot. She waved hello to Chief Leary as their paths crossed. Leary turned to watch her walk away and then used a keychain remote to unlock his truck. As Alex climbed into the passenger seat, she fervently hoped he hadn't seen the kiss.

When Leary climbed into the cab a few seconds later, he motioned at the retreating doctor with his head. "What'd the doc want?"

"Um...she...talk. She, uh, wanted to talk."

Leary glanced at her and smirked. "Too bad she couldn't find anyone who spoke fluent English."

Alex rolled her eyes and smiled indulgently. "Just drive, Chief."

Leary parked and climbed out, grabbing a bag from the back of the truck before heading toward the garage doors. Alex trailed behind him, figuring there was no time like the present to ask for a favor. "Chief, if you don't mind, could I beg off the cleaning duties? I was kind of hoping to get Lancaster out of the way tonight so tomorrow morning would be all clear."

"Yeah, all right," Leary said. He turned and started walking backwards so he could face her as he continued speaking. "Murray and Jones probably took care of all the cleaning by now anyway."

"Because they're so responsible."

Leary snorted, waving at her before he disappeared around the wall. Alex fished her cell phone out of her pocket as she headed for her Jeep. She dialed Lancaster's number from memory as she slid behind the wheel, leaving the door open as she listened to the phone ring in her ear. Grumbling about the fact that she had this jerk's number memorized, Alex searched for a pen. She found a napkin on the passenger seat and wrote, *Rachel Tom — Dinner, Seven*. She stuck the note into the sun visor as the ringing suddenly stopped.

A clipped voice announced, "Martin Lancaster."

"Mr. Lancaster, this is Alexandra Crawford with the Shepherd Fire Department. I was wondering if now would be a good time for the inspection you contacted us about."

"Oh. Alex!"

She cringed at the familiar use of her first name, but decided not to waste her time correcting him. She knew it would do no good. "Yes, Mr. Lancaster. I meant to stop by earlier, but—"

"Don't be silly. I saw on the news. Is everyone all right?"

"Yes, for the most part." She glanced at her bandaged wrist. She had an SFD windbreaker in the backseat she could use to cover the injury and avoid any expressions of sympathy from Lancaster. "I was thinking I could swing by now if you had the address..."

"Oh, yes, certainly."

She pulled the reminder from the sun visor and wrote the address below Rachel Tom's name.

He was still talking. "I'm a bit tied up right now, you know how meetings can get, but I can meet you there in a half hour, if that's all right."

"No problem."

"Good, good. See you then, Alex."

Fighting the urge to curse, she snapped the cell phone shut. She took a deep breath, started the Jeep, and pulled calmly out of her space.

Martin Lancaster was the CEO of Lancaster Building & Development, an architectural firm that was responsible for designing forty to fifty percent of the buildings in Shepherd. Martin was the grandson of the company's founder and had only recently been promoted to his current position. Like his father before him, Martin complied with all the fire safety regulations and welcomed the fire department's routine inspections of his company's newest projects.

Typically, such building inspections were done by official investigators, but the town of Shepherd had decided that it would save the city that expense by having firefighters rotate the duty. After all, they would be the ones with their asses on the line if the building wasn't up to code and something happened as a result.

When her turn had come around, Alex had welcomed the break in her day and headed out to give the new building her typical once-over. Unfortunately, Martin Lancaster had fallen head-over-heels for her at first sight. Since that first inspection, he had been requesting that Firefighter Alex Crawford be the one to inspect his buildings. Seeing no way to refuse without drawing undue attention to herself, Alex bit the bullet and went out.

She parked in front of the newest building, the banner hanging over the front door proclaiming that it was the FUTURE HOME of something called Langford, Taggart, and Warren, which she assumed was either a law firm or accounting group. She really didn't care either way. She paused by the door of her Jeep to pull on a windbreaker and make sure the sleeve extended far enough to cover her wrist bandage. That done, she went up to the door and pushed the temporary buzzer.

A few seconds after she announced her arrival, she saw a silhouette moving on the other side of the plastic sheet covering the door. Martin Lancaster brushed aside the sheet like a stage magician and smiled at her like a five-year-old presented with a new toy. He unlocked the door and pushed it open. "Alex! I was watching out the window and saw you drive up. Welcome."

"Thank you, Mr. Lancaster." She hoped by keeping it formal, he would get the hint and keep the meeting strictly business. As she stepped into the closed environment of the lobby, she realized that she still reeked of smoke. Normally, she was self-conscious about that sort of thing, but if it kept Lancaster at arm's length...

Lancaster was a thin, bookish man with wire-framed glasses, the collar of his shirt looking a little wide around his neck. He wore a suit that had obviously been tailored for someone a little bulkier, and his brown hair was slicked back against his skull. He looked like a high school kid on career day. Alex tepidly shook his outstretched hand before scanning the lobby of the building. She had a checkpoint list to follow. A few high points, and bing, bang, boom, she was out of there.

"So, where would you like to begin, Alex?"

Same place we always begin, you nebbish little nerd, she thought. Out loud, she said, "I just need your forms."

He opened his briefcase, balancing it against his thigh as he searched through the pockets. He handed her the building permit and construction documents, all of which were required for the file. She stuck them on her clipboard without checking them. She knew Lancaster; everything would be in order.

She was just thankful she didn't have the task of doing all the inspections for his buildings. The foundation, plumbing and electrical, floor system, preliminary framing and electrical systems all required their own inspections at various stages of construction. Firefighters weren't necessary at those inspections, but Lancaster didn't attend them. If he did, he would most likely have requested Alex be there, too.

All she had to do was tour the building, make sure the fire exits were clearly marked, sprinklers and smoke detectors were present and working, and walk the perimeter of the roof. Easy as pie.

If only Martin Lancaster wasn't dogging her every step, she might actually find the procedure relaxing.

They finished their tour where they'd started, in the lobby, and Alex signed the certificate that gave Lancaster a passing grade. He placed it in his briefcase, squared his shoulders, and gave her a wide smile. "Thank you for your time, Alex. It was, as always, a pleasure to see you."

Ignoring the repeated use of her first name, she summoned her best professional demeanor. "No trouble, Mr. Lancaster," she said briefly, and made a beeline for the door. Unfortunately, Lancaster was quicker than he looked and kept up with her.

"I was wondering, if you have a few moments free, if you'd like to grab a coffee or—"

"I'm sorry. I'm due back at the firehouse."

"Oh. Well, I was just thinking that since you finished the inspection so quickly, you might have a little leeway on when—"

"I'm on duty; I really should get going."

Lancaster followed her onto the sidewalk. "Perhaps after your shift, then."

"I'm sorry, Mr. Lancaster, but I'm afraid I have to decline."

His smile seemed to collapse under its own weight and he nodded. "Okay. Well, yes, of course. I'm sorry to have imposed, Alex."

She forced a smile as she climbed into her Jeep. "Have a good day, Mr. Lancaster."

"And you."

He went back inside, and she started the engine and breathed a sigh of relief. She'd been wondering when he would make the jump and broach the topic of actually going out on a date. Now that it was out there, and she'd flat rejected him, there was a chance he'd back off. It was a small chance, and she wasn't confident, but it was still there.

As she pulled away from the curb, she realized she'd just been asked out twice in one shift. It was a new personal record and, she would have to check with Murray, but it might also be a departmental record. Even though one of the potential suitors was Martin Lancaster, it was still an ego boost. Smiling, she drove back to the firehouse to brag about her double proposal.

By the time she got back to the firehouse, the ladder and medic truck were both absent, most likely responding to an aid call. The engine stood in the center of the garage, looking lonely and abandoned. Alex walked past it, heading for the back of the apparatus bay. Three rooms were tucked against the back wall. The game room, with a pool table and a few donated arcade games, was the center of them. To her right was the den, where they gathered to watch TV or listen to the occasional ball game on the radio. To her left were the bathrooms and the stairs to the bunk area.

The chief's office was separate from the other rooms, on the side of the bay opposite the cubbies. She could see Leary through the glass, speaking to someone on the phone. She headed over, knocking on the doorframe and miming writing a signature. He held up the clipboard to let her know he'd signed her in. She nodded and waved before turning to head back to the den. She could hear Murray inside cursing out the coach of his favorite team. She paused in the doorway and watched Jones laugh as another player struck out.

"Keep laughing, Probie," Murray grumbled. "I'll get you back in the playoffs."

"You have a serious gambling problem, Murray." Jones shook his head. "But as long as I'm reaping the benefits, I say — live how you wanna live." He was looking back at Murray to deliver his worldly wisdom and spotted Alex in the doorway. "Hey, Crawford. How's the Weasel doing?"

Murray craned his neck to look back over the top of his head at her. "Hey, Crawford. You're upside down again."

She put her hand over his face as she walked past and took her regular seat in the recliner. "Don't worry about Weasel," she said. "Worry about the poor nurses assigned to his wing."

Murray shook his head, eyes glued to the TV. "Nah. Nothing to worry about."

Alex arched an eyebrow. "You have met Wizell, right?"

"I ain't saying he ain't flirting," Murray said, "just that it's not going anywhere. These nurses are dressing his wounds, dealing with his burns, peeling off skin if the burns're bad enough." He shook his head again. "Trust me. The second someone does something like that to your body, they're never anything more than a lab jacket to you."

Alex absently touched her bandage through the windbreaker and thought of Rachel Tom's invitation. Murray interrupted her reverie by spewing a string of curses at the television.

"Fucking chumps! Every last one of them, their mothers and their fathers, all of 'em, chumps."

"How much?" Alex asked Jones, nodding toward Murray.

"Fifty." Jones smirked.

Murray slapped the arm of his chair and shot to his feet; both Alex and Jones jumped back. He stared at the TV for a few seconds, nostrils flaring, before he turned and stormed out of the den.

"Ooh, he's steamed," Jones said unnecessarily.

Alex grinned. "What about you? You think what he said is true?"

"About what? Chumps?"

"No, doctors. Do you think you could date a doctor who treated you?"

Jones shrugged. "Depends on what they treated me for. Broken arm, some heroic derring-do, yeah, I think I could date someone who put me back together. STD, though. I'd most likely steer clear of the doc who helped me out there."

Alex raised an eyebrow and Jones's eyes widened. He shifted uncomfortably and hastened to add, "I mean, I would if it ever came up. Hypothetically, right? The whole thing was..." He cleared his throat. "Hey, I, uh...you know, never had..."

"Okay, Jones, I know you're pure," Alex said. She stood and headed for the door, pausing to pat him on the shoulder. "You have to have sex before you can get an STD."

"Aw, geez," Jones muttered. He stood and followed her from the den. "I'm not a virgin, you know."

"I'll put it in the newsletter," Franklin said, overhearing the last bit as he crossed the bay to his cubby.

"Lieutenant! I... Aw, damn it, Crawford."

Alex laughed as she went into the kitchen. Murray was banging the cabinet doors open and shut without really bothering to search inside. She put one hand on his shoulder and said, "Murray. Sit. Take a deep breath. I'll cook you something. What're you in the mood for?"

"Beef stew?" Leary said from the door. He looked past her at Murray. "What's with the banging around, Godzilla?" His office shared a wall with the kitchen, meaning Murray's tantrum may have interrupted his phone call.

"Sorry, Chief," Murray muttered. "Bad bet."

Leary winced and shook his head. He moved toward the other end of the table. "I told you not to go with your gut. What's your gut ever gotten you, other than an ulcer?" He patted Murray on the shoulder and took a seat.

Alex searched the cupboard for the cans of beef stew. She found a red and white can and had just taken it down when Jones walked in. He saw it in her hand and snatched it away without saying anything. Alex arched an eyebrow at him. "Whoa, Probie. Know your boundaries."

"Sorry." He smiled. "I thought I'd cook tonight. After all, it's my fault Murray's trying to punch through the walls, right?"

"You're damn right," Murray said over his shoulder. He was still pouting, but seemed to have brightened a bit at the knowledge the new guy would be cooking for him.

Eager to hand off the cooking duties, Alex took a few more cans of stew from the cupboard and placed them next to the stove. She stepped back and took a seat next to the pouting Murray. "Where'd our other truck get off to?"

Leary waved dismissively at the doors. "Some demonstration downtown. They're having pyrotechnics, wanted some firefighters on hand just in case. If we get a call, Ladder 8 over in Greensboro will back us up." He looked around and said, "Where's Holt?"

With Wizell out of commission, a lieutenant named Robert Holt had been pulled in from another company in another town. Alex hadn't paid much attention to the details.

Murray answered. "He's downstairs pumping iron. Said he wanted to check out our set-up. Flannigan is down there with him playing coach. It's like *Rocky* down there. Holt's gonna 'eat lightnin' and crap thundah'." This last bit was said with a very passable impression of Burgess Meredith's raspy shout.

"Where's the can opener?" Jones asked.

"Hand crank in the drawer by the fridge," Leary replied. He returned to the Holt topic. "Our set-up? What, like becoming a firefighter is really just an excuse to bulk up while at work?"

Murray rolled up the sleeve of his t-shirt and flexed his bicep. "It is for me."

"Hand crank?" Jones said when he found the old-fashioned can opener. "What is this, the Dark Ages?"

Leary raised an eyebrow. "I have a penknife on my keychain you could use if you prefer."

Jones grumbled and turned the hand crank over in his hands, trying to figure out how it worked.

Alex slapped her thighs and stood. "Okay, since I was saved from cook duties, you guys want something to drink? I can run across the street."

"Something orange flavored," Leary said. "Don't care about brand, so long as it's got sugar."

Murray asked for a root beer and Jones made it two. As she passed Jones, Alex saw him try and fail to hook the hand crank to the can. She took both can and tool from him, set the can on the counter and effortlessly attached the opener to the side. With a few quick, strong twists, the top came loose. The lid was tilted up at a slight angle, allowing her to get her trimmed thumbnail under the edge and lift it up. She handed the can back to Jones with a smirk. "Learn to use it. Your life in the kitchen will be much easier."

"All I'm saying is an electric can opener is, like, twenty bucks. Who needs this hassle?"

Murray shook his head. "If you'd been born thirty years ago, wolves would have eaten yo' ass when you was a baby."

She left the squabbling boys behind and headed to her cubby. Taking her wallet from her coat, she headed out. The store was literally across the street, kitty corner from the station. She trotted up the hill and jogged across the street. Inside the store, she greeted the clerk by name, and headed for the coolers at the back.

Alex grabbed a six-pack of root beers and then found something orange-flavored for Leary. By the time she started for the cash register, two kids had entered. They were each carrying a skateboard under their arm and laughing about the scrapes on the taller boy's knees. A girl trailed behind them, obviously bored out of her skull by whatever the boys were talking about. Alex gave them a nod as they crossed paths and smiled at the clerk as she put the bottles on the counter.

She heard a voice behind her as the clerk totaled up her purchases. "You a firefighter?"

She turned and saw the teen skater girl standing behind her. The skater boys were at the frozen drink machine, unaware their female hanger-on had detoured. Alex was wearing her department t-shirt, so it wasn't a surprise she'd been spotted. "Yeah, I am."

"Cool," the girl said. "So they, like, let women actually hang off the truck and stuff?"

"We stopped hanging off the truck a good while back," Alex said with a smile. "The boys started letting us sit up front with them."

The girl nodded absently. "So, you like, sleep with all the guys? That's what I heard, I mean, that you guys all sleep together in the station."

"Well," Alex said, "we do have separate beds. Bunk beds."

"So there's no sex?"

"I can't speak for anyone else," Alex said, "but no, nothing happens."

The girl gave a half-hearted shrug. "That's cool, though, being a firefighter."

"I think so." Alex gave her a smile. "What's your name?"

"Michelle."

"Nice to meet you, Michelle."

The boys had moved over to the candy aisle and the one with skinned knees finally realized his girlfriend had wandered. He joined in the conversation, nodding at Alex. "So, do you guys have, like, a dog?"

She turned and looked at him. He looked half-baked and was smiling like a moron. He repeated his question and Alex said, "Yeah. We call him Weasel."

"Huh." The kid stuttered a laugh. "Cool. Weasel."

Alex paid for her drinks and took her bag. "Nice meeting you, Michelle." The girl waved after her. Alex headed back across the street, careful not to jostle the bag too much. Once, she'd gotten Murray's soda shaken too much and it had sprayed all over everything when he opened it. The resulting spray war had become nearly legendary and, while fun, she didn't want a repeat of it.

She carried the bag into the firehouse, the smell of stew rising from the kitchen area and making her mouth water. She was halfway across the bay when she realized there was a woman's voice among all the chatter. She slowed her steps, and craned her neck to see into the room.

Her back to the door, sitting at the head of the table in the seat previously occupied by Murray, was Dr. Rachel Tom.

Alex fought the sudden urge to run to her cubby and change into something nicer. She proceeded into the kitchen, ignoring the nerves that started jangling like a five-alarm bell. Leary saw her coming and smirked. Rachel paused and looked over her shoulder.

"Alex! They said you were out."

"Yeah." She set the bag of drinks down on the table, avoiding the playful grins of her co-workers and trying to focus on forming coherent sentences. "Um...hi."

"Hi," Rachel said.

Jones stepped between the two of them. He grabbed the bag and fished for the bottles inside. He pulled his root beer free, flashed a smile at Alex, and went back to the stove.

"Probably need some help with the spices, eh, Probie?" Murray gave Alex a wink and joined Jones at the stove. Both men stood with their backs to the room, neither of them even bothering to pretend they were working.

Leary also stood, moving around the table. "You guys don't use enough cayenne. Let me see if I can find some." He stood next to Murray, joining the wall of silence.

Alex shifted uncomfortably from one foot to the other, very aware of the three men crowded behind her. From the lack of sound coming from their "preparations", she knew they were just trying to give the illusion of privacy. She cleared her throat and motioned at the apparatus bay with her head. "Wanna take a walk?"

"Sure," Rachel said.

As she led the doctor out of the kitchen, Alex looked over her shoulder and said, "Save me some of the stew, would ya?"

"The way Murray eats, we'll have to open another can, at least," Leary said.

"Anyone wanna give me odds that Probie'll cut off one of his fingers?" Murray asked.

"No bet," Leary said.

Alex joined Rachel in the bay, smiling apologetically like a teenager embarrassed by her family's appearance on the front porch before a date. "Sorry about that," she said, keeping her voice low. She put her hand on the small of Rachel's back and guided her toward the open garage doors. She noticed that Rachel tensed at the touch and was about to pull her hand away when the other woman suddenly relaxed. They stepped out into the chilly air, the streetlight on the corner casting a glow over the driveway.

They stood awkwardly facing each other, each waiting for the other to begin the conversation. Rachel had zipped a jacket over her clothes, and had her arms wrapped around her abdomen. Her hair was in a loose ponytail and a few strands had fallen free to whip about her face. After a few seconds, Rachel nodded at the empty section of the bay.

"Was there a fire?"

"Not yet," Alex said. "The ladder is just on hand at some demonstration downtown."

"Oh, okay." She looked into the bay again. "So, y-you're not on the ladder?"

Alex shook her head. "No, I'm with the engine."

Rachel smiled, obviously embarrassed. "Okay...uh, I don't..."

Alex grinned. "Not a lot of people know the difference. The engine carries the water supply and a whole bevy of tools like ladders, axes, the fans, stuff like that. We lay the hoses, help with ventilation; we do search-and-rescue inside the building. The ladder guys help do search and rescue involving ladders, vent the building from the roof and use big fans to clear the smoke."

"Which one is better?"

"They're both great, equally good," Alex said. A moment later, she said, "But the engine is so much better." They both laughed, and Alex gestured at the bay. "Would you like a tour?"

"No, that's... I just got off duty and got to thinking, so I came by to let you know that...um, you don't have to meet me for drinks or anything if you don't want to."

Alex felt her stomach drop. *She changed her mind,* she thought. *Decided she was just caught up in the moment, is rethinking it. No problem.* She managed to nod. "Well, I guess we could call it off if you wanted to..."

"No!" Rachel put her hand on Alex's arm. Alex wondered if she'd just imagined there was a spark from their contact. "I-I didn't mean that. It was just... I ambushed you and I was thinking that you really couldn't say no without embarrassing me. I wanted to say that I wouldn't...I mean, if you still want to go, I'd be thrilled."

"I still want to go."

Rachel looked relieved. "Great. That's... Thank you for not laughing in my face."

Alex smiled. "I'm looking forward to it. Tomorrow at seven."

"Right. So I'll...I'll see you then?"

"Count on it."

Rachel shifted her feet and then looked back into the bay. "I'm sorry if I embarrassed you back there."

"Oh, please," Alex said. She laughed and nodded toward the kitchen. "I apologize for anything these pigs said before I showed up."

"They're sweet. Especially Mr. Murray."

Alex fought the urge to laugh harder. "Yes, he...he is darling."

"Okay, then, I should go. I'll see you tomorrow at seven."

"It's a date," Alex said. She extended her hand as Rachel moved in for a hug. They awkwardly shifted until they were shaking with one hand and embracing with the other. When they pulled back, Rachel grinned and Alex chuckled. "Okay, that wasn't weird at all."

Rachel smiled nervously. "Sorry."

"It's okay. We'll figure it out." She couldn't swear to it in the dim light, but she thought that Rachel blushed.

"Okay. Well, I should probably let you get back to your dinner."

"Right. Have a nice night."

"You, too."

Alex watched Rachel walk back to her car, waving as she drove past. Once the taillights faded over the rise, she turned and went back into the bay. She froze in the doorway of the kitchen.

Leary, Murray, and Jones had moved the table so they could all sit at the long end facing the door. Each of them had a bowl of stew in front of him, but no one was eating; they were too busy smiling at her. Murray was the first to speak, holding his hands out palms up.

"Well?" he said, affecting an effeminate tone. "Dish, girl."

Alex rolled her eyes and went to the stove. She found a bowl that wasn't too dirty and served herself. She shook her head as she paused at the table long enough to snag her root beer. "You guys seriously need to get a life."

They booed her playfully as she walked out of the kitchen with her root beer. She stepped outside and took a seat in the lawn chair Leary had occupied earlier. She cracked the top off her drink and set it on the ground. From the kitchen, she could hear loud scraping noises as the guys moved the table back where it belonged. A few minutes later, Leary came outside and leaned against the bay doors.

"Date?" he asked.

She thought for a moment and then nodded.

"She's cute."

Alex smirked. "Yep."

"Want the guys to ease up on you?"

"The guys?" she asked. "So you were against moving the table?"

"Kicking and screaming," he said, but his smirk gave him away.

"It's all right, Chief. I can take it."

He nodded. "Enjoy your stew."

She raised her spoon and saluted him with it as he went back into the building. She crossed her leg over her knee and watched the sparse traffic flow by the firehouse. Truth be told, she was a little touched by their playfulness. She had joined the academy with a class of four other women. The guys had been dismissive, harsh, and misogynistic. It was torture and only abated slightly when she was assigned to this house. Leary was surprisingly open-minded about having a woman on his team, and the other guys seemed willing to follow his lead.

Slowly but surely, she'd gained their respect. They had seen what she was capable of and, by God, they were starting to trust her. And now, here she was, the night after fighting a fire, sitting outside of her firehouse, a war wound on her arm and eating a hot bowl of stew. And she had a date tomorrow night.

Things were definitely on the upswing.

His footsteps echoed through the abandoned corridors, reverberating off the bare walls. The offices had long been empty. All of the storage closets he'd checked were crammed full of empty copy paper boxes, long dead electronics, and sundry junk. He'd shoved some more loose paper into the cracks, making sure the closets were as full as they could possibly be. Then he poured a small Mason jar of gasoline over the mess and closed the door. The fumes would build up in the cramped space and he'd get an even bigger bang for his buck.

His tote bag carried seven more jars, protected from banging against each other by fluffy towels. The fumes were bad, but he was used to them from his games as a boy. Other boys may have played with matches or lit ants on fire; his games involved setting fires in abandoned houses. He hardly even noticed the fumes anymore, although the headaches he got afterward told him that his body still noticed. He tried to move fast and he wore a white rag around his nose and mouth like a bandit in some old Western, but the headaches still came. An unfortunate by-product of his mission, but one he felt he could deal with.

Opening the stairwell door, he walked to the edge of the landing and peered down. There was a wide window on each landing, so the long abandoned stairs were illuminated ghostly white by the moon. It looked as if the stairway circled down into Hell. He poured the contents of another Mason jar down the stairs, watching as the gasoline seemed to jump from step to step, splashing out to either side as if thankful to be free of its glass prison.

He was humming a tune, something by Bruce Springsteen, and tried to remember the name of the song. The title escaped him, as did the lyrics, so he continued humming. He was sure it was something about fire.

He left the stairwell and walked back the way he'd come. Gas fumes assaulted him from all sides, from the bag on his side, from the closets he'd already rigged. It smelled like ambrosia to him now, but he knew his body would rebel later. At the end of the hallway, he knelt and carefully spilled another pool beneath the windowsill.

One floor down, two to go. He'd used three jars here, which left him only five for the other two floors. He'd have to scrimp on one of them, most likely the topmost floor. Unless... If the bottom and top floors were both inflamed, there was a chance the second floor would be engulfed with them. He regretted not thinking of that before he wasted three jars on the second floor, but no use crying over spilt gas.

He threw open the stairwell door without worrying about the rudimentary alarms he'd already disabled and, ignoring the fumes, rushed up the stairs to the topmost level.

Alex lay down in the bottom bunk, still wearing her t-shirt but stripped to her boxers below. Her turnout pants were pooled next to her bed, her boots standing up beneath them. Should the alarm go off, all she needed to do was swing her legs over the edge and step into them, yank the pants up and hook the suspenders on her shoulders. Easy as pie; took her about three seconds to do it.

The lights were out, save for the main lights in the apparatus bay. The ladder had returned around ten and the guys who weren't sleeping around her were watching a video in the den. Knowing Captain Sawyer, it was probably a porno.

Murray was on the bed above hers, stressing the struts holding his mattress up and snoring loud enough to keep her awake. Alex had one arm tucked behind her head, the other draped across her stomach. All she could think about was her date with Rachel the next day. In — she checked her watch and did the math — eighteen hours, they would be sitting together and having a meal.

It had been ages since she'd been on a date. Her shift work didn't totally preclude a social life, but it didn't exactly help, either. Her last date had been with a police officer named Tania. Fifteen minutes into the date, Tania had pretty much insulted every angle of firefighting she could think of. Firefighters were, in Tania's opinion, lazy and shiftless, being paid a king's ransom to sit around the firehouse, watch TV and play pool, and occasionally get a little soot on their faces. "My job," she'd said, eyes locked firmly down her nose, "is a real job; people shoot at me."

Alex's opinion was that people would shoot at Tania even if she was a dentist.

She rolled onto her side and saw Jones sprawled in the next bunk, hand covering his face. He had yet to get used to sleeping in the same room as a bunch of other people, especially people who slept as loud as Murray did.

She closed her eyes, finally about to drift off, when the alarm began to sound.

Captain Franklin, who had the night watch, spoke over the intercom: "Ladder, Engine, respond to warehouse fire, three-three-one-four Pine, fully involved, Class-B." He repeated the message and by the time he finished, Alex had slid down the pole and was chasing Murray across the apparatus bay.

Rachel was curled in the corner of her couch, reading a few pages before slipping into bed for the night. She'd always been a night owl, something that had proved to be a lifesaver during her residency, and seldom climbed into bed before three. Tonight, however, she was having more than a little trouble concentrating.

She kept re-reading the same paragraph, trying to absorb the action on the page and finding herself unable to focus. Finally, she slipped the bookmark between the pages and put the book on her lap. All she could think about was her upcoming date with Alex. A firefighter. She grinned and took off her reading glasses, checking her watch as she reached for the remote. She was certain there would be something on TV Land that she could lose herself in for half an hour.

The television came to life, the screen filling the living room with pale blue light. She was about to turn on the DirecTV when she realized what she was watching.

At first, she'd thought the local news was rerunning its eleven o'clock broadcast. Then she spotted the small LIVE banner in the bottom right corner, next to the address — 3314 Pine Street, in the warehouse district.

"...continues to blaze out of control. Two firefighting companies are on hand battling this inferno, but they seem to be making absolutely no headway." She watched with a sharp, almost overwhelming sense of horror as a man in full turnouts swept past the reporter on the ground. The reporter caught up with him.

"Sir, excuse me. Excuse me, sir?"

The chiseled, aged-but-not-old face of Chief John Leary turned toward the camera, teeth bared, eyes flashing with anger. His gray-white hair stood on end, obviously a result of removing the helmet he was carrying under his arm. Rachel saw only the smiling man blowing on a spoonful of fresh beef stew, telling her that Alex would "be back in just a jiffy". He snapped something that the reporter's microphone didn't pick up and headed back to the building. The reporter stammered something about how the chief was "obviously very busy" and promised to get a statement later.

Slim chance, Rachel thought.

The TV feed cut back to the studio, where a harried looking anchor was sifting through papers on his desk. He obviously wasn't used to being on the air so late and his discomfort was evident. He looked up at the camera, probably making sure he was still on. "If you're just joining us, we're continuing coverage of a fire that was first reported around 1:30 this morning. Since our crew has been on the ground, the fire team has managed to keep the fire from spreading to surrounding buildings..."

Rachel was intent on the picture-in-picture shot of the fire. Her heart was pounding and the palms of her hands were sweaty. Just the sight of such an involved conflagration, the knowledge that it was happening so nearby, was enough to cause a panic attack. But she wouldn't run, she wouldn't hide. Not this time. If Leary was on the grounds, it stood to reason that Alex was there as well. It might be superstitious nonsense, but she wasn't going to turn her back while Alex was potentially in danger.

The second fire in one shift; she honestly didn't know the odds, but it couldn't be all that common. She scanned the dark background — it was hard to tell one silhouette from another —

and tried to read the reflective tape on the back of the firefighters' jackets as they sped to and fro.

"We're getting word now," this from the reporter on the scene, "that a firefighter may — I repeat, may be trapped inside the building. We don't have any details at the moment, but as soon as we can obtain confirmation..."

Rachel refused to believe what she was hearing. Her mind taunted her, assuring her that it was definitely Alex. Alex had come into her life only to be snatched away in a blaze of fire in the middle of the night. Wasn't that ironic? Fate poked her in the side, laughing when she jumped. She stood up, halfway decided on changing into street clothes and heading to the hospital. She wanted to go; she wanted to stay and hear the rest of the news; she wanted to scream at the reporter to go away and let the firefighters do their damn jobs.

She dropped back onto the couch and hugged her knees to her chest, staring at the television and praying for good news.

Alex Crawford lay on her belly, one hand against the wall to orient herself in her environment of screaming swirls of yellows, blacks, and grays. There was a bell ringing in her ear, the air pack's five-minute warning siren mixing with the wail of a motionless PASS device somewhere in front of her. The fire roared above her and she was suddenly aware that the screaming was coming from inside her own mask.

Fingers wrapped around the collar of her turnout coat and she felt herself hauled up off the floor. Someone was half-dragging, half-carrying her back the way she'd come in. She tried to walk, but her feet refused to cooperate and she fell to her knees. The person who'd saved her picked her up again, letting her walk this time as he moved her toward the engine. "You all right?" he asked, helping her pull her mask off. "Where's your partner?"

She didn't recognize the man; he was from the Greensboro station and had responded to the same call. "He's in there," Alex managed, coughing a bit as she watched the doorway dissolve into a wall of flame. "Oh, my God, he's still in there!"

Flames, smoke, oxygen burning her lungs if she tried to breathe... Rachel had her eyes closed, fists pressed against her forehead, trying to block out the images on the television as well as her memories of fire. When she looked up again, her eyes were wet with tears. The reporter was giving another recap of the situation, turning to indicate the three-story inferno behind him. He'd just paused to take a breath when there was an ear-piercing scream. A woman's scream. *Alex?*

Rachel's heart jumped and she forgot to breathe as she frantically searched the background for signs of the woman she'd met that morning. *Nothing. Damn it, nothing!* She couldn't see anything in the dark; the smoke and the idiot reporter were in her way. A part of her knew she was getting carried away. She would never be able to sleep if she kept watching, but she didn't think she could stop watching. *I have to know she's all right; I can't just sit here and do nothing. I have to see if I can help.*

She stood up and turned off the TV, the sudden darkness causing her a moment's blindness as she swept her hand across the coffee table for her car keys. She wasn't going to just sit and wait; she couldn't. They would appreciate the extra hands at work, anyway.

Rachel changed into an old pair of jeans and a sweater before she drove to the hospital. She was on autopilot, following the same route she always took and blessing the lateness of the hour for the lack of traffic. Since she didn't have to pay attention to other cars, she kept her eyes on the horizon for smoke or the orange glow of flames.

When she entered through the sliding doors, the emergency room was astoundingly serene. Rachel directed her steps toward the elevators, looking around for signs she had missed the commotion, but everything seemed to be business as usual.

She rode the elevator to the third floor, and found that was where the real drama was happening. The steel doors parted to reveal Wizell in his wheelchair, his bandaged head swiveling back and forth between the two nurses who flanked him. He bared his teeth like an attack dog and his face turned deep crimson. "I don't care. I don't care. I'm going down to that building and..."

"You're staying right where you are, Mr. Wizell," Rachel said as she stormed onto the floor. Despite the panic that had propelled her the entire way to the hospital, she felt a kind of relief. Here, finally, was a problem she could deal with head on. Wizell snapped his mouth shut and turned his wide eyes on her.

"D-Dr. Tom," one of the nurses said.

Rachel recognized her: Mary Evanov, a recently hired young nurse who had probably never had to deal with a patient like Wizell before. Her brow creased in confusion, but she didn't have the nerve to question the doctor's presence. She had, after all, just cowed the most belligerent patient on the floor.

Rachel stood in front of Wizell's chair and glared down at him. "You will go right back to your room, get back into bed, and you will calm yourself. Am I understood?"

"Yes, ma'am," he said meekly.

Rachel exhaled. "Good." She looked at Mary. "Nurse Evanov, please escort Mr. Wizell back to his room. And make sure the restraints are well secured to the bed, just in case we have to use them."

"Yes, Dr. Tom." Under her breath, she added, "I'm so glad you showed up. I was afraid we would have to sedate him."

"Hear that, Mr. Wizell?" Rachel asked.

"I'll be good, I promise." Wizell sighed, holding up his hands in surrender as Mary wheeled him away. "Geez, make one little ruckus and suddenly you're on *America's Most Wanted*."

"What are you doing here so late, Dr. Tom?" the remaining nurse asked.

Rachel held up her hand, watching until Wizell was wheeled back into his room. She guided the nurse over to the desk, keeping her voice hushed. "How long has he been awake?"

"Since he heard the sirens. He turned on the news and initiated his great escape right afterward, so he didn't get a chance to see how bad it is. None of us did. Is it bad?"

"The fire is out of control from the looks of it. His..." She paused and looked over her shoulder to make sure he wasn't in earshot. "His company may have lost someone."

"Oh, God!"

Rachel shushed her and said, "I'm here just in case we get a sudden burst of admissions. Couldn't hurt to have an extra pair of hands."

"Right, of course, Doctor. If it does get crazy, I'll get on my knees and worship your foresight."

"Well, that probably won't be necessary," Rachel said. She tried to cover her fear with a smile as she took off her coat. "I do, however, accept cash gifts."

Alex sat in the back of the medic truck for the second time in the same day, watching as the other firefighters doused the building. The fire was burning itself out; all they were doing for the moment was limiting its advance on the neighboring buildings. She couldn't believe the similarities to the afternoon's fire. It was another warehouse, this one three stories tall with offices on the upper two levels. She and her partner had gone in looking for squatters and had again found no one.

Instead, another door had opened on a fireball. It was burned into Alex's vision. And along with it, the image of a helmet engulfed in bright yellow flame.

The bumper of the truck sagged and she blinked herself back to her present surroundings, focusing on Leary's haggard face. He sat across from her, his hand on her shoulder.

"What happened in there?" he asked softly.

"He's gone, sir," Alex choked out. "Right in front of me. He..." She gnawed at her lip and shook her head. "He just...disappeared. No one could have survived it."

Leary squeezed her shoulder just once and withdrew his hand. He turned to look out of the open doors at the smoldering building. "When the fire dies down, we're going in and we're going to pull him out. We will find him, Crawford. Got that?"

"Yes, sir."

"His PASS device..."

"Ringing loud and clear, sir," she said. She turned her head back to the building. The PASS device hooked on their jackets signaled when the wearer was immobile for a certain length of time. No one liked to admit that its primary purpose was to facilitate the recovery of corpses. Over the calls of other firefighters, over the sirens that were still blaring and all the horrendous noise caused by the media circus, she swore she could still hear it ringing, a persistent, monotonous sound calling for them to come and find it. "Can you hear it, too?" she asked.

Leary was quiet for a minute, obviously trying to mask out the ambient noises. "Yeah," he finally said. "I can hear it."

He sat with her for a long time, watching out the back of the medic truck as their team and Greensboro's guys drowned the fire until it was out.

"Gas," she muttered. "I smelled gas in there. Really strong."

"Yeah. This was set."

"Bastards," she spat.

By the time the fire had been contained, the sun was starting to color the sky at the edge of town. Leary helped Alex out of the truck and stood aside as she pulled her gear back on. The purported objective was to overhaul the building — clear out all the flammable materials and snuff out any remaining heat pockets that could rekindle the blaze. The true objective was to find their missing firefighter.

Somewhere under all this debris, Alfred Jones was waiting to be found, and Engine 12 would not go home without him.

Chapter Four
Just Bugs, No Bunny

"Excuse me," he repeated, trying to get the attention of a reporter on the scene.

One of the talking heads, someone he vaguely recognized from the evening news but couldn't name, was wrapping a microphone cord around her hand. She glanced up at the sound of his voice but didn't really look at him. To her, he was just another rubbernecker. "I'm sorry, sir, you can't be here."

The arsonist fought the urge to smirk, wondering how many times firefighters had said the exact same thing to her. "I-I live around here," he said. "I saw the fire. I hope no one was hurt…"

The reporter sighed and continued to gather the tools of her trade. She turned her back to him, hoping that would fend him off. "We heard that maybe a firefighter was trapped inside. That's all they're saying right now. Please, I'll have to ask you to step back."

He fought the urge to smile at the news, struggling to keep his expression neutral even though the woman hadn't looked at him once. "Oh," he managed. "Oh, dear, that is horrible."

He started to walk away, not getting too close to anyone lest they smell the gasoline stink that clung to him like a second skin. He shoved his hands into his pockets, ducking his head and finally allowing the snicker that had been building up since the trucks had first arrived. He'd done it. A firefighter had gone down.

Looking over his shoulder, his mind's eye saw the smoking husk whirling in the maelstrom of flame that had consumed it earlier. Perhaps he'd gone overboard with this one. Between the first fire, which had been too weak, and this one, he needed to find a middle ground.

It would be fine, though. The next fire would be a masterpiece. Snickering again, he turned and hurried away from the scene.

They pulled Jones from the rubble a few minutes past six in the morning. His mask had melted into his charred skin and his uniform was a deep charcoal color. His arms were up around his face in the classic boxing pose, his knees drawn to his chest as if trying to protect himself from the fire.

The medics loaded him onto a gurney, zipping him into a body bag before they removed him from the shell of a building. Leary passed Murray and Alex, handing each of them a corner of a sheet.

They nodded their understanding and took up positions a few feet apart.

When the medics carried the gurney over the debris littering the floor, setting it on its wheels once they were outside, Murray climbed onto the bumper of the engine and lifted his portion of the sheet over his head. Alex did the same on the bumper of the ladder. The reporters, who were out in full force, had to scramble to the side in an attempt to get a halfway decent shot around the impromptu screen. Once Jones had been loaded into the ambulance, the firefighters dropped the sheet and went back to attend to their duties. The building still wasn't safe.

Alex watched the bounce of the ambulance as it rolled over the TV camera cords and other various pieces of equipment the reporters had left lying around. Several of the talking heads tried to get their equipment out of the way, but the truck wasn't giving them time to clear out. Alex managed a weak smile and picked up her axe, following Murray back into the smoky husk of the building.

Since she was there anyway, Rachel helped out with whatever the staff needed, but she spent most of her time leaning against the doorway of the waiting room and watching the fire coverage on the news. One of the reporters announced that they were bringing the body out, at which point the camera spun back toward the building.

"What the hell are they thinking?" Rachel muttered. She hated the fact that she was glued to the screen. The reporters were just getting in the way, and why? So people like her could sit at home and gawk. She crossed her arms over her chest and cursed herself for being unable to look away.

At that moment, two firefighters each stood on the bumper of the truck nearest to them — Rachel saw that one was the engine and the other was the ladder — and held up a wet, smoke damaged sheet. She smiled, fighting the urge to applaud. When the sheet was dropped again, the firefighter that had stepped onto the ladder turned and slipped around the edge of the truck.

Rachel felt her breath catch when she read the CRAW written in reflective tape over the tail of the jacket. "Alex," she whispered, as she clutched the pendant hanging from her necklace. "Thank God, Alex."

A few minutes later, the reporter back in the studio — the replacement for the one who had been in at 2 AM — broke in. "We have an update for you at this time. Our sources tell us that the casualty was a probationary firefighter, which means he had only recently graduated from the academy."

Rachel flashed on the man standing at the stove earlier in the evening, ladling stew into a bowl. He had offered her some. She could practically still hear him say, "You're sure? There's plenty to go around." She could see his Marine-length hair, his thin face, and a smile that she was sure had melted hearts all around town. He was so young. She'd seen young people die; it was a fact of life in the hospital. But he'd been so...alive earlier. Making stew and joking with the guys, and now he was gone.

"Ma'am?"

She looked into the dark waiting room, straightening slightly. The speaker was a young man — probably the same age as the firefighter who died — sitting on the couch. He looked concerned. She cleared her throat. "Um, yes, sorry, yes?"

"Are you all right? Would you like me to get a nurse?"

She realized that she was crying, and then a moment later remembered that she was still wearing her street clothes. "No, that's all right," she said, forcing a smile. "Thank you."

She turned and went back to the nurses' station, resting her hands on the edge of the counter until Mary looked up from her crocheting. "Things have obviously calmed down here. I'm going to go home," she said softly. "I have to get some sleep before my shift tomorrow."

"All right, Dr. Tom. Do you want us to give you a call if someone from the fire is sent in?"

"No," she said. "I don't think I'd be in the best shape to deal with that right now." She smiled and thanked the nurse before she headed to the elevator.

In front of the elevators, the corridor branched off, stretching out to either side in two short halls. It was for the benefit of their more mobile patients, so they could look out the windows. Convalescing patients were walked from their rooms to the windows as a part of their exercises. Even though the view was mostly of a parking lot and the strip mall across the street, everyone still seemed fond of coming down and looking at the evergreens on the mountains outside of town. It was also an area used by nurses who wanted to have their coffee breaks without going all the way to the ground floor.

As she passed, she spotted Wizell sitting in his wheelchair, staring blankly through the glass. Following his gaze, she saw the rolling black cloud at the edge of town. She started over, thought better of it, and stayed where she was. She wondered if he knew, if he'd heard the news. He most likely had; hard to believe he hadn't been watching the news broadcast of his friends doing their jobs.

She pressed the down button on the elevator and left Wizell to his thoughts.

At the firehouse, Alex headed to the edge of the apparatus bay and turned on the faucet. The truck needed to be hosed down and there was no reason why she shouldn't get it done with as soon as possible. Leary and Franklin were heading for the chief's office and the loathsome task of notifying Jones's family. She pulled a couple of sponges from the cabinet and went to find the hose.

Murray joined Alex and she automatically handed him a sponge. He took it without comment, turning to look over at the chief's office while Alex picked up the bucket and carried it over to the truck.

"Twenty-one, man. Shit."

She knew he was talking about Jones's age.

They'd managed to salvage his helmet. All of the singe marks had been confined to the front. She'd noticed the cross he'd drawn with a marker hadn't been touched and she wanted to take an axe to it. Jones had prayed on the way to this fire, the way he did on every call. A lot of good it had done.

Alex motioned at the rig and said to Murray, "C'mon. Let's get this done. You want to hang the hose to dry?"

"Sure." He pulled some of the equipment from the truck, setting it aside to be washed. Glancing over his shoulder at the chief's office, he asked, "Who do y'think they'll put with us?"

She shrugged. "One of the twins, probably."

"You'd like that, huh, Crawford?"

She could tell by the tone of his voice he was trying to lighten the mood, but she shot him a weary look. "Not today, Murray."

He nodded and sprayed water from the hose at the side of the truck. A wave of soot and dirt immediately cascaded down the red flank. Alex watched the stream for a moment before she dunked her sponge into the bucket and got to work.

Alex and Murray finished washing the truck and restocked it with all of the now gleaming equipment. The hose was hung up to dry in the hose bed, and they were finally taking a few minutes to decompress in the den. Alex was seated so that she could see the front of the bay.

Jones's replacement arrived two hours before the end of shift. As Alex had predicted, Administration had sent one of the twins.

Alex guessed it was Heather, but there was no real way to tell just by looking, at least not any that she was aware of.

The twins were stationed with Engine 4, a company on the other side of town, and had become widely known in the department after an encounter at a fire ground. Then-Chief Goldberg, having never seen either of the Riley twins at a fire, had spotted one of them laying a hose line. A few minutes later, he glanced at the roof and saw what he thought to be the same firefighter assisting in ventilation. Over the course of the fire, Heather and her sister Helen had inadvertently caused the old man more than a bit of confusion.

Afterward, when he found out the truth, he began referring to them as Bugs and Bunny, a reference to the old cartoon where the rabbit had played all the positions in a baseball game. The name had stuck and, although it had never been specified, everyone agreed that Heather was Bugs and Helen was Bunny.

Alex kicked Murray's shin when the replacement arrived. "Look who's here."

"Really? Figured she wouldn't get in 'til next shift," he said.

"Probably just wants to touch base, get her stuff in the cubby, save herself time getting acclimated."

Murray nodded, watching as she entered the chief's office. Her blond hair was in a ponytail that reached mid-shoulder. She was wearing an Engine 4 shirt and navy blue trousers, carrying a set of turnouts over one arm and her helmet tucked under the other.

Murray raised an eyebrow. "Damn, she's fine. And there's a carbon copy of her running around?"

"Down, boy," Alex said with a smile.

"Hey, you got the doctor yesterday. Can't I call dibs on this one?"

"She's not a drumstick at Thanksgiving dinner, Murray."

He shrugged. "All right, all right." The twin had left the office and was carrying her stuff across the bay to the stairs. Alex knew she was eventually going to be assigned to Jones's cubby, but until it was cleaned out she would keep her stuff in one of the lockers in the gym. "Okay, what do you think?" Murray asked. "Bugs or Bunny?"

Alex tilted her head slightly and spotted something on the woman's helmet. "My money is on Bugs."

"Why?"

"Trade secret."

Murray watched the woman stow her gear and then said, "All right, then. I'll say she's Bunny. Fifty-fifty odds, right?" He scratched his chin. "Wanna start slow? Say, thirty bucks?"

"No way," Alex said. "I'm not getting pulled into your gambling net like…" She hesitated, worried that saying his name would shatter the business-as-usual façade they had going. "No bet."

"Yeah, all right," Murray said.

The blonde spotted them and headed over, extending her hand with a smile. "Hi. Heather Riley. You can call me Bugs; just Bugs, no Bunny."

"Bugs," Alex said, taking the other woman's hand. "I should've made the bet."

Bugs smiled and looked at Murray. "Yeah, I've gotten so used to the betting about me and my sister that I wrote Bugs on the back of my helmet to avoid confusion." She indicated the helmet she'd just carried across the apparatus bay.

Alex winked at Murray, who was suddenly glad she hadn't taken his odds. "It's nice to meet you," he said, standing and shaking her hand then resuming his seat.

"The boys won't mind working with an extra woman on the team, will they?" Bugs asked, raising an eyebrow.

"No worries," Alex said. "We hardly even think of Murray as a woman anymore."

From his chair, Murray kicked her in the ass.

Alex tossed her leather backpack onto the couch and shrugged out of her jacket. She draped it over the back of her recliner as she passed and ran her fingers through her still wet hair. She'd showered at the station, getting all the soot and grime out of her hair, but she still smelled of smoke when she climbed into her Jeep. She had stayed an extra hour to give Bugs — their second replacement firefighter in the same fucking shift — the grand tour and answer any questions she had, and Alex was exhausted. Stifling a yawn, she stripped down to her underwear, not bothering with pajamas before collapsing on top of her comforter.

Her next shift was in forty-eight hours and she planned to be unconscious for at least half of the interim. Her eyes closed as soon as her head hit the pillow, her bed seeming to catch her as she fell into it. Just before sleep claimed her, she thought of how lucky she was to not have anything to do for two whole days.

When she woke, the light was dim in the bedroom and she realized it was closing in on evening. She pulled the blankets up to her chest and rolled onto her side. *Might as well sleep through until dawn.* Outside, a car horn honked. *Stupid people with lives,* she thought. *Would be nice if they let those of us without plans get some...*

Her eyes snapped open and she nearly fell out of bed. She hurried into the living room, shuffling her bare feet on the carpet and cursing herself as she checked her watch. 7:45 PM. She'd slept for almost six hours. Just fucking fantastic.

She grabbed her jacket off the back of the chair and turned the pockets inside out. No phone. Her backpack had fallen over and spilled across the couch cushions, saving her the trouble of dumping it. She finally found her cell phone at the bottom of the pile. She turned it on and fumbled with her keys until she found her voice mail in box.

No new messages.

She frowned and checked her watch. She and Rachel had made plans to meet at seven. She was forty-five minutes late, so why no call? She recognized the irony of her being offended, but still couldn't bring herself to ignore the twinge of aggravation. Kicking herself for not getting Rachel's phone number, Alex went back into the bedroom. She pulled on a blouse and found a pair of jeans in the hamper. As she buttoned the blouse, she tried to think of the most likely place to intercept the doctor. Not the hospital, Rachel had been off duty for almost three hours. Unfortunately, that was the only place in Rachel Tom's life that Alex knew about.

She sat on the edge of the bed feeling like she'd missed the opportunity of a lifetime. It was silly, some woman she'd spent a grand total of fifteen minutes with over the course of a single day... Who cared? There were other women. Theoretically, there were other women. She groaned and ran a hand through her short black hair. The one woman in years who'd actually made her feel something, the one woman who'd made her excited about the prospect of eating a meal across from someone, and she'd missed it.

She stared at the phone, tapping her thumb against the display screen and shocked into yelping when it began to vibrate in her hand. She derided herself for being so jumpy, then answered the call when Murray's cell phone number appeared on the display.

"Murray?" she said. "Why...what's up?"

"Hey, Alex, got a minute?"

She really didn't want to deal with whatever he was calling about, but maybe with what happened to Jones, he just needed to talk. "Yeah, I have some time. Where are you?"

"Still at the station. The chief, he...he wanted me to kind of go through Jones's things and... You know..."

He trailed off, leaving the unpleasant details to Alex's imagination. It was a fact of life: Jones had died and his replacement would likely need the space. Didn't make the process of cleaning his cubby out any more enjoyable.

Murray cleared his throat and moved on. "Anyway, you know that doctor from last night?" Alex's heart rate kicked up a notch. "She stopped by, wanted to know if we could give her your phone number. I wasn't sure if I—"

"Yes! She...it's all right, Murray. Is she there now?"

"Yeah. Want me to put her on?"

"Yes!"

After a pause, Rachel's voice came over the line. "Alex?"

"I was just trying to figure out how to get hold of you." She paused to collect herself. She was out of breath, smiling like an idiot, and in danger of making a very big fool out of herself. She cleared her throat. "I, uh...thought you were going to call."

"After last night, I wasn't sure if you still wanted..." There was a long pause and Alex thought they'd been disconnected. After a moment, Rachel quietly said, "The man whose phone I borrowed is standing right here smiling at me. I-Is there someplace we can meet?"

Alex gave her the address of Peter's Café and gave her directions. When Murray got the phone back he said, "Hey, Alex. Need a chaperone?"

"Goodbye, Murray."

"Make sure she doesn't get too handsy?"

"Goodbye, Murray."

"Will you take some pictures for me if she does get too handsy?"

Alex snapped the phone shut without bothering to say goodbye again, but she smiled at Murray's sense of humor. One five minute phone call and she was revitalized and cheerful. She gathered up the scattered contents and stuffed them back in her backpack then headed out the door, hoping to get to the café before Rachel did.

Alex sat nervously in the booth next to the front door of Peter's Café, fiddling with her coffee cup as she watched the sidewalk out the front window. *How long could it possibly take to get here from the firehouse?* she wondered. *Don't be stupid.* She exhaled sharply. *Why would she go out of her way to contact you just to blow you off?* A few customers came and went, but due to the lateness of the hour, the place was quiet enough that Peter had time to come and stand next to her table.

"Waiting for someone?" When she smiled nervously, he gasped and slid into the seat across from her. "Alex has a girlfriend." He grinned. "Who is she? How long has this been going on?"

"I met her yesterday."

"Ooh, she moves fast."

Alex shrugged. "Well, she was the doctor I saw after the first fire—"

He shushed her and moved forward, touching her unburned arm. "Honey, that reminds me, no talk of the fire around Michael. The sirens woke him up last night and we watched the whole horrid thing on the news. He was terrified. And then the sad news about the death of that young man..." He squeezed her arm. "I just wanted you to know, he's fragile right now."

She glanced toward the kitchen door. "Is he all right?"

"He really likes you. Your job scares him a lot. Me too, for that matter. It may be old hat to you, but he isn't used to having a friend with such a dangerous job."

"Why don't you guys come over some night for dinner? My treat. I'll soothe his nerves."

"He'd really appreciate that. So would I." He looked past her shoulder and said hurriedly, "We'll set it up later, all right?"

"Sure." Alex turned to follow his gaze. Rachel was standing behind her, looking flushed and smiling brightly. She was looking nervously between Alex and Peter, as if trying to figure out whether to stay or make tracks. "Rachel. Hi. This is—"

Peter stood. "This is a man who's just vacating your seat. I'll leave you two ladies alone, unless you'd like something to drink?"

Rachel slid into the seat he'd just vacated. "Yes, um...could I get some water?"

"Flavored or plain? We have Clearly Canadian: cherry, blackberry, orange pineapple, peach?"

"Plain would be fantastic, thank you."

He went behind the counter, poured a bottle of water into a glass, and dropped a few cubes of ice into it. He smiled at Alex when he brought the glass back to the table. "If you ladies need anything else, let me know." He went around the counter and settled himself as far from their booth as he could.

Alex knew he would do his best not to eavesdrop, but she still lowered her volume a notch. "I was so relieved when you called."

"I wasn't going to," Rachel said. "I followed everything on the news and I knew you were having..." She swallowed the rest of her sentence and began again. "I just thought that coffee would be the furthest thing from your mind tonight."

Alex shrugged. "You were right. I have to confess, I'd forgotten all about it until just before you called. Why, uh...why did you need Murray? I gave you my—"

"I lost it," Rachel sheepishly admitted. "I had it in my jacket pocket and when I rushed out I...when I saw the fire on the news, I kind of rushed to the hospital in case they needed me. Anyway, the paper must have fallen out between my apartment and the hospital. I looked in my car, but..."

"Oh." Alex looked down at Rachel's fingers wrapped around the bottom of her glass. The sweat from the ice water was condensing around Rachel's fingertips and Alex found herself hypnotized by it. She blinked a few times and said, "So what made you decided to go ahead and call me up?"

"I had to see for myself that you were okay. I'm so glad you weren't injured. I mean, I would've hated for my handiwork on your wrist to be for nothing."

Her tone was light, but Alex could see there was real relief in her eyes. She was telling the truth about being worried. The knowledge that this woman already cared so much for her was humbling. She shrugged and looked down at her own hands. "Well, truth be told, I'm glad to have the excuse to ignore everything that happened this morning, even for a little while."

Rachel took the hint and dropped the subject. After a beat, she said, "You look exhausted; are you sure you don't want to reschedule?"

"You know, it's silly, but, I'm afraid if we call off our first date, it'll jinx us."

"First date," Rachel repeated with a smile. "Us?"

Alex looked out the window and smiled nervously. "I suck at relationship stuff."

"Eh, you get at least a passing grade."

Alex looked at Rachel's glass. "Tell you what, take a drink of your water." Rachel took a slow swallow as Alex drank what was left of her cappuccino and tried not to watch the movement of liquid down Rachel's throat. They put their drinks down at the same time and Alex said, "Okay, there. Our date is over. Would you like to walk me home?"

"Are your dates always this short?"

"Only when I'm saving the best for later."

"Good answer."

They slid out of the booth and Alex reached for her wallet. Peter exposed his eavesdropping by rushing over and waving her off. "No, honey. First dates are always free in Peter's Café."

Alex chuckled. "Thanks, Peter." As Rachel stood, Alex put her hand against the small of the other woman's back, a gesture she'd done only once before but was already finding quite comfortable. Apparently she wasn't alone; this time, Rachel didn't tense at all. She guided Rachel out of the café and pointed down the street. "It's just a few blocks this way."

"Few blocks? My car is right here." Rachel indicated a sedan parked at the curb.

"Oh." Alex's face fell as she saw her romantic plan collapsing around her. "I didn't think about your car."

"It's the thought that counts, I think is the saying," Rachel said. "Look, you just got off a hell of a shift; you've got to be exhausted. We should try this again another time."

"Okay. It's a deal. Can I have your cell number?"

"Oh, right," Rachel said. She pulled her purse around and dug inside. Withdrawing a pen and pad, she wrote her numbers. "This is my cell and my home. I don't want another scavenger hunt like today."

"Yes, and the less exposure you have to Murray, the better," Alex said with a nod.

Rachel smiled. "Okay. And I lost yours, so..."

Alex scribbled her home and cell numbers down as well. As she capped the pen, she avoided Rachel's eyes. "I'm really glad you went to the trouble of finding me. It was a really bad morning and..."

"It was an entirely selfish move, trust me," Rachel said softly. She slid her hand across Alex's shoulder and moved in close. She pecked Alex's cheek and hesitated, obviously debating whether or not to move to the lips. Before she could decide, too much time had passed for a kiss to be spontaneous, so she stepped back. "Want a ride home?"

"I think I'd better walk off that kiss," Alex said, still avoiding Rachel's eyes.

Rachel laughed. "Okay. When is your next day off?"

"Tomorrow, actually," Alex said. "Twenty-four on, forty-eight off."

"Oh, right, right. Well, do you want to...?"

"Dinner. Tomorrow, if you're off."

Rachel laughed. "I get off at five again tomorrow. Say...maybe eight? Give me time to gussy myself up."

"You look just fine," Alex said. She laughed at herself and shook her head. "Anyway. I'll call you around lunchtime."

"You'd better," Rachel said playfully.

Alex watched Rachel climb into her sedan, waving at her through the windshield as she started the car. When she'd pulled away from the curb, Alex turned and caught movement inside Peter's Café out of the corner of her eye. She turned and saw Peter and Michael both in a window booth, smiling at her through the glass. Peter made a heart shape with his fingers and Michael mimed a heart pounding against his chest.

Alex gave them another hand gesture, but she only used one finger.

Alex stretched out on her bed again, this time in a pair of boxers and a tank top. She threw an arm over her face and settled in, hoping for a good, peaceful sleep, at least for a couple of hours. She had Rachel's phone number safely transferred to the pad by her house phone, so she wouldn't accidentally throw it out or lose it when she dug for change at the store.

The problem now was that every time she closed her eyes, she saw Jones opening that door, saw the flames engulfing him.

He should have been behind her. She should've been the one to open that door. Letting him lead the way had been a show of faith, a reward for his excellent progress. Instead...instead, she had signed his death warrant. It was just like Wizell's accident, only...

She opened her eyes, moving her arm and staring up at the ceiling.

It was just like Wizell's accident, except the flame was bigger. She got out of bed and went into the kitchen, searching until she found one of the street maps she'd stocked up on while studying to be a driver. Unfolding it onto the dining room table, she found the sites of the fires and placed a finger on one and a thumb on the other. They were just a few blocks from each other.

She sat down, thinking back to Wizell's accident. He had opened the door and the backdraft had knocked him down and burnt him badly. The second fire, less than a day later, had been only a few blocks away. It had been bigger, it had been badder, and it had actually killed the firefighter that was caught in it.

Someone was torching these buildings. Worse, they seemed to be traps set to catch reporting firefighters off guard. She stood up so fast she nearly toppled her chair. She had to call Leary and tell him what she suspected.

Chapter Five
Peaches and Cream, Baby

Despite the late hour, the phone was answered on the second ring. "Shepherd Fire Department, Deputy Chief Hawkes speaking."

Alex was caught off guard. "Oh. Chief. I was trying to get Chief Leary. This is Alexandra Crawford."

The cold, business-like voice disappeared, replaced by the "beloved uncle" tone. "Crawford. Hey. Hell of a thing, huh, your last shift?"

"Yeah," she agreed. "Pretty awful. Is Chief Leary...?"

"Sorry, Crawford. Leary's long gone. Anything I can help you with?"

She hesitated. Hawkes was a capable fireman and a great administrator, but she wasn't keen on sharing her theory with him. On the one hand, if she was right, the higher ups needed all the information as soon as possible to make sure the arsonist didn't strike again. On the other, if she was wrong, she would prefer it stayed between her and Leary. She didn't want to get a reputation as someone who saw conspiracies around every corner. Besides, Leary had seen both fires first hand. If he said they were unrelated, she would trust his judgment.

She thought about calling him at home, but that was off limits. He was a family man, with a wife and a young daughter, and she didn't want to intrude on private time. "No, that's all right, Chief. Could you leave Chief Leary a message to call me if he does come in?"

"Sure thing, Crawford."

They exchanged a few more pleasantries before Alex was able to hang up.

She went to bed and stretched out on top of the covers. She stared at the ceiling, half hoping for sleep and half dreading the nightmares that were sure to come.

She and Jones were crawling down the corridor, Jones in the lead with the hose dragging the ground beside him. They reached a bank of doors and Jones slid his hand up the wall. Alex knew what he felt; her shoulder was against the wall and she could feel the heat even through her gear.

He gave her the okay sign over his shoulder, half lost in the cloud of smoke. She slapped the back of Jones's leg. "Okay, keep moving."

It was a fully involved fire, which meant others outside were already applying streams to the open windows. Alex looked up at the ceiling as they rounded a corner, watching the smoke. It had seemed wrong the first time, now it was even worse. It was like a giant, flaming sign that said "Turn Back Now". She ignored it now, as she had the first time, and followed Jones deeper into the building.

She'd seen what he was doing wrong the first time and shouted at him. But even in her dream, it was already too late. She still saw sheets of smoke flowing into the cracks around the door as if the room was alive and taking a deep breath. And the exhalation would be the envy of every fire-breathing dragon since the days of King Arthur.

Jones knelt in front of the door, either not hearing her or just ignoring her as he reached for the knob rather than feeling the heat of the door. The same mistake Wizell had made. She remembered cursing and grabbing the leg of his turnouts, trying to pull him back as he twisted the knob in his hand.

She pulled her hand back at the last moment, right before the door opened and Jones was engulfed. The wave of flame looked so wrong, so unreal. Instead of exhaling, as she had in the actual fire, she inhaled to scream. Where the hell was her mask? The flames followed the oxygen, and by the time she realized what she'd done, it was too late. Her lungs had become superheated, fried, and useless as she gasped futilely for air. Her throat now burnt, her lungs twin lumps of charcoal, her insides felt like she had swallowed a match. And just before she burst into flames, she jerked awake in bed, breathing deep and hard with her healthy lungs.

She had screamed instead of inhaling. She had survived; Jones was dead. Her face and pillow were wet. She brushed off her cheeks and slipped out of bed on shaky legs. She stood for a moment, making sure her knees would support her, and then went to the shower.

Alex turned the cold water as high as it would go, stripped out of her underwear, and unwound the dressing on her wrist. She got into the stall and stood motionless under the spray. Goosebumps rose on her flesh; her hair slicked back against her skull as she simply stood there and willed herself to become a block of ice. After a few moments, when her hands and knees were shaking with the freezing temperature, she finally turned on the hot water and soaped up.

She couldn't smell the smoke anymore, but that didn't mean the odor was gone. One of her ex-girlfriends had broken up with her because she "couldn't be with someone who smoked, so how could she sleep next to someone who reeked of the stuff?"

When Alex finally felt clean, she shut off the shower. She toweled off, redressed her wrist, and put on a set of fire department sweats. The apartment felt a little too warm after her freezing cold shower, so she padded barefoot to the window and pushed it open to let in some fresh air.

Her apartment was a spartan one-bedroom over a pawn shop and a Korean hairdresser. She had a few neighbors, but they were private and never stayed very long. It was nothing to do with her and everything to do with the kids who were, at that moment, closing a deal down on the corner. Her longest lasting neighbor was a sweet old man who claimed his name was Mr. Round and that his rotund waist was just a coincidence.

Down in the street, someone was screaming for someone else named Michelle to unlock the car door. The screech of tires immediately thereafter hinted that maybe Michelle had decided to leave the door locked. Despite the darkness, the streetlights on each corner cast a bright red-yellow glow on the tableau of her street. Like actors on a stage, her late-night neighbors slipped across the stage, each focused on their own scripts.

Alex watched the teenagers on the corner exchange a very complicated hand gesture and then part to go their separate ways. An angry young man in ripped jeans appeared, maybe Michelle's jilted boyfriend, and stormed across the street muttering to himself. He passed a limping yellow dog as it exited the alley. The dog paused to push his muzzle around an overflowing trash can before loping down the street and disappearing into the darkness.

Despite its many faults, Alex loved the neighborhood, loved Mr. and Mrs. Ki-hyun who ran the hairdresser shop downstairs. She hated what was happening to her street — the car theft, the broken windows, the graffiti on every surface — but what could she do? Call the police and give them another paper to shuffle at the end of the day? She sighed and moved away from the window. She had enough worries; she could put the world outside her window out of her mind for the day.

It was almost midnight. The sun long since set, and her apartment was filled with shadows. Alex stumbled over her backpack and kicked it out of her way as she wandered toward the kitchen. She turned on the light over the sink and, as she filled a glass from the tap, caught a glimpse of the map still unfolded on the dining room table. She prayed she was wrong. The thought of someone setting fires to kill firefighters, it nauseated her just thinking about someone sick enough to do that.

She carried her water into the living room and sat on the couch in the dark, put her feet up and closed her eyes. She hated waking up so late; it threw off her internal clock. In a few hours, it would be bedtime. She could already see herself, still awake at two in the morning, watching some Eighties sitcom on Nick-at-Nite. The past few weeks, it had been *Family Ties*, so she was hoping for a bit of variety tonight. Maybe Dick Van Dyke or one of Bob Newhart's shows.

Alex loved watching those old shows; just hearing the theme songs reminded her of being nestled under her dad's arm, smelling his cigar smoke, laughing just because he was laughing. She wanted someone to curl up next to during her trips down Memory Lane, but so far no one she'd gone out with could get past the fact that the shows were so old. Nick-At-Nite and TV Land were wastes of cable television, as far as they were concerned. Alex, on the other hand, couldn't imagine Bob Newhart's staccato, stuttering delivery ever becoming passé. He still killed her each and every time.

The phone rang and she grumbled, picking up a cushion off the couch and covering her face with it. "Shut up and leave me alone." After a moment, the fourth ring was silenced and her voice issued from the answering machine: "This is Alex. Go for it."

There was a beep and then she heard, "Alex. Alex. Alex. Alex. Alex."

She tossed the pillow away and grabbed the phone on the ninth "Alex" and shut off the machine. "Hey, Weasel."

"Oh, Alex, did I wake you?"

"What do you think?" she asked. "How are you doing?"

"I'm in a hospital bed with a catheter in a very uncomfortable location. The nurse that I spent half the shift working on just went off duty so I have to start all over with the new one, and the food here sucks."

She sat back and teased, "But other than that?"

"Peaches and cream, baby. The doc wants to keep me another day, claims I have some kind of infection. They just want to keep the ol' Weasel around a little longer. This place is Dullsville, so I really don't blame them for lying to keep me here."

"How dare they?" Alex said, feigning indignation. "You're our entertainment."

He laughed and said, "How about you, girl? Your wrist all right?"

She looked at the wrist she'd burned the day before and worked it back and forth, watching the bandage wrinkle and twist but feeling nothing too bad below. "It's healing nicely, I think. No loss of mobility."

"Good," he said. "Hate to think you were permanently injured trying to save my sorry ass."

Jones's face flashed in front of her, along with the memory of being lifted bodily from the corridor and carried out. She didn't even know who it was that saved her life. She knew he was a Greensboro firefighter, but she hadn't had a chance to learn his name. "I would've stayed," she said softly. "To save Jones. Someone picked me up, carried me out of there."

"From what I've heard, it was a flashover. That Greensboro guy shouldn't even have been in there, but if he hadn't... You know as well as I do that if you'd stayed another ten...hell, if you'd stayed another two seconds you would've roasted alongside Jones. Come on, you saw his body, kid. Wasn't nothing you could've done differently. You think Jones would've wanted someone to die alongside him?"

"We were partners. He was a probie. If anyone was supposed to die..."

"No one is supposed to die. Haven't we taught you anything?" He sighed. "We have a dumbass job where we run into a fire and put it out. Up until, what, twenty or twenty-five years ago, firemen didn't even wear masks into fires. Some people think firefighters have a death wish and a lot of times I can't find a way to disagree with 'em. Alex—"

"Jones shouldn't have been in front of me. I should have been leading the way and—"

"And nothing. You could have gone in first. You could've strapped his turnout gear on for him, too. Helped him aim when he peed. Jones was twenty-one years old. He was a little green, sure, but he was a damned good firefighter. You should feel proud that you gave him a chance to lead the hose."

"He died," Alex repeated. "It was his first time leading and—"

"He lost the Lotto, kid. Could've just as easily been me that let him go first. He might've died on his second entry or his fifth or his ten-thousandth. No use second-guessing, no point in playing what-might-have-been. What happened is what happened and we've got to deal with that."

Alex took a deep breath and turned back to the window. She could see the glow of the downstairs pawn shop all around her window, neon flashing brightly at random intervals. "He prayed. Going to this fire, going to all of them. Guess no one was listening."

"You think he just prayed for himself? You knew Jones. If he was praying for himself, he followed it up with 'and keep an eye on my fellow firemen'. Someone coming through the smoke to yank you out? Maybe someone was listening, you know?"

After a moment, she said, "Thanks, Eric."

"No problem, Alex. I spent about six hours this morning staring out the window coming to the same conclusion. Thought I'd...I don't know, share my wisdom."

"It's appreciated."

"Well, bits of wisdom are so rare for me that I had to tell somebody. And no one else at the firehouse takes my calls anymore."

She smiled again, glancing toward the TV. Bob Newhart was talking with Marcia Wallace. "Thanks, Wizell. You're a good friend. Have there been any more fires today?"

"None I've heard of. Heard sirens earlier, probably just an aid call since there wasn't any smoke I could see."

She nodded. "Here's hoping."

After a moment, he said, "Alex, can I ask you a question?"

"Sure."

"You don't even feel a little guilty for when I got burnt?"

She rolled her eyes and laughed. "No, I don't feel any guilt whatsoever for that."

He sighed wearily into the phone and then said, "Oh. Oh, nurse, hurry. My poor little heart is breaking. Oh, no, nurse!"

Alex laughed and touched her face, surprised to find it dry. "Weasel, I'm glad you're... I'm glad you made it."

"And I'm glad you weren't hurt worse than you were. All us guys, we...you're our sister, you know?"

She found herself oddly touched by that sentiment. When she'd first signed on with the department, she had gotten the cold shoulder from everyone. She had her own bathroom and some other women in a neighboring firehouse had started a petition to get separate changing rooms, too. Alex had passed on signing, instead stringing up a sheet to block her corner cubby from the rest of the room. After that, the guys started to realize she didn't expect or want special treatment. When Murray had instigated a water war with her, she knew they were coming around. But this...calling her "sister". She smiled at the phone. "Thanks, Weasel."

"Okay. I gotta go. The redheaded nurse is coming back and I want her to think I'm at death's door. They tend to play fast and loose with the sponge baths when they think you're gonna die."

"Just make sure they don't shave anything."

He was quiet for a moment and then sheepishly asked, "W-what would they...they shave?"

She laughed and said goodbye, hanging up on him and stretching out on the couch again. A five-minute phone call from Weasel and, all of a sudden, she didn't feel quite so bad about everything. She was alive, barely injured, she had a date with a beautiful woman in less than twenty-four hours, and Bob Newhart was on TV. What was there to complain about?

He had the plans laid out in front of him, the perfect spots for his presentation marked. The fire would look small, easy to extinguish, but the hot spots. They would prove most deadly if the firefighters weren't extremely careful. And they had no reason to be cautious. He guesstimated where the fire engine would park, figuring what the collapse zone would be. What was it, one-and-a-half times the height of the building? He wasn't sure. He figured two times, just to be on the safe side.

The news was replaying their late-night footage of the fire and he paused, riveted by the coverage of his handiwork. He drummed his fingertips on the edge of the table as they pulled the body out; cursing the damn firemen who'd held a sheet up to block the shot. Way to ruin the moment. He sighed and moved closer to the TV, getting a closer look at them. The big one's jacket said Murray. The other one...

Alexandra Crawford. The media had talked about her earlier in the day, saying that she'd been inches away from death herself. Apparently, she'd been on her hands and knees behind the male firefighter, escaping death only because of the order in which they'd gone into the building. Irony. He was a huge fan of it. He grinned. "Alexandra Crawford," he said quietly. "I promise to aim for you next time." If she survived, he would know she was worthy of his attention. If not, well, if not, then he'd have his sacrifice.

When the newscast moved on to other local news, he returned to his table and sat down, arranging his toys. He put a toy fire truck on the plans, wondering how tall the ladder actually was. It would have to reach the roof, of course, so they could ventilate.

The roof... He checked the information on the building and smiled. The rafters. The firefighters would be very careful when cutting ventilation. They would be certain not to cut any rafters. But if the rafters were already severed...well, then, that would make for a very interesting chain reaction, wouldn't it?

He stifled a laugh and began to outline his new plan.

"Ki-hyun Hair and Nails," the high pitched female voice crackled. "How I help you?"

"Hey, Moon, it's Alex."

"Alex. How nice of you to call."

Alex smiled at how much Moon's accent diminished when she realized she was talking to a friend. The way Moon explained it, people had a certain expectation of what a Korean hairdresser should sound like. She didn't want to be the one to disappoint them. "I may need your services."

Moon half gasped, half groaned into the phone. "That mop you call hair? Shave it all off; say you're a boy until it starts to grow out some. We'll start from scratch."

"Hey, come on," Alex said. She bent down and looked at her reflection in the door of the microwave. She plucked a few of the strands off her forehead and wrinkled her nose. "It's not that bad." And it was much better than tying her hair into pigtails on the way to a fire. It was easier to just cut it short and ignore it. "I h-have a date tonight."

Another sound from Moon, this time half laughter and half shriek. "Ooh, Alex finally found someone who meets all the requirements? Wonders never cease. And if your hair is 'not that bad', why're you calling me before a big date to make you look good?"

"Good?" Alex asked, surprised.

"Marvelous, dear; I meant to say marvelous. Sorry, I forgot who I was for a minute. Won't happen again. Now, you're off all day today, so all afternoon is the window, yes?"

"Any time, yeah. Earlier is better..."

There was a shuffling of papers and then Moon said, "Okay, and when are you meeting this big, life-changing, soul mate of a person?"

"Tonight at eight."

"Excellent, excellent. Hmm, well, okay. I can get you in at four in the afternoon. With your disaster of a hairstyle — if I may take the liberty of calling it that — it'll take about an hour to get done. Good?"

Alex nodded and made a note. Three hours before the big date. It wouldn't give her much time to ruin all the work Moon did. "Okay. Sounds perfect."

Her voice dropping into a teasing cadence, Moon asked, "And you have a nice dress for the date, yes?"

She rolled her eyes. "Moon, I'm going to wear slacks."

Moon grunted. "Such a lady."

Alex laughed. "I'll see you this afternoon."

"Four o'clock. Don't be late. I'm going to need every second of it. Oh, the horrors I'll be facing..."

"Goodbye, Moon. Say hello to your husband for me."

"Kim will be here this afternoon, tell him yourself. He misses you."

"I'll be sure and bring him a tuna sandwich."

Moon gasped and said, "Trollop! Home wrecker! I'm hanging up on you!"

The call was disconnected and Alex laughed, shaking her head. First Weasel, then Moon. Nothing like a couple of phone calls with good friends to make her forget the hell she'd been through twenty-four hours ago. She hung up and looked at her reflection again and ruffled her black hair. "It's not that bad," she repeated as she headed for the front door.

She'd spent most of the night on the couch, dozing, while Bob Newhart ran an inn, and finally going to bed while Ted Danson tried to free Shelley Long from the floor of his bar. She'd slept almost until noon, stretching her tired muscles the entire time she'd been setting the hair appointment with Moon. Now it was time for some real exercise. She dressed in her department sweats and went out for a jog.

She parked a few extra blocks from her jogging trail to make up for missing the day before. She had her iPod playing, but she was mostly using the music to block the outside world. As soon as her sneakers began pounding out their familiar rhythm, her mind shifted back to thoughts of arson.

Two fires in one twenty-four hour period; it couldn't be a coincidence. The only explanation was that Shepherd had a firebug. The thought of someone intentionally setting fires made her want to hunt the guy down and force him to inhale several lungfuls of smoke. Serve him right.

Of course, she thought, watching a couple of people light up cigarettes near the pond, *some people might not find that to be a very painful torture.* She shook her head as she followed the trail into the woods, checking her time and smiling at the result.

Leary still hadn't returned her call, but she wasn't surprised. Days off were for family. There was no big hurry. The town had gone twenty-four whole hours without a third fire. Maybe the guy had been scared off by how big the second one had gotten. Her heart told her that wasn't the case. These guys liked the big booms, and they really got off on the fires that killed someone. They were freaks who thrived on destruction.

She remembered once, when she was still a probie herself, when they'd all been out drinking at a local pub. Murray and Franklin left early and spotted a kid playing with a firecracker in the alley. She wasn't exactly sure what transpired afterward, but Leary had assured her that the kid would never even see another match without twitching.

Maybe when she became a chief she'd force them to tell her.

As she was heading for the cool down portion of her jog, she realized her cell phone was vibrating against her hip. She slowed, checking the readout — Unknown Caller — before she yanked out the earplugs and answered the phone. "Alex Crawford."

"Um, Alex? Rachel Tom."

"Rachel, hi!" She stopped completely and bent forward, resting her hand on one knee.

"Am I...interrupting something?"

Alex realized then that she was panting into the mouthpiece like some late-night pervert. "Sorry, uh, you caught me while I was jogging. I've been thinking about where we should go tonight. I mean, if you still want to go to the Lumber, then by all means—"

"No, I'm not married to the place. Have you thought of someplace better?"

"There's a place not far from the firehouse. It's..." She swallowed and shrugged. "Well, it's a theme restaurant." Rachel laughed and Alex wondered how she could save that sound as her ring tone.

"It wouldn't happen to be a firefighter theme, would it?"

"Well, it just so happens..." Rachel laughed again. "A priest, a rabbi, and a snake walked into a bar..."

"Wait, what?" Rachel asked, sounding confused.

"Nothing. I just wanted to hear you laugh again." She blushed at how corny that sounded — she seemed to be making a habit of saying corny things to this woman — but it seemed to work.

"Fresh," Rachel said with a chuckle. "Okay, I'll meet you at..."

Alex grinned. "It's called Vollie's."

"Mm hmm," Rachel said. "Maybe over dinner you can explain to me why it's called that. Is eight still a good time?"

"Yeah. Eight would be wonderful. Do...do you need me to pick you up or..."

"That would be fine. Do you know Spring Creek Apartments?" Alex didn't, so Rachel gave her directions. "I'm in Apartment 4-B. I'm looking forward to it."

"Same here. See you then."

"All right."

Alex hung up and was about to hook the phone back onto her waistband when a thought struck her. She opened the phone again and dialed the police station, moving from one foot to the other as she waited for the dispatcher to answer. "Shepherd Police Department, this is Nancy. How may I direct your call?"

"Hey, Nancy, this is Alex Crawford."

"Oh, hi."

Alex spoke quickly before the receptionist could get sidetracked into small talk. "Listen, is Bill Von Elm around?" Von Elm was the fire marshal for Shepherd and would most likely have already snooped around both sites at least a little.

Nancy checked and came back quickly. "I think he just headed out to look at one of your fires from yesterday." After a hesitation, she asked, "Were you at either of those?"

"Both, actually," Alex said, leaving out the part about being with both of the firefighters who'd been injured.

"Oh my goodness; how awful."

"It's the job," she said, her mood darkening a bit. "Listen, Nancy, just let Bill know I'm looking for him. It's not urgent, but—"

"I understand. I'll let him know, hon."

Alex thanked her and hooked the phone back on her waistband. She looked down the path. The end seemed to be miles away. As fast as her heart had been racing during the conversation with Rachel, she decided maybe she didn't need to run the rest of the way. The thought of Rachel banished the unpleasant thoughts her chat with Nancy had brought back and, smiling, Alex started to walk the path.

He couldn't very well contract anyone to do it for him, so he was forced to take matters into his own hands. His neighbor had a reciprocating saw that would be perfect. He searched the man's tool shed for what felt like ages, disturbing several generations of hobo spiders and finally locating the tool in a box marked "Sawzall." Though he'd seen it in action, it took him about half an hour to figure out how to work the damn thing properly. He could have asked his neighbor, but then the man would know he'd taken it. Couldn't have that, not at this early date.

He took the tool home with him and practiced cutting. He used two-by-fours from his garage to determine how to wield it, how deep to cut and at what angle. Then he nailed a few boards to the ceiling and practiced cutting upside-down, since he would be applying the blade to ceiling rafters.

When he finished his experimentation, he smiled at his handiwork and pulled off his safety glasses. Sawdust covered his shoes and the floor around him, and he sat down, crossing his legs Indian-style. He used his finger to draw in the sawdust like a child with finger paints. Only his drawing would, hopefully, lead to the death of a firefighter.

Chapter Six
Next to the P in SOUP

Rachel lifted her leg from the tub and watched the water slide down her calf before she submerged it again. She shifted in the water and let herself sink a little to get her hair wet. She'd started the bath immediately upon getting home from work and had been soaking for almost half an hour, her toes and fingers already hopelessly pruned. She'd started out reading, but found herself unable to concentrate on the words. Her mind kept going back to the date she had in a few hours. With a firefighter.

She'd spent the last few hours trying to remember what had possessed her to make the first move, but it was hopeless. Alex Crawford was not her typical date. She tended to go for intellectual types, the kind she found in libraries with their noses buried in a giant book. She liked shy women, women who wore glasses and frumpy sweaters; the kind that really came out of their shells given the right prompting.

She shuddered in the bath and smiled at herself.

Alex definitely wasn't her typical shrinking violet, but something about the way she had looked at the hospital... Rachel wasn't a believer in love at first sight; in her mind, nothing stronger than lust at first sight was possible. The only time she'd ever been in love, it had taken her a long time to realize it. Almost too long. She brought her hand out of the water and brushed her cheek, leaving a wet trail behind anyway. The hurt of that relationship's end had caused her to be careful, safe, when it came to dating. But it seemed she was determined to change that with Alex. Maybe she had been playing it safe too long. And, really, wasn't "careful" the dumbest word in the world to describe a relationship?

Whatever the reason, she was drawn to Alex Crawford, firefighter with nerves of steel and a quiet demeanor, and was powerless to stop herself.

She craned her neck and looked at the clock next to the sink. She had plenty of time, but she decided bath time was over. She had to get ready for her date.

The front window of Ki-hyun Hair & Nails was half covered by the ornate sign that Kim had painted himself, showing a sunset over what Alex assumed to be a Korean beach. Inside, the shop was long and narrow. Vanities lined the wall to the left and right, separated from the waiting area at the front of the shop by a waist-high counter. The vanities had tables that could swing out from the wall so the stylist could work on nails without moving to a different station.

Kim, a sweet old man with snow white hair and an eternal smile on his face, had his back to Alex when she came through the front door. He was singing under his breath as he swept hair from the floor around the chairs. He wore a bright pink shirt underneath his pale white apron and moved the broom with quick, short movements. Alex held up a bag from the Subway down the street and said, "Hey, Kim, ready for a break?"

He looked up, eyes shining when he saw Alex and his jaw dropping when he saw the sandwich. "Six-inch tuna?"

"On wheat. Do I know you, or what?"

He put down the broom and hurried over, taking the bag and pecking her on the cheek. "You're too good to me, too good. You should come in here more often."

"That's what I tell her, all the good it does," Moon said. She was walking out of the back room of the store, pushing aside the curtain that covered the entrance, and shook her head when she saw Alex's hair. "It's so much worse than I thought. You, what, rub soot on your head when you're at fires? This is what you do to cause poor Moon to have a heart attack?"

"You should hear her when someone comes in with split ends." Kim chuckled as he took a seat and carefully unfolded the paper from around his sub sandwich. "End of the world time."

Moon went to the nearest seat and swiveled it around, patting the back. "Okay, Firelady, you come and sit here. I have another appointment at five minutes past five and I am going to need every minute between now and then on your atrocity of a head."

"Sweet talker." Alex grinned as she walked over and took her seat.

Moon looked at her husband. "I thought you were sweeping."

He put a hand over his heart. "And miss watching my wife work a miracle? Never."

Moon tutted and turned to face Alex. "Sweet talker, eh?"

"He knows how to get on your good side, that's for sure."

Kim took a big bite of his sandwich and grinned at them both.

Thirty minutes later, Moon turned the chair around for Alex to face the mirror and held out her hands. "There and voilá." She clapped once and then planted both hands on her hips. "How do you think about your hair now, Firelady?"

Alex turned her head to look at the sides. "It's...um...nice."

"Nice?"

"And, I don't know, a little shorter than usual?" She laughed at Moon's stricken look. "What? I'm sorry. I really don't... I really can't tell what you did."

Moon gasped and snapped her fingers at her husband. "Get me the clippers. I shave her head."

"No, no, just...what? Point it out to me."

Moon sighed and stepped around Alex's chair. She picked up a bottle off her table and pointed it at Alex like a gun. "First, this is a miracle product. Very important. You should try to find a bottle of this that you can afford on your salary, because it's very, very expensive and rare. It's called conditioner."

"I use shampoo," Alex said, but she took the bottle from the irate Korean.

"Shampoo. Okay. Fine and dandy. Next time you go to a fire, I hand you a little bitty fire extinguisher and have you go to work with just that." She walked around behind Alex and clutched her head with both hands. "Your hair, it cries to me, Alex. It cries and I can't bear it. Oh, the screams of terror from your poor, neglected hairs. Each one, like a screaming banshee to me." Throughout her tirade, she whipped Alex's head back and forth, forcing her to hold on to the armrests to keep from falling to the floor.

When Moon released her, Alex said, "Okay, okay, fine." She looked again at her reflection. "So this is all just from conditioner?"

"It's not really a miracle gel, sweetheart. I also highlighted it." She put her face next to Alex's, gesturing to the mirror. "Here, here...it's a little lighter brown. Brings out your eyes."

"My eyes are blue," Alex said.

"You want I should give you blue highlights? Punk rocker blue or little old lady blue? I have both." She feathered Alex's hair, motioning at the mirror when she finished. "You see? Moon worked miracle. Made you look delicious and oh so irresistible. Your date, bah, won't know what hit her."

Alex grinned. "Thanks, Moon; how much do I owe you?"

"One promise. You will put on make-up before you go on your date. A little lipstick, even. Maybe eyeliner. Just something, because your date, she deserves to be proud of the woman she's with, right?"

"Okay, Moon, I promise."

"And details. That will be my tip. I want all the details. Tomorrow."

"I'm back on duty tomorrow."

Moon's eyes widened and she took a step back. "You will put my masterpiece under a helmet? With smoke? Oh, why do you torture me so, Alex? Why do you let my beauties live only one day?"

Alex grinned and leaned in, pecking Moon on the cheek. "I'll give you all the juicy details as soon as I can. And I'll do my best to keep the hair from getting too mussed."

"On the job," Kim called from the back room. He'd finished his sandwich long ago and was watching TV. He pushed aside the curtain and said, "Avoid mussing it on the job. Finger mussing during the date is okay."

"Dirty old man," Alex and Moon muttered in stereo.

Alex went upstairs and practically emptied out her closet searching for something appropriate to wear. She finally settled on a white dress shirt under a black blazer. She added a pair of jeans, hoping to give the date a casual air. She soaked in a long bath, knowing Moon would murder her slowly if she ruined her hair. After the bath, she rubbed lotion into her hands and elbows. She loved her job, but it wasn't exactly kind to her hands. The fingernails that weren't chewed short had dirt underneath them. She found the clippers and trimmed them all to a more or less uniform length.

She dressed and went to the bathroom vanity to eye the archaeological remains of the last time she'd worn make-up. A few clear nail polishes, a lipstick here and there, and one or two eyeliner pens were all that remained from her last date.

Alex nervously applied some lipstick and fiddled with some eyeliner, kicking herself for feeling so anxious. This was high school graduation, her first kiss, and coming out to her best friend all over again. She messed with her hair again, finally seeing the highlights Moon had added. She exhaled sharply. "You'll do fine. She asked you out. She's already interested. Ball is in her court."

She checked her wallet, made sure her cell phone was charged, and turned on her answering machine before she stepped out into the hallway. It was six-thirty. She had an hour and a half to get to Rachel's apartment.

Spring Creek Apartments stood four stories tall, a narrow slip of brick building nestled between two others. Alex approached from the west and looked up the alley next to the building. Her mind

immediately began calculating the problems they would face
fighting a fire here: a narrow alley, and close proximity to the
neighboring buildings that could cause the fire to spread more
easily. With a strong enough wind, the entire block would be in
danger.

She put the thoughts out of her mind and pressed the buzzer
marked "TOM". After a moment, Rachel's voice came through the
tinny speaker box.

"Alex?"

"Hi, it's me, Alex." *Which she'd know, since she just said your
name*, she growled at herself. She looked at her watch and added,
"I'm a little early..."

"No, it's fine. Come on up."

The buzzer sounded and Alex stepped into the air-conditioned
foyer. The building didn't just seem cool, it seemed chill. She
repressed the shudder and moved across the artfully faded yellow
tile. There was a flight of stairs leading up, but she walked past
them to the antiquated elevator in the corner. Taking the stairs
would give Rachel a few extra seconds to get ready, but four flights
of stairs also increased the risk that Alex would start sweating. The
risk of sweating was already bad, considering how she reacted
around this woman, so she didn't want to tempt Fate.

As she rode the elevator up, she second- and third-guessed
herself about her decision not to bring flowers or chocolates. She
just wasn't sure whether that was in style anymore, or if Rachel
only ate healthy things or, God forbid, if she had allergies. At that
thought, she sniffed her unbandaged wrist and prayed her perfume
was all right.

The elevator deposited her at the fourth floor. The staircase
was to her left, and she looked at it as if noting an escape route.
Always a firefighter, she thought as she turned her mind toward
the date. The short landing offered her only two options; the first
and closest door, to the immediate right of the elevator, was
unpainted and unmarked. Straight ahead, however, was a lovingly
maintained green door with a gold 4-B hanging above the
peephole. Alex stepped up, rapped her knuckles just below the
number, and stepped back. She tugged the cuff of her jacket down
in a futile attempt to hide her bandage. She didn't know why she
bothered; Rachel obviously knew about the wound. But her vanity
got the better of her and she continued to adjust the sleeve when it
rode up a bit.

"Just a second."

The voice came from deep inside the apartment, so Alex relaxed a bit. She looked down at her hands, wondering whether to put them in her pockets or clasp her wrist behind her back or... She sighed. Holding flowers or chocolates at least would have given her something to do with her hands. It was probably why the practice had begun in the first place.

She fiddled with the edge of her jacket and wondered if she should have heeded Moon's suggestion of a dress. *No*, she told herself firmly. *Not at Vollie's. It's bad enough I'll be there with a date. If someone spotted me in a dress, I would never hear the end of it.*

She was considering taking the jacket off when the door suddenly swung open and Rachel appeared in her robe. She held up one hand and held the robe closed with the other. "No, no, before you ask, you're right on time. I'm just a little rushed here. Sorry. Come on in; make yourself comfortable."

Rachel opened the door a little wider and Alex stepped inside. Motioning toward the living room, Rachel said, "I'll just be a minute."

She disappeared down a dark corridor that branched off to the left of the front door and a few seconds later, Alex heard a door close. Alex wandered past the wall that divided the hall and the living room, impressed at the size of the apartment.

The living room took up the majority of the apartment's space, being combined with the dining room to leave more area for the kitchen. The only light came from two lamps on either side of the room, which made Alex want to kick off her shoes and curl up for a nap. The couch and armchairs were focused on the picture window rather than the television. Alex walked across the room, her eye drawn to the ceiling as she stepped over the threshold. A nearly opaque skylight dominated, directly over the couch. Alex resisted the urge to whistle at the sight and instead examined Rachel's bookshelf.

Books swarmed the four shelves, some crammed diagonally across the tops of others. She recognized a few author names, one or two books she'd been meaning to look for at the library and more than a couple that she'd bought herself. She heard the bedroom door open and smiled, turning to Rachel. "You have great... Wow!"

"Great wow?" Rachel smiled. She was wearing a red kimono-style blouse, the sleeves ending just below her shoulders and leaving her arms mostly bare. The high neck of the shirt was just barely touched by the loose strands of Rachel's raven black hair, her eyes dancing in the weak light of the living room. She wore a black skirt, cut just below the knee. "What were you going to say?"

"I..." Alex swallowed. "I'm sorry. It was something about books."

Rachel laughed again. "So I guess I look all right?"

"Understatement," Alex said dryly.

"So, shall we?" Rachel motioned at the front door. Alex stepped forward and followed Rachel from the apartment. Rachel locked the apartment door while Alex pressed the elevator call button. The doors swished open almost immediately and Alex rested her hand against the small of Rachel's back to usher her into the car. Rachel tensed again, but only for an instant. Alex shifted her hand to Rachel's hip as they moved to stand side-by-side in the small car.

Rachel said, "You look really great tonight."

Alex scoffed, "Next to you, I probably shouldn't have bothered. You look outstanding."

"I think you mentioned something about that," Rachel said with a chuckle. "But no, I'm serious. You did something with your hair, right?"

Alex grinned in spite of herself. "You just made an overly dramatic Korean woman very, very happy. Yes, I did get some highlights."

"It suits you." The elevator doors opened and they stepped out. Rachel said goodnight to someone passing by them in the lobby and let Alex hold the door for her as they went out into the night. There was a chill in the air and, without thinking, Alex put her arm around Rachel and drew her in.

Rachel smiled. "Thank you."

Alex didn't reply, but rubbed Rachel's bare shoulder to keep it warm until they reached the Jeep.

"That thing you do with your hand," Rachel said.

"What, putting my hand on your back?"

"Yeah, that." Rachel smiled for a moment and then nodded, as if coming to a conclusion about something. "I like that."

"Oh." Alex opened the door for Rachel and jogged around the front of the car, sliding behind the wheel. "You buckled?"

Rachel patted the seatbelt. "Yep. I'm starved. I skipped lunch in anticipation of tonight. What kind of food does Vollie's serve?"

"Steak, a lobster plate..." Her face paled and she looked at Rachel. "Oh, God, you're not a vegetarian, are you?"

"Once, in college. But I was drunk and it didn't mean anything."

Alex laughed out loud. "God. I'm so nervous about everything being perfect for tonight. I even decided against bringing chocolates because I didn't know if you were a health food nut or... N-not that I'm calling you a nut."

Rachel laughed. "Alex, relax. This is a date. If it goes perfectly, it goes perfectly. If not, we'll have a funny story to tell our friends at dinner parties. First dates do not make or break a relationship. Oh, second date. Excuse me. This is our second date."

"Is it?" Alex thought for a moment and remembered their conversation at Peter's. "Right. I guess it is. I just keep feeling like I'm on a job interview. That if I don't impress you, I won't have another chance and I'll lose you." She exhaled. "And now I'm scaring you off."

Rachel smiled in the darkness. "Alex? What are you doing next Saturday?"

"What?"

"Humor me."

"I think...I think I'm working."

"Friday, then?"

"I don't know. I'm probably going to be off one of those days."

Rachel nodded. "Okay, then. Either Friday or Saturday, you're going to come to my apartment and I'll cook for you. You don't have to worry about getting another date with me, which means that the outcome of this date is a moot point. Does that make you feel better?"

Alex took a deep breath and exhaled slowly. "Strangely enough, it does."

Rachel reached over and rested her hand on Alex's forearm, squeezing once before pulling her hand back. Alex shuddered, forcing herself to keep her face neutral.

Riding a few blocks in silence, Alex stole a glance at Rachel and saw the other woman smiling absently. "What?" she asked.

"Hmm?"

"You're smiling."

"Oh, sorry. I've...it's been a while since I've been on a date."

Alex nodded. "Ah. So, shouldn't you be the nervous one, then?"

"I don't know," Rachel said. "Sometimes I feel like I'm just sleepwalking."

When Alex looked over again, she saw pain in Rachel's eyes before she turned away. She wanted to know more, but there seemed to be a barrier between them that hadn't existed a few minutes earlier. Alex hesitated, then reached over and put her hand on Rachel's thigh. "I'd like to wake you up."

She pulled her hand away, kicking herself for sounding like such an idiot, such a moronic cliché. She turned to apologize and saw a tear on Rachel's cheek. "I'm sorry, I shouldn't—"

"No, it was the right thing to say," Rachel said softly. "Thank you."

They continued the ride in silence until a tan brick building rolled into view. "Okay, here we are," Alex said as she pulled into the parking lot, passing an antique fire truck that was on display like the newest SUV at a car lot. Two bright lights were focused on either side of the truck, revealing banners that said "VOLLIE'S". A smaller font went on to warn that this was "Restaurant Parking Only" and that "Violators Will Be Torched".

"You were going to tell me what that means."

"Vollie's," Alex said. "It's what we call volunteer firefighters. Like the new guy is a probie. It's firefighter lingo."

"Oh, okay," Rachel said. "And you said they have steak?"

Alex nodded. "Some of the best, melt-in-your-mouth, steak in town."

"I can't wait."

Alex parked near the fire truck and took a moment to get her things together. Rachel took the opportunity to get an up close look at the display truck. The cab was open air, with a hose wound on one side and a ladder neatly folded on top. She tried to imagine such a dinosaur responding to a fire in this day and age and couldn't. When she turned, Alex was standing at the back of her Jeep, smiling over at her.

Rachel gestured at the truck over her shoulder as she walked back over. "You get to ride one of these every day?"

"On a bad day, I ride it three or four times. Of course, ours is a tad more modern."

Rachel stepped off the platform and accepted the hand that Alex offered. "I would hope so. But still, it's impressive; such an elaborate display for a restaurant."

"Wait until you see inside," Alex said as she guided Rachel up the sidewalk.

The building was designed to look like a firehouse. The windows were framed by faux garage doors. A stone Dalmatian stood guard at the front door and Alex rubbed his head as she passed. "For luck at my next fire," she said.

Rachel pulled her hand from Alex's and went back to rub both hands over the cold, gray head of the statue. She walked back to

Alex with a grin. "That should take care of you for the next few fires."

Alex laughed and opened the door to the main restaurant.

There was a line, but the hostess spotted Alex and waved her forward. "Alex," the girl said with a bright smile. She turned to the next couple in line and said, "Folks, this woman is a Shepherd firefighter. Would you mind if we allowed her and her companion...?"

She didn't have a chance to finish; heads started nodding immediately. The hostess guided them through the main restaurant to a secondary room.

It was smaller, more intimate, with more space between the tables. Each table had a black lantern with a small candle burning inside, transforming the dining area into an intimate dining room. The hostess sat them in one of the back booths where they could have a little bit of extra privacy, and promised to send a waiter over to take their order.

"This place is fantastic," Rachel said, lowering her voice despite their solitude. "I don't know why I've never heard of it before."

"Firefighters really keep it afloat. A lot of citizens get perturbed by the long line; others are irritated when we get to jump right to the front." She shook her head. "They'll eat at a restaurant devised in our honor, but show us a little bit of courtesy..."

Rachel picked up the menu. "My father used to pay for civil servants when he saw them in restaurants. If someone was wearing an official t-shirt or a uniform of some kind, he'd discreetly ask the waitress to bring him their check and he would pay for it. Ninety percent of the time, we were gone before they had any idea what he'd done."

"That happens sometimes, but don't order the steak and lobster and then cross your fingers."

"Yes, ma'am." Rachel smiled as she opened the menu and saw that newspaper clippings and official department photographs framed the list of entrees. She scanned the photographs at the top and said, "These are fantastic pictures."

Alex glanced up from her menu and gasped when she saw what page Rachel was on. "Rachel, don't look at the—"

"Oh, my God," Rachel whispered.

"...soup page," Alex finished. She sagged in her seat and closed her eyes in anticipation of Rachel's reaction to what she was seeing.

Next to the P in "SOUP", Alex Crawford was standing on a sidewalk in a soaked, formerly white shirt. Her shirt was drenched and see-through, her white bra standing out in vivid relief against the dark of her skin. Her hair was plastered to her skull from the spray behind her and she was looking off to her right like someone on the cover of a romance novel. Her sleeves were rolled up to her elbows, showing off muscular forearms that were wet and glistening in the sun. She had both hands in front of her, holding a limp stretch of hose. There was a brick building behind her, the windows broken out and smoke still rising from them. The photo was in sepia, the edges given the same charred effect the rest of the menu had.

Rachel covered her mouth and looked up at the mortified Alex. "Oh, my God," she repeated.

"That was taken at a charity event. We were supposed to be demonstrating firefighting techniques, but it turned into a bit of a water fight instead. Murray drenched me with the hose and I was looking for some payback. I didn't know anyone had taken a picture. Well, I mean, I saw the flash, but I didn't know it was for something that so many people would see time and again. I only agreed to let it be in the menu in the interest of charity." A red flush was rising in her cheeks. "Can we please move past the mocking stage?"

"Mocking?" Rachel echoed, looking at the picture again. "Dear me, you're hot."

Alex looked up. "What?"

"Can I buy one of these menus?"

Alex's blush deepened and she tried to snatch the menu away from Rachel. "Give me that."

"Unh uh." Rachel turned in her seat so Alex couldn't reach it. "I'm taking this home. I'm having it framed." She clicked her tongue. "My date is a celebrity. I don't know if I'll be able to contain myself."

Alex sighed. "Do you want me to order for you, or are you just going to have soup?"

Rachel turned the page and said, "All right, all right." She scanned the photos in the rest of the menu, all of them local firefighters.

The waitress approached to take their drink orders. She was dressed in custom made turnout pants, extra wide red suspenders and a t-shirt that read *Vollie's Fire Department* over the left breast. She was a perky redhead whose nametag read Sheila. They ordered their drinks — a house wine — and salad — Caesars for both — and sat back to wait for Sheila to return.

Rachel smiled. "So. The picture, do you still model?"

Alex groaned and put her head down on the table as Rachel laughed.

Chapter Seven
Don't Be That Jackass

During the entire meal, only two other couples were seated in the special dining area, but they were strategically placed so that each party was as far as possible from the others. Alex insisted Rachel order the goat eyes, refusing to tell her what they were. When they arrived, Alex fed one of the grilled mushrooms to her date, laughing when Rachel snapped at her fingers.

Over their salads, Alex talked about her parents, her time in the academy, and some of the more memorable pranks she'd played and that had been played on her. Rachel, in turn, told about her family and residency, during the main course.

Halfway through the meal, Rachel excused herself to use the restroom. The waitress pointed her to a small corridor branching off the main dining area. She told Alex she'd be right back and weaved through the tables, taking time to gaze at all the marvelous memorabilia throughout the restaurant. There were dozens of framed newspaper stories. Most of the stories showed the hometown boys and girls in action, but some were of historic fires: The Great Chicago Fire of 1871, the Tillamook Burn of Oregon, the burning of Atlanta in 1864.

There were hoses on the walls, long hooks, and a variety of SCBA facepieces. On a shelf that ran the length of the room just below the ceiling, rows of helmets stood like soldiers awaiting roll call. The shields on the front of the helmets represented the various firefighting companies in Shepherd.

When she turned the corner for the bathroom, she caught sight of the most elaborate piece of memorabilia. The wall between the men's room and the women's was dominated by a full firefighter uniform. The helmet was flat against the wall, the crown facing out. The rest of it was arranged as if an invisible man were occupying the pants and jacket.

Rachel stepped up to the disembodied uniform, imagining she could smell the smoke coming off the material. On either side of the suit hung more framed newspaper clippings from the local paper detailing rescues and fires. She recognized a few of the names. Leary and Franklin jumped out at her, but she saw no mention of Alex in any of the pieces. She was about to read one of the articles when she remembered why she'd gotten up in the first place. Casting a final glance at the phantom fireman, she went into the ladies room.

By the time Rachel paid — she insisted, and actually slapped Alex's hand when she reached for the check — the restaurant had pretty much cleared out. They thanked the hostess and headed out into the night. Rachel immediately hugged herself against the cold wind. Alex put her arm around her date, amazed at how automatic the move already was. She kissed Rachel's temple as they parted to get into the Jeep.

Rachel scanned the empty parking lot. "Wow, how long were we sitting there talking?"

Alex checked her watch. "It's just gone eleven."

Rachel whistled. "I'm so sorry. I didn't realize I was being such a chatterbox."

"Yes, well, you should have paid attention to all my complaints," Alex said with a grin. "I don't have to be in until noon tomorrow. When do you have to be at work?"

"Ten AM."

"Oh, so not so bad," Alex said.

"Not bad at all."

Back in the Jeep, Rachel made use of the headrest, closed her eyes and let herself sway with the motion of the car as Alex drove her home. When the Jeep came to a stop, she pretended to be asleep just to see what Alex would do. She felt Alex's knuckles brush her cheek, felt a hand cup the side of her head.

"Hey," Alex said softly.

She opened her eyes. "Am I home?"

"I got you here safely," Alex said.

The streetlight on the corner illuminated half of Alex's face and gave her a halo.

Rachel straightened in her seat and, reluctant to end the date so soon, said, "I had a great time. We're going to have to try Vollie's again."

"We?" Alex smiled and raised an eyebrow. "So, with you cooking for me next week, would that be our third date?"

Rachel grinned and said, "Mm, I don't know. With the coffee and tonight, yes, that would be the third."

Alex caressed Rachel's cheek again and leaned across the console. Rachel closed her eyes and her lips parted slightly as Alex slid closer to her. Alex captured Rachel's bottom lip between both of hers. Rachel cupped the back of Alex's head and moaned softly as she angled her mouth against Alex's. They held each other for a moment before they parted. Rachel's tongue flitted out and touched her top lip as she sank back into her seat.

"Mmm." She smiled dreamily and looked up at Alex.

"Was that okay?"

"Hm, ho, yes." Rachel looked up at Alex. "Yeah. Yeah, that was...yeah."

Alex smiled. "Well, you made me speechless at the beginning of the night. Looks like we're even."

"Looks like," Rachel said happily.

Alex climbed out of the car and opened Rachel's door for her. Rachel led the way to the front door and punched in a code on the call button pad. The door buzzed, Rachel opened it, and ushered Alex inside. They walked into the dimly lit lobby and Alex waited by the elevator with her. Rachel pressed the button and smiled up at Alex. "I had a lovely time tonight."

"I'm glad. I was afraid it might have been all one-sided."

"No," Rachel assured her. The elevator doors opened with a ding and Rachel looked into the car, reluctance in her eyes. "I'd invite you in for tea, but we probably wouldn't end up drinking very much tea."

"What makes you so sure?"

"I don't have any tea."

Alex laughed and kissed Rachel again, just to the left of her eyebrow. "That's okay. I really should get home and get some sleep."

"Just so long as you want to come upstairs," Rachel teased.

Alex touched a loose strand of Rachel's hair and bent down to kiss her again. She slid her hand from Rachel's shoulder down to the small of her back, settling her fingers just above the curve of her ass. Her tongue flicked against Rachel's teeth, her arms tightening around the other woman before releasing her. Rachel staggered back a step, touched her bottom lip and nodded. "Okay. So you're willing to come upstairs."

"When you're ready for me," Alex said softly.

Rachel rose again and kissed the corner of Alex's mouth. "I'll call you about next weekend."

"Okay."

"Thank you for dinner."

"You paid for dinner."

"But you made it worth paying for."

Alex laughed. "Well, thank you for asking me out."

Rachel laughed as she stepped into the elevator. As the doors began to close, Alex put her hand out and stopped them. "Oh. I meant to ask, I know it's kind of weird, but the higher ups are planning Jones's funeral. I'll understand if you don't want to go, it being a funeral and all, but..."

"I'd love to be there for you," Rachel said solemnly. "Just give me a call and let me know where and when."

"Great." Alex thought a moment and then added, "You know, we've basically just booked ourselves into at least a month long relationship."

Rachel laughed. "I'll restrain my cry of horror until I'm safely in my apartment."

They exchanged their goodnights and Alex stepped back. She hated feeling needy, but she was a little down even before the elevator doors fully closed. Once the doors bumped shut and the light above the door disappeared, indicating that Rachel was on her way up, Alex turned away. She made it as far as the stairs before an idea hit her.

With little thought as to how it would look, she suddenly dashed to her left. She used the banister to whip herself around at each landing, taking the stairs three at a time, huffing and puffing until she came to a stop outside the fourth floor elevators. She made it with nearly a whole second to spare. The doors opened on Rachel's smiling face and she stepped forward before she realized there was someone in front of her.

"What—"

Alex didn't give Rachel time to ponder what was happening. She stepped into the elevator car, gathered Rachel in her arms, and pressed her against the back wall. Rachel sagged into Alex's assault, sighing into her mouth as they kissed. Alex felt sweat beading on her forehead and under her shirt, felt her heart pounding a rhythm against her ribs, but she didn't care. Rachel's hands slid under Alex's jacket and held on tight until Alex pulled away with a gasp.

They gazed at one another for a moment, faces inches apart, before Alex said, "I'm sorry. Had to do that..."

"Do you need mouth-to-mouth?" Rachel asked with a laugh.

Alex smiled as she stepped back and released Rachel. "Goodnight, Rachel."

"Goodnight, Alex."

Alex leaned against the wall and let Rachel leave, for real this time. The elevator doors closed on her and she touched her lips. *All in all, a marvelous date.* She rode down, still feeling ten feet tall after that last kiss, and went out to her car. The night was still freezing, but she felt it a little more keenly since she was alone.

Wishing she'd brought a heavier jacket, she climbed into the Jeep and started the engine.

As the heater started to circulate warm air, Alex stared down at the LCD radio display and smiled. "A relationship," she muttered. "Who would've thought?"

She started the car and pulled away from the curb. She barely noticed the ride home or the trek up to her apartment. She moved like a sleepwalker and dropped onto the edge of her bed in a state of bliss. She saw the blinking light on her answering machine, meaning she had a message, but decided to ignore it. Anything worth hearing could wait until the morning.

Murray came into the chief's office the next morning as Alex was signing in. She glanced up at him catching his quizzical look. "What's up, Murray?"

"What the hell happened to your hair?"

"Jealous?" she asked as she walked out of the room. She jumped up to slap his bald dome as she passed him.

Murray scribbled his name into the log and hurried to catch up with her. "I can't tell what's different. Did you, did you cut it?"

"I changed it a little," Alex said. "I had a...a thing last night."

This only served to confuse Murray further. "What kind of thing? The Fireman's Ball isn't until January, right? What kind of thing did you have?"

Alex rolled her eyes and went into the den. Bugs Riley was already there, having taken control of the remote and refusing to hand it over. Alex dropped onto the couch and put her feet up on the coffee table. Some Oprah clone was on the television, talking about relationships and how there was no "me" in "relationship". Alex made a face. "This is what we're watching?"

"Better than what Sawyer had in mind," Bugs said.

Alex had no doubt about that and settled in without further complaint. Murray stepped over Alex's legs and sat across from her, staring hard. "Hey, Bugs, you're a woman."

"God, he's observant," Bugs said flatly.

"What the hell did Crawford do to her hair?"

Bugs glanced over and said, "She got highlights, I think. Right?"

Alex shrugged, smiling a little.

"O-oh. Did you have a...a date?" Murray asked, eyes gleaming.

"Murray..." Alex hoped she sounded threatening.

Bugs slid to the edge of the couch, suddenly intrigued. "Ooh, gossip, I love it. Who was the lucky guy?"

Murray barked a laugh. "Every guy on the planet Earth is the lucky guy when Crawford goes out on a date."

Alex slapped his leg and Murray hooted, rubbing the spot where she'd hit him.

"What?" Bugs asked.

"It wasn't a guy," Murray said in a stage whisper.

"Wayne," Alex said sternly, unleashing the man's seldom used first name. It was the equivalent of a mother using all three names to call her child. He jumped as if she'd slapped his face, eyes wide. "Would you please—"

He held up his hands. "I'm sorry, Alex."

Alex sighed and shrugged. She looked at Bugs and held her hands out in surrender. "It was a woman."

"Oh," Bugs said. Realization dawned on her face as she leaned back. "Oh, I see. Well...uh, w-what did...oh, I'm sorry, I didn't..."

Murray scratched the back of his head and tried to make a dignified exit, muttering "Excuse me," as he stepped over Alex's legs. He was halfway out of the den before he turned around. "Hey, Alex, didn't you wanna talk to Leary about something?"

"Oh. Right," Alex had half forgotten the arsonist in the afterglow of her date with Rachel. "Is he here?"

"Right outside."

She stood and followed Murray into the apparatus bay, surprised to see Leary was speaking with the second person she'd been trying to contact. Fire Marshal Bill Von Elm was standing with the chief in the garage doorway. Von Elm was an older man, with a shock of white hair rising from the crown of his head, swept back in a way reminiscent of an aging rooster. He had a pair of round eyeglasses perpetually perched on the edge of his nose, and his pear-shaped middle threatened every belt she'd ever seen him wear.

She approached carefully, giving Leary the opportunity to see her and wave her off if necessary. He glanced over and, instead of asking for a moment, motioned her forward. "Crawford. Bill tells me you were trying to get hold of him."

"Yeah, and you, too, Chief," Alex said.

"Oh. I had a—"

"It's all right, I know," Alex said. She looked at Von Elm. "But if this is a bad time..."

Von Elm shook his head. "No, we were actually trying to find you last night. What do you know about Martin Lancaster?"

Alex blinked. Of all the questions she'd expected, that one was nowhere on the list. "Well, I really don't know much. He took over his father's development company a few years back when his father was declared non compos mentis. Guess it's been about a decade or so now. He's maybe overly concerned with fire inspections."

"Has a little crush on you, doesn't he?" Leary asked.

Alex stifled a groan. She was hoping that would never come up officially. "Well...he likes me. Requests me to do the routine inspections of his new buildings. Did something happen to him?"

"No, no," Von Elm said. "He came into the office today, had some information about the last two fires. Apparently, both of the buildings were Lancaster Development projects back in the day. They were built before he took over, but he thought there might be some kind of connection."

"Have you determined the fires were deliberately set?" Leary asked.

"Looks that way. Gas all over the place, down the stairs, in pretty much every nook and cranny. The back doors in both buildings were forced open, so we're thinking a group or two of kids were messing around, wanted to see a building burn. You guys have any kids in your lookie-loos?"

"Who knows?" Leary sighed. "Everybody looks suspicious to me at an arson."

"I didn't see anyone," Alex said. "Lancaster thinks someone is targeting his buildings specifically?"

Von Elm shrugged. "Yeah, well, he's probably just paranoid." He sniffed and leaned against the wall. "Does he strike you as the kind of guy someone would target?"

Alex sighed. "I don't know; I don't think so. He's a pest, but going to these lengths just to get back at him or annoy him? I doubt it. Plus, fifty-some percent of the buildings in this town are Lancaster developments. The odds in favor of picking a Lancaster building to torch aren't that out of the ordinary."

"Well, just kind of wanted a character witness, you know. Make sure we weren't just dismissing this theory out of hand." He shook Leary's hand, making it disappear within his own meaty mitt and nodded at Alex. "Nice to see you again, Ms. Crawford."

Alex thought about bringing up her arsonist theory, but knowing Lancaster had come up with the same idea was enough to silence her. She didn't want to say anything that might make Von Elm paint her with the same brush as Lancaster. She said goodbye to him and walked with Leary toward his office.

He heard her following him and turned to face her. "That take care of what you called me about?" he asked.

"Not really," Alex said. She waited until they were behind the truck, lowering her voice to keep anyone from overhearing. "I wanted to talk to you about the possibility that the buildings aren't the target of these fires. We might be."

Leary frowned. "What makes you say that?" he asked as he guided her toward his office. He shut the door behind them and offered her a seat on the couch while he moved behind the desk.

"Jones was killed in a flashover. Wizell was injured in one, but it was a midget in comparison."

"You're certain it was a flashover?" Leary asked.

Alex nodded. "I saw the smoke seeping in around the door, but it was too late to do anything about it. As soon as he's had time to go over the investigation, I want to ask Von Elm about the rooms where the flashover started."

"Well, if you're thinking the fires were flashovers, you already know what the rooms looked like: trash on top of trash, probably on top of old furniture, all of it on fire. It ate up all the oxygen in the room and when Wizell and Jones opened the doors..."

"It's not the floor plan I'm interested in," she said. "It'll probably look normal, but if you look at it from the point of view of someone setting a trap..."

"A trap?"

Alex pressed her lips together. "Wizell was only burnt. It was bad, yes, but he survived and he'll be back in a week."

"Actually, a couple of days," Leary said. "But that doesn't mean anything. I've been in most every house you have and I know what you've seen — piles of newspaper, piles of clothes, chimneys that have never had the dignity of being cleaned. Half the people in this town are living in tinderboxes without even knowing it. If you were looking specifically for a trap, every one of those fires would look suspicious."

"It's not just the flashover part. I'll concede that the majority of rooms I've seen have been less than fire-safe. But the escalation, surely you have to see that. The second fire, less than a day later, was like the first one on steroids. Someone was watching and saw that they didn't have enough oomph behind their blast. So they doubled up and made sure they took someone out."

"Okay, say this is true. We're trained to see things like evidence of a flashover. The firefighters we send in are supposed to see it like a big, flashing neon sign that says 'stay out'. Unless the arsonist was..." He caught himself and looked away.

Alex picked up. "Unless the arsonist was counting on someone screwing up or letting the probie go first."

"I didn't say that."

"Doesn't make it any less true. I know I screwed up, Chief. Jones is dead because of me and I have to live with that. Maybe whoever set the fire knows enough to set the trap, but not enough to know we look for those signs. Maybe he didn't realize the trap would be so obvious."

"You're saying he just got lucky with Jones?"

As much as it sickened her to admit, Alex nodded. "Yes. The fact that I let Jones go in first played right into this sick bastard's plan."

Leary rested his chin in his hand, staring blankly at the wall above her head. "Okay. So this guy isn't targeting Lancaster, he's trying to kill firefighters. Why?"

"We won't know why until we know who. Maybe not even then."

"Okay. Then get Holt down here and get everyone into the kitchen. Gonna have a little meeting."

She stood. "Where is Holt?"

"Weight room," Leary said.

She whistled. "Again?"

Leary shrugged. "Some say he only took Weasel's shifts so he could use our equipment."

Alex was laughing as she left the office. She gathered Bugs and Murray before heading to the stairs to grab Holt and Flannigan from the gym. He grunted when she told him there was a meeting in the kitchen, but he followed her like a trained bear. As she took her seat at the table, Leary clapped both hands together and said, "All right, the reason I asked you all here—"

"One of us killed old lady Hargrove for her fortune," Murray said with a surprisingly convincing British accent.

Before Leary could reply, the alarm sounded. Captain Franklin, again fielding the calls, intoned the information on address and situation. Nothing major, but enough that the ladder and engine were both going. Alex slid into her turnouts like a second skin, climbed onto the truck and took her regular seat.

As the truck pulled from the garage, she took a look around and saw half of her crew had been replaced since their last shift. Robert Holt was in Wizell's normal position up front, while Bugs Riley was sitting next to her in the back of the cab. It felt foreign, as if she was hitching a ride with a bunch of strangers.

Flannigan, however, made it feel like home. He pounded the roof with his fist and whooped, making Alex smile and making Holt blanch. Murray returned Flannigan's cheer and added his fist to the pounding symphony. The radio crackled and Leary came over the air. "Okay, I'm going to have to do it this way. I want everyone to be on their toes on this call. We lost two guys this week; I'm not losing any more."

"You heard Franklin, Chief," Flannigan said. "Gas leak. Easy-peasy."

"They're all easy until some jackass lets his guard down." He paused and then added, "Murray, you listening to me? Don't be that jackass."

Murray laughed and said, "I will do my level best, Chief."

Ignoring Murray's laughter, Alex checked her helmet to make sure it was held tight. Securing the strap, she prayed that staying safe would be as simple as paying a little extra attention for a while. A little hyper-vigilance never hurt anyone. She crossed her fingers and, in honor of her fallen partner, closed her eyes to whisper a quick prayer.

The gas leak was routine stuff: get the truck in the street; go door to door and get the people out; sit around and wait for the gas company to come out and fix the problem. After evacuating a few apartments, Alex and Bugs started venturing inside to open a few windows to air out the building. They repeated what little information they had over and over again as they ushered the residents out of their homes and down the stairs.

"It's all right, ma'am," Alex was saying, helping an elderly lady out of her apartment. "Your knitting will be right there when you get back."

"Well, that Mr. Preston a few doors down, he sometimes likes to get into things that aren't his. You'll take care of that, right? You'll make sure he doesn't take anything of mine, Officer?"

Alex nodded, not bothering to correct the woman. If the first five corrections hadn't stuck... She simply said, "Mr. Preston will be escorted out just like you are. We're getting everyone out and then my friend and I will come out, too. All right? All your belongings will be fine."

"Okay, but if Mr. Preston gets back in first, he better not come into my apartment."

"If he robs you, call the police station and ask for Officer Alex, okay?"

Bugs stifled a laugh as she pulled the old woman's door shut. Once the resident was waddling down the stairs, Alex turned and exhaled with a shake of her head. "How odd. Mr. Preston warned me that the woman in this apartment probably tried to set the fire."

"Nice to know that people still trust their neighbors," Bugs said. She followed Alex up to the next level. "Have you noticed how many people try to do chores before you evacuate them? You tell people their home is in danger of bursting into flames, and they suddenly have all these things they simply must do before they can evacuate. Do they not understand that if the apartment explodes, it won't matter whether or not their clothes are in the washing machine?"

"It's the 'never-happen-to-me' syndrome," Alex said. "No one believes it will be their building because that only happens in the movies and on the news. It's up to us to get that reality across to them."

Bugs sighed and said, "Yeah, well, it'd be much easier to just stand on the street with a megaphone and say, 'Come out now. We'll meet you down here and offer you cookies.'"

Alex laughed. At daytime, low danger calls like this, more often than not, housewives and older ladies in the neighborhood brought out cookies, lemonade, and other refreshments for the firefighters. The elderly were looking for someone to mother, while the housewives were checking out the hot male firefighters. "Oh, yeah. What do you bet Murray rushes through his part of the building and bogarts all the cookies?"

"Hell, I barely know the man and even I'm not taking that bet," Bugs said. They reached the landing and branched out, each heading to a different apartment.

They knocked and simultaneously called, "Fire Department!"

Despite the disparaging tone most people adopted when speaking about public transportation, Rachel loved taking the bus. Most days she left her car at home or in the hospital parking garage and hopped on the cross town just to relax a little. It gave her time to read or, on days when her shift had been particularly relentless, take a quick nap. This morning — or afternoon, really, since it was inching toward two o'clock — she was going to get some lunch after spending a hectic morning shift trying to calm and reassure a man who'd accidentally nailed his hand to a board with a nail gun. As she rode, Rachel was taking the time to enjoy an intriguing historical novel she'd recently found at the library.

She was so involved in her current chapter that she hardly noticed how long they had been sitting at what she assumed to be a red light. She finally looked up when the man in front of her turned around and sighed, "Can you believe this?"

When Rachel realized he was speaking directly to her, she marked her place in the book, then looked around and asked, "Why? What's going on?"

"Firemen have the whole street shut down. Traffic's backed up. It's going to take forever to clear this mess up." He checked his watch and twisted in his seat, turning to look fully at her. He looked her up and down and puffed out his chest a bit. "This is just irritating, you know. I've got a big meeting to get to and, wouldn't you know it, my Lexus picks today to break down."

Rachel smiled with patently false sympathy. "Aw, that's a shame. I'll be sure to tell my firefighter girlfriend what a terrible, terrible day you had." His eyes widened at the emphasis on "girl", and Rachel smiled sweetly at him.

His attempt at a love connection fizzled, he faced front again and slumped down in his seat. Rachel slid out of her seat and moved to the opposite side of the bus to look down at the disturbance.

Firefighters were swarming around a brownstone a few hundred yards ahead, beyond the roadblock. She couldn't really tell what the firefighters were doing, since there didn't seem to be any smoke or flames, but if she squinted she could just barely make out the names on the backs of their coats. She spotted a Riley and then Murray — with his size, he was almost unmistakable, even at this distance — and...

There, she saw a firefighter exit the building and move to stand with Murray and Riley. Something in the way the new arrival moved, as the old song said, but the coat confirmed it: Crawford. That was Alex. She smiled and resisted the urge to slap the window like some giddy schoolgirl trying to get the attention of her crush. The bus inched forward and she moved her head as a light pole moved in to disturb her view. Alex spoke with her coworkers for a few moments and then she and Riley strode down the sidewalk toward the traffic jam.

"She's walking this way," Rachel whispered.

"Who?" the Lexus owner asked.

"Never mind."

As the two firefighters approached, Rachel was surprised to see that Riley was also a woman. She could tell that she and Alex were talking, but the distance was too great to make out any words. When the two women made it within three car lengths of the bus, Rachel reached up to open the window and shout, but then she thought better of it. She'd never seen Alex at work, never seen her in full uniform for that matter. The urge to spy on her was too great to resist.

Two men in jumpsuits with the gas company logo met them halfway and the little group paused next to the bus driver's window. Alex seemed close enough to touch, but she looked like such a different woman. The helmet overshadowed her face; the high collar of her coat reached up and brushed her cheek when she turned to indicate the building.

As Alex and Riley turned to lead the gas company men down the street, Rachel felt a surge of pride. She felt like every proud parent who had ever seen their child in a school play, every sideline father who saw his son score the winning touchdown. She wanted to grab the Lexus jerk and point out the window and tell him that was her girlfriend.

That was her girlfriend.

Chapter Eight
Your Brain Damage is Kicking In

The rest of the day, Alex wandered the firehouse going through the motions and trying her best to ignore the feeling of walking on air that she'd had since waking up that morning. Every thought ran back toward Rachel, every comment reminded her of something Rachel had said or done the night before. When she wasn't pining for Rachel, she was trying to remember the exact tone of her laugh or the way the skin around her eyes wrinkled when she smiled. When she wasn't doing that, she was kicking herself for acting like a complete and utter high school kid.

Other than the gas leak, they didn't have a call the entire shift. After dinner, Leary reiterated his radio speech, letting them know that there were special concerns about their safety at fires and making sure they were on their toes for the next couple of calls. Holt merely grunted and headed upstairs to the weight room, probably upset that a call had interrupted his workout.

Everyone else was trying to ignore the fact that Jones's funeral was set to coincide with the end of their shift the next day at noon. Jones's mother had worked out the schedule with Chief Leary to be certain that all of her son's new friends could attend. Almost everyone had brought their dress uniforms to work, planning to change at the end of shift. The wool uniforms were hanging in their cubbies to avoid getting wrinkled, identical suits hanging breast-to-back along the wall in the dark cubby area.

The only cubby lacking the dress uniform belonged to Bugs. Alex assumed she was going to skip the service and didn't particularly blame her. She understood that going to the funeral of the man you were replacing would feel a little weird. A little past seven in the morning the day of the funeral, however, Leary called Bugs into his office and had a short discussion with her. Afterward, she made some noise about needing to head home sometime before noon to pick up her dress uniform.

When she had a spare moment, Alex headed outside with her cell phone to call Rachel and let her know the final details for the funeral. Murray hadn't been giving her a moment's peace and, to keep him and the others from eavesdropping, she'd finally decided to just move it outside. She leaned against the wall, facing the street as she dialed Rachel's number. The phone rang a handful of times before she heard a murmured, "Hello?"

"Rachel? It's Alex. I didn't wake you, did I?"

"No, you didn't. I was just napping," Rachel said, contradicting herself. There was a rustling sound and then she said, "What's the plan?"

"The funeral starts at 1:30. Can you get off?"

"Actually, I'm off for the rest of the day. I took Dr. Tennant's early shift this morning so I could be off the rest of the day. I wanted to be there for you."

Alex had to take a few seconds to compose herself. She was touched beyond belief that Rachel would do something like that for her.

"Alex? You still there?"

"Yeah," Alex said. "Uh, so I was thinking I would swing by your place about an hour before that."

"That sounds perfect. I'll be ready to go by 12:30," Rachel said. After a moment, she added, "You know, I saw you on my way to lunch yesterday afternoon."

"Oh, yeah? Where? You drive by the house or something?"

"No, it was downtown. You were working. I guess it was a gas leak or something?"

"Oh." Alex watched an SUV pull into the firehouse parking lot as she tried to remember that afternoon's call. She watched until the truck moved out of sight before she asked, "Where were you?"

"On the bus."

Alex thought for a second, trying to remember a bus. "Bus...oh, yeah, I saw that. Bugs and I were right by it. Why didn't you try to get my attention? It would've been nice to see you."

"I don't know. I just...I'd never seen you in your uniform and looking all...hot."

Alex was glad she'd moved outside; she would never have lived down the deep crimson blush she currently had going. "So you were spying on me?"

"A little," Rachel admitted.

Alex smiled. "Well, I'll just have to remember that. See about getting some payback."

"I'll be on the lookout."

"Doesn't that kind of defeat the purpose?"

"Maybe. Maybe if I know you're looking, I'll put on a show."

Alex laughed and covered her mouth. "Good God, woman."

"I know," Rachel said. "I'm sitting here covering my eyes because I can't believe I just said that."

"No, it was good. I liked it."

"Okay. Well, I'm going to hang up before I say anything more humiliating."

"Okay. Bye, Doctor Tom."

Rachel chuckled. "Bye, Firefighter Crawford."

Alex slipped the phone into her pocket and went back into the station. She was so wrapped up in her thoughts that she didn't notice Murray moving to intercept her until his arm was around her shoulders. He turned her around and steered her back out of the apparatus bay. "Hey, Crawford, what's up; how you doing, fancy a soda, me too, let's walk to the store, my treat."

She glanced sideways at him. "Murray, your brain damage is starting to kick in."

"Just walk," he said with a furtive look over his shoulder.

"You're freaking me out, Murray."

They were halfway to the big garage doors when she heard someone shout "Alex!" from the kitchen.

Alex groaned when she recognized the voice. She stopped and looked at Murray, patting his arm. She whispered, "Bless you for trying," then turned and faced Martin Lancaster with a fake smile plastered on her lips. "Mr. Lancaster. What a pleasant surprise."

"A pleasant surprise, I hope," he said, walking toward her. He wore his typical tailored suit but his hair stuck up in wild curls. It had been slicked back the last time she'd seen him, but she wasn't sure this was an improvement.

"It's definitely a... surprise," Alex said, forcing herself to approach him. "What are you doing here?"

"I simply wished to express my condolences for your fallen brother. If your Mr. Von Elm determines that these fires are indeed aimed at me or my company, I feel it would be my duty to make amends for—"

Alex held up her hands to stop him. "We're just doing our jobs, Mr. Lancaster. There's no need for—"

"Oh, please. I insist. And with the funeral being today—"

"You're not coming to the funeral." Alex was unable to stop the words before they were out. "I mean, i-it's going to be a family affair. The people he worked with, his family, people like that. I don't think his mother wants a big spectacle."

"Well, I'm sure one more person—"

"It really wouldn't be right. I'm sorry, Mr. Lancaster, but we have to ask that you not attend."

He appeared crushed, but nodded slowly. "Okay. I understand. Thank you for your candor, Alex."

As long as she was being a bitch... "Ms. Crawford."

He pinched a smile. "Yes, of course. Well, I should get going. Thank you for your time, Al...Ms. Crawford. Mr. Murray."

Murray grinned. "Not a problem, Mr. Lancaster."

Martin slipped between them and headed for the door. When he was gone, Murray whistled. "Ooh, boy howdy, that was harsh."

"The man has been harassing me for close to a year," Alex said as she walked toward the kitchen. "Maybe now he'll stop requesting me for his inspections. I don't mind doing my share, but..." She froze when she saw the food on the kitchen table. "What's all this?"

"Lancaster brought it," Bugs said as she buttered a bagel. "He's a good guy."

"Yeah," Alex said. "I'll let you take a couple hundred of his inspections, see how much you like him then." Nevertheless, she was a little awed by the spread. The table was covered with boxes of bagels, bags of doughnuts, a bowl of fresh fruit, two tall cartons of orange juice, a gallon of milk, and bags of Pepperidge Farm bread. The firehouse was set for at least a week's worth of breakfasts. Or two days, depending on how much restraint Murray was able to display. Alex took a seat, picking up a bunch of grapes and plucking one from the stem.

"Okay, I've only met him the once, but you gotta admit," Bugs motioned with her butter drenched bagel, "the guy knows how to say thank you. Once, at Engine 4, we pulled this guy out of a smoky apartment. Wasn't breathing, had to perform CPR, I think they even put him in that hyperbole chamber."

"Hyperbaric chamber," Murray corrected.

"Right." Bugs nodded. "Anyway, once he was all better, he shows up at the firehouse with a brand new, big screen TV. Just in time for the World Series, too. We got to watch the Red Sox break the curse in style, I tell ya."

"Never mention those rat bastards again," Murray said, eyes aflame with hatred.

Eyes wide, Bugs looked to Alex for help. She smiled and explained. "Murray had to give everyone in the firehouse fifty bucks the day after the 2004 World Series."

"Because?"

"We're not allowed to say why." Alex winked. "It wasn't the most charitable donation we've ever received."

Murray grumbled, "It was a sure thing. Eighty damn years and they go and break their tradition the day I try to make some dough." He went back to devouring a banana.

"What are you doing after this?" Bugs asked.

"Toilets," Alex said. "When I took the test to become a firefighter, I had no idea the job description included cleaning toilets."

"Or windows," Murray said. "Man, maids don't even do the windows anymore."

"Neither do you, Streaky," Alex said. "Why d'you ask, Bugs?"

She shook her head. "I need to run back to my apartment and pick up my dress uniform."

"I thought you went already?" Alex said.

"I did. It was a little wrinkled, so my fiancé offered to get it pressed for me."

"Your fiancé does your laundry?" Murray asked, incredulous.

Bugs held her hands out in a "what-do-you-want-from-me" gesture. "He offered; I needed it done, what's the problem?"

"Man no use iron," Alex grunted. "Man make fire. Man kill things, keep wife barefoot and pregnant."

Murray held up his hands. "Whoa, now, whoa. Don't make me out to be some chauvinist. I'm modern, I'm a sensitive guy, but it just seems weird that the future Mr. Bugs is standing at home wearing an apron, hunched over an ironing board while his bride-to-be is out fighting fires. It's topsy-turvy is all."

Alex shrugged. "This isn't your grandfather's fire department."

"No, it ain't. Because my grandfather wouldn't have been very welcome in a firehouse."

Alex held up her hands in concession. He definitely had a point. Aside from women, Blacks and Hispanics had the hardest time breaking into the firefighting profession. She was about to say something when Robert Holt wandered into the kitchen.

He was dripping with sweat, his t-shirt sleeves cut off at the shoulders. He glanced at the food on the table, not saying a word as the three people seated there followed him with their eyes. He opened the fridge, withdrew a jug of fruit punch and chugged half the bottle. Alex was about to complain about backwash when she saw "HOLT" written on a strip of tape on the side of the jug.

Releasing a healthy belch, he screwed the cap back on and replaced it in the fridge. He wiped his mouth on his forearm and left the kitchen again.

Murray shook his head. "That dude is weird."

"Talking about me behind my back, are ya?"

Alex jumped. She hadn't even seen the new arrival until his arm was around Murray's neck, his free hand flat on top of his captive's bald head. Murray froze; eyes wide, lips pressed out as if he was trying to whistle as his hands went to the arm wrapped around his throat. "Holy..." Murray gasped.

Bugs and Alex were out of their seats. Alex could barely believe her eyes. "Weasel!"

"One and the same, darling," he said, grinning brightly. He released Murray, who gasped and spun around to confirm the owner of the voice. Wizell reached out and clasped Alex's hand, chuckling evilly. "How's the No-Boys-Allowed Firehouse doing without me?"

"We're dragging ourselves through each day," Alex assured him, moving around Murray for her own hug.

"My trachea is fine, by the way," Murray rasped.

"Big baby," Wizell muttered with a grin. He slapped Murray on the back and turned to Bugs. He squinted and pointed a finger at her. "Now, I know you're one of the twins, and you've got to be...uh..." He snapped his fingers and said, "Aw, man, just tell me."

"Heather Riley."

Wizell clapped once and said, "Ah, Bugs. We got Bugs in the firehouse." He shook her hand and said, "Eric Wizell. Weasel to those who know me. Pleased to meet you."

Alex shook her head as she examined the lieutenant. He was wearing his dress uniform, buttons polished and every crease precisely where it belonged. His gloves were tucked into the jacket pocket, the fingers sticking out and draping over the edge. His cap was the only thing missing, but it was most likely out in the apparatus bay. The only incongruous parts of the outfit were the bandages wrapping his neck and ears. "They finally kicked you out of the hospital, huh?"

"Oh, well, special occasion and all," he said, indicating his uniform. "I gave them my puppy dog eyes and a little bit of the bottom lip." He turned to Bugs, widening his eyes and puffing his bottom lip out to Oliver Twist levels. "I got a day pass. They're not letting me come back to work until next week. The bastards. I'm fine now. I'll find an excuse to hang out here; you got my word on that."

"Yeah, but I don't want to be behind you in a fire when that fancy new skin of yours starts flaking off," Alex said.

Wizell scoffed. "Women." He sighed and patted Murray on the shoulder. "Is Leary around?"

Alex nodded. "He should be nearby. C'mon, Bugs, we'll go see if we can round him up."

"Okay," Bugs said, unsure of why she had to go. They headed out into the apparatus bay. Alex glanced back and saw Wizell put his hands on Murray's shoulders as he claimed Bugs' seat. Wizell knew how close Murray and Jones had been, knew how the death had to be hitting the big man. Alex moved on, giving the men their privacy.

Wizell and Leary sat in the lawn chairs out front and sipped root beers while they talked about the calls the truck had taken in the past few days. From the cubbies, Alex could hear them laughing and joking about Holt's constant weight room presence. She and Bugs were in the curtained off space, which had been enlarged to accommodate a second woman.

Alex took off her t-shirt and was reaching for her dress blouse when Bugs said, "Can I ask you a personal question?"

Alex tensed slightly, but said, "Sure."

"Murray's little slip the other day. About you being...you know."

"Do you want me to leave until you're dressed?" Alex asked sincerely. They were both in their bras, but Alex had her trousers on. Bugs was standing just behind her in a pair of boxer shorts.

Bugs laughed. "Don't be silly. I was just wondering if it made it easier or harder to be in the department."

Alex frowned. "What do you mean?"

"Well, for one thing, you probably don't have guys hitting on you all the time. That's gotta be pleasant."

Alex scoffed, "Oh, please. The fact that I'm not interested doesn't deter them one iota. If anything, it makes them more determined. A couple of guys think that I'm only gay because I haven't spread my legs for the right guy yet."

"Right," Bugs said. "Just like Murray and Leary are only straight because they haven't found the right queen to bend them over a chair."

Laughing, Alex choked out, "Oh, God, do not let them hear you say that." She pulled her dress shirt out of the closet and shook her head. "Wearing a shirt and tie, cleaning toilets, and here I thought running into burning buildings would be the worst part of my job."

"I know what you mean. I'd give anything to be running into a burning building right now," Bugs said as she worked her hair into a bun. "So it doesn't give you any, I don't know, special camaraderie with the guys?"

"Just because we happen to like sleeping with the same gender?" She shrugged. "At first, they tolerated me, but I didn't start getting respect until I dragged Murray through a window. Not only saved his life, but showed the boys I could do all the stuff they could. They warmed to me after that, and after I strung up this sheet so they wouldn't have to sacrifice their entire den."

"Why would they?"

"The bigwigs down at city hall wanted to give me my own changing room. If the measure had passed, they would have converted the den into a women's changing room. So I went out and campaigned against it, making sure the bill didn't get voted in and then I just put this up. It showed them I was a team player."

"So it's all political, huh?"

"Yeah, pretty much." Alex sighed. "You just have to roll with the punches."

Bugs nodded. "I know. It just sometimes feels like we're gonna keep taking the punches until the guy hitting us gets a sore shoulder."

Alex grinned and finished buttoning her blouse. "Very apt."

"So, are you seeing anyone?"

A picture of Rachel popped into her mind, but Alex hedged. "I have someone I'm currently very fond of, yes." She pulled on her trousers, tucked the shirt into the waistband and fastened the belt. Wiggling her toes in the tight black socks, she half-turned. "Can you imagine if we got a call right now?"

"Oh, yeah." Bugs laughed. "I can see the headlines now: 'The Dapper Department'. Firefighters responding to a blaze in suits and ties."

"Screw that," Alex said. "This suit cost me over three hundred bucks. If I have to go into a fire, I'm going in naked before I'm getting this thing dirty." She angled the mirror on the wall of her cubby and bent down, trying to watch as she wound the tie around itself. "Damn things. Most departments in this day and age have clip-on ties. It's the wave of the future. Keeping these horrific little — tying ties — is like keeping a typewriter when a computer will do a better job."

"Or having laces when Velcro tightens your shoes just as well," Bugs said as she stepped in front of Alex. "Here. You're hopeless; let me get it." She reached up and undid the sloppy knot Alex had made, redoing it in a few seconds. She looped and knotted the tie, then pulled the knot tight against Alex's throat. "Too tight?"

"No, it's good. Thanks."

Bugs stepped back to her cubby and pulled her jacket off the hanger. "Does your girlfriend usually tie your tie for you?"

"There's no 'usually' with us. I mean, we just started going out."

"Oh, I see," Bugs said. "Well, before it gets too serious, you'd better make sure she can tie a tie. I've seen relationships crumble for lesser reasons."

Alex laughed. "I'll keep that in mind."

Rachel, unsure of what to wear, went online and did a search for pictures taken at fire department funerals. All the images she could find showed scores of firemen in identical black suits and caps, the picture of formality. All the firefighters seemed to be wearing a regulation dress uniform. She didn't see many civilians in any of the photos she found, so she had to decide what to wear based on the dress uniforms. She headed to her closet and summarily disqualified almost everything she owned.

After about twenty minutes of debating with her inner fashionista, she withdrew a simple maroon gown and laid it out on the bed. The dress was an appropriate length for a funeral, wide shouldered and not too low cut. The only markings on the dress were the narrow threads breaking up the smooth expanse from the bottom of her breasts down to her waist and a smattering of violets running along the hem. She shed her robe and slipped into the dress.

She stood in front of the mirror and cast a critical eye over the drape of it. She reached up to gather her hair, testing it both up and down to see which complimented her better.

She primped and preened for a few minutes, then told herself to stop being silly. Alex, after all, probably wasn't acting like a giddy high school senior on her way to the prom. She sighed and let the dress fall, slipped out of her underwear and went to the run the water for her bath.

Leary stepped out of his office with both arms held out in front of him, his wrists turned out as if he was expecting to be handcuffed. "Would someone give me a damn hand here?" he asked. Alex walked past, her hand deliberately over her eyes. "Crawford, would you mind?"

"Sorry, Chief," she said, keeping her hand firmly over her eyes. "If I look at you in your dress uniform, I may have to reconsider my homosexuality."

"'Cause you look so damn fine." Murray grinned as he stepped up to fasten Leary's cufflinks for him. Leary sighed as Murray's thick fingers managed the small holes with ease.

Bugs walked by, fitting her cap over her bun. "Ooh, men dressing men. Does he tie your shoes for you, too, Chief?"

"I'm just not that good at manipulating small things, that's all," Leary said.

"Then how do you aim in the bathroom?" Wizell asked.

Leary snapped, "Are you still here, Charcoal?"

Wizell held up his hands. "Whoa, whoa, not nice making fun of the nearly fried guy over here. Channel 6 called me a hero."

"Channel 6 also airs *Jerry Springer* in the afternoons," Leary pointed out. "I'm not exactly holding my breath until they get a Pulitzer or Tony or whatever the hell award they give TV stations. Now come on, let's get a move on, gals and fellas."

He pulled his cap on as Alex glanced back at him. All joking aside, the man was built to wear the dress uniform. He was enough to make any woman take a second look.

They each spread out to their own car. Leary paused to talk with the incoming lieutenant before he joined them in the parking lot. "Flannigan is picking up Jones's parents. The rest of us, we gonna convoy to the church?"

"I can't," Alex said. "I have to pick up Rachel."

He gave her a thumbs up. "Everyone else?"

"Sounds good to me," Wizell said. "I don't know where the church is."

Murray banged the roof of his trunk and called, "Carpool with me, Weasel."

Wizell hurried to catch up and slid into the passenger seat of Murray's truck. The company lined up behind Leary's Suburban and then pulled out in a queue. When Alex's Jeep turned off toward Rachel's apartment, Murray and Leary sounded their horns in farewell. She waved at them through the window, honked her own horn in response, and laughed when she saw the other motorists' looks of confusion.

Rachel was putting the finishing touches on her make-up when there was a knock on the door. "Perfect timing." She smiled at her reflection. She shut off the lamp and hurried down the dark hallway, her bare feet making shush-shush noises against the carpet. "Just a minute," she said, pausing in the foyer to slip into her flats. She smoothed the bodice of the dress, grabbed her purse, and opened the door. "Oh, wow!" she gasped, unable to restrain herself.

She'd seen the photos online, but nothing could have prepared her for the sight of Alexandra Crawford standing at her door in full dress uniform. The jacket was jet black, save for two yellow stripes circling each wrist. Six gold buttons marked with SFD gleamed on her chest, while the black tie was perfectly knotted under her chin. A military style cap shielded her eyes, her dark hair feathering out from beneath the rim.

When Alex brought one hand up to fiddle nervously with her collar, Rachel saw that she was wearing fine white gloves with three pleats on the back running from her wrist down her fingers. She exhaled and finally blinked, taking a step back. "You look magnificent."

Alex shifted from one foot to the other, looking down at herself. "I look like the guy in those ads trying to get kids to join the Marines." She gave Rachel an appreciative once over. "You, on the other hand..."

"Is this all right? I-I wasn't sure what was appropriate."

"This is more than appropriate," Alex said. "You look gorgeous. Gorgeous." She tilted her head and then amended, "If I could just..."

In response to Rachel's nod, Alex stepped forward and brought her hands up. Rachel bowed her head as Alex reached around and cupped the back of her head. Her fingers moved expertly for a moment and when she stepped back, Rachel's hair fell loose onto her shoulders. Alex brushed her fingers through the freed tresses. "Perfect."

"Thank you." Rachel extended her arm. "Shall we?"

Alex took the arm and tucked it against her side as she escorted Rachel to the elevator. Despite their somber destination, Rachel couldn't help smiling. After a lifetime of being the background, being the blood-smeared anonymous face in an emergency room, now she felt wanted, attractive, loved. She covered Alex's hand with her own and rested her head on the uniformed shoulder.

He couldn't stay away. It was just too sweet. Too perfect.

He sat in the back pew and tried to remain inconspicuous. The family was already there — the mother in tears, while the father stood stoic, proud. He thought his son had died a hero. Yeah. Hero. He died trying to save a room filled with ratty furniture. Big whoop. Bring on the tickertape parade. The daughter, the dead fireman's sister, was a mess. Make-up streaking down her face, sobbing against her mother's shoulder. It was truly a spectacle. Someone should've done something about it, but no one did. Stupid people with their boundaries.

The firefighters arrived en masse, sweeping into the room like the Knights of the friggin' Round Table. Crisp black suits, hats pulled low to hide their eyes. They looked more like the Mafia, now that he thought about it. Here to bury one of their own, a very insular fraternal organization. Yeah, just like the Mafia.

He supposed that made him Eliot Ness — cleaning up the city, one dirty mobster at a time. He repressed a smile and scanned the crowd of firemen for his special project, panicking when he didn't see her. Had she decided not to come? He knew she'd been right behind Jones when he died. Maybe guilt had gotten to her.

Fuming, he stood and headed for the back of the sanctuary. No one saw him go, which was fortunate; not many people stormed out of a funeral muttering curses. He'd wanted a few more fires to play with Crawford. If she was going to crumble so easily, he'd been sorely mistaken in choosing her for his pet project.

He climbed into his car, ready to burn rubber out of the lot, when he spotted a Jeep sliding into one of the few empty spaces. Not wanting to draw attention to himself, he waited for the occupants to go into the church.

Alex Crawford got out of the driver's side, went around the front of the car, and opened the passenger door. She put her arm around an attractive woman with long dark hair, guiding her toward the church. What was this? Jones's wife? Or perhaps...

He looked again at how Crawford's hand rested against the small of the other woman's back. It was such a natural gesture, so easy, so...intimate.

His eyes widened and he pressed back against the seat, watching the door of the church long after Crawford and her...her...the other woman had gone inside. This changed things, he told himself. This changed things dramatically.

Rachel was allowed to sit with Alex and the rest of the company in the front pew reserved for pallbearers. Leary, Alex, Wizell, and Murray were four of those who would carry the coffin, while Alfred's brother and father were to take up the front positions. Rachel sat between Alex and Jones's brother, a beefy twenty-something kid with eyeglasses and a pencil-thin mustache. He continually lifted his glasses and blotted his eyes with a handkerchief. Wizell, Rachel noticed, had become the epitome of class. His evil grin, the playful gleam in his eye, everything that made him "Weasel" was hidden behind a veil of reverence and dignity. She was highly impressed by his about face.

As the service began, Rachel reached over and took Alex's hand. Alex squeezed it, her hand like steel through her cotton gloves. The priest spoke of Alfred's contributions to the community, of his devotion to the church, and the programs he ran with the kids. He revealed that Alfred had approached him about a Junior Firefighter Program in the church, which would teach elementary school children how to observe basic fire safety in their homes.

When the priest asked if anyone wished to say a few words about the deceased, the man beside Rachel stood. He walked to the stage and replaced the priest at the podium.

"Hi. I'm Alfred's brother, Mike." He sniffled softly and looked down at his hands for a moment while he regained his composure. "Alfie...man, he always wanted to be a fireman. When we were kids and we were playing with matches, he was always the one who squirted us with the water hose." He cleared his throat. "Sorry, Mom, by the way."

The audience laughed softly.

"I heard that when he died, Alfie was serving as the nozzle man; he was leading the way into that fire. It was fate that he happened to die on that assignment, but I know that he died proud. And whoever gave him that opportunity, well, I just want to thank you."

Rachel felt Alex's hand tighten around her own and looked up and saw tears glistening in Alex's eyes. Rachel reached over and patted Alex's bicep. Alex smiled weakly.

Mike Jones finished his speech and took his seat in the pew.

The priest resumed his place and said, "Would anyone else care to speak?"

Leary stood, and every firefighter in the room turned and looked at him in surprise. He straightened his jacket and stepped up on stage, his shiny-as-new shoes squeaking on the wooden floor as he took his place.

He cleared his throat and whispered, "Thank you," to the priest. Gripping the lectern with both gloved hands, Leary flexed his fingers before he spoke. "I'm going to give the people who know me a few seconds to close their mouths." That drew a laugh from the gallery. "I'm Chief John Leary. I was Alfred's boss for the four months he was on the ladder and also after he recently transferred to the engine. Before he moved over to the engine, I had a talk with him and asked him what he wanted to do. He said, 'Fight fires.' I asked him if he wanted to be a hero and he looked me in the eye and said, 'I want to be a fireman, sir.'

"Alfred wasn't a firefighter for very long, but we will never forget that he was a firefighter." He pursed his lips, flexed his fingers on the edge of the podium again, and then shrugged. "That's it. That — that's all." He turned, shoes squeaking as he stepped off the stage.

After a few moments of silence, the priest returned to the lectern. "Thank you, Chief. If no one else would like to speak, Alfred's sister, June, requested that she be allowed to sing a special song for her brother. June?"

A lovely teenage girl with flowing blond hair stepped onto the stage, taking a microphone from the stand. She waited as the organist played the introduction and then began singing a hymn that Rachel vaguely remembered from her days in church. She couldn't quite recall the words, simply getting a flashback to sitting in a pew and squirming in her least favorite gingham dress, doodling on the bulletin and wondering how long it was until lunch.

She looked over at Alex, who had her eyes closed and her lips pressed tightly together. Her jaw was working convulsively, her brow furrowed and her nostrils flaring. She squeezed Rachel's hand, then released it and rose suddenly. She stayed low, ducking her head down and hurrying down the aisle until she exploded out the back doors of the sanctuary. A few people turned to mark her passage, but June Jones showed no sign of being disturbed.

When the song was finished, there was a smattering of polite applause. Rachel stood, eased down the row, and followed Alex to the back of the church. She found Alex in the foyer, hugging herself tightly and looking out the glass doors at the parking lot. "Are you okay?" she asked softly.

Alex turned and looked at her with red-rimmed eyes. "I got pulled out of a fire when I was six. Our apartment was on fire and they got my parents out. They came back and got me, saved my life. I thought the fireman was a monster at first, but he saved me. And then I saw him without his helmet and he was just an ordinary man." She looked out the door again, her hands balled into fists. "When I was seventeen, that fireman died. House fire. Ceiling collapsed. It was eleven damn years, but I've never been able to shake the feeling that he died in exchange for me. He died so I could live. It's why I became a firefighter, to make up for his life. Now, Jones is dead for me, too."

"He didn't die because of you, Alex. There's no way to know what will happen in a fire or, hell, walking down the street. Would you have felt guilty if that first fireman had died of a heart attack?"

"But he didn't. He died in a fire."

"That doesn't matter." Rachel put her arms around Alex and held her tightly. "You've already repaid what that man did for you. You've saved the lives of others. Fate is balanced."

The doors to the sanctuary opened and the priest stepped out. "Ms. Crawford? They're ready for the pallbearers."

Rachel turned her head until her lips were against Alex's ear. "Will you be okay?"

"Yeah," Alex whispered. She pecked Rachel on the cheek and slipped from her arms. "Okay, I'm coming," she said to the priest. She let her hand trail down Rachel's arm, keeping physical contact with her as long as possible. She turned at the sanctuary door and tossed Rachel her keys. "You can wait in the Jeep for me if you want. I'll be there in a few minutes."

Rachel nodded and mouthed, "Okay," as Alex ducked back into the sanctuary. She left the church and walked toward Alex's Jeep, turning when she heard the doors open. She stopped and watched as two teenaged ushers held the door for the family. Jones's fiancée, mother, and sister were the first ones out. They waited outside as the rest of the mourners filed out into the suddenly chilly afternoon. Lastly, the pallbearers appeared.

She felt a surge of sadness and pride as she watched Alex bearing the right center section of the casket. The firefighters, resplendent in their dress uniforms, were a sharp contrast to the Jones family members dressed in somber suits.

Rachel finally keyed the remote entry button and climbed inside, turning to watch as Jones was loaded into the hearse. When she turned back, she spotted several CDs tucked between the driver's seat and the console. She looked over her shoulder to make sure Alex wasn't coming, then pulled them out and perused Alex's music choices. The Who, Rolling Stones, nothing too surprising until... She chuckled when she found Billy Joel's *Greatest Hits*, giggling as she turned the case over to read the track listing.

When the door opened and Alex climbed in, Rachel held up the CD. "Busted," she said.

Alex glanced at the case, took it from Rachel, and tucked it back between the seats. "A former girlfriend got that for me. I should toss it out or trade it in."

"I wasn't making fun of you," Rachel said. "I like Billy Joel. 'Piano Man' might be my favorite song."

Alex held the wheel for a second and stared out the windshield. "Who is the real estate novelist?"

"Let's see..." Rachel had to run through the song in her head until she came up with, "Paul. And he never had time for a wife."

Alex turned in her seat and lowered her voice. "No one hears about this."

"Not from me," Rachel assured her.

"Okay," Alex said. "If you swear." She took the disc from the case and fed it into the player. When she started the Jeep, the harmonica signaled the intro to "Piano Man". Rachel grinned and fastened her seatbelt.

They joined the procession, behind the chief's Suburban and directly in front of Murray's SUV. Rachel turned in her seat, waving her fingers at Murray. He leaned forward and pushed his nose up with his thumb, poking his tongue out at her. She laughed. "Mr. Murray and Mr. Wizell look unexpectedly grown up in their dress uniforms."

"Yeah, it has a maturing effect on us all," Alex said with a smile. "Because every minute wearing them feels like an hour to us."

Rachel stroked the sleeve of Alex's jacket. "Still, you have to admit, it's very appealing."

Alex looked down at Rachel's hand, looked at Rachel, then looked back out at the road. She cleared her throat and murmured, "Mm hmm."

"What are your plans for after the cemetery? You're off duty, right?"

"Mm hmm. Why, did you have something in mind?"

"Nothing in particular." Rachel leaned back in the seat and shrugged. "I just... I don't want to leave you."

Alex smiled. "Well, I'll see if I can think of something."

"Try your hardest," Rachel said. "If I have to, I'll go to the firehouse and wash the trucks with you."

Laughing, Alex reached over and squeezed Rachel's hand. "Thank you. I never would have believed I'd be laughing today."

The rest of the brief trip, they listened to the CD. When "Piano Man" ended, Alex skipped forward a few tracks to "She's Always a Woman". When they pulled into the cemetery, Alex reached over and silenced the piano man. They parked along a narrow gravel road, the doors of every car in the procession seeming to open as if on cue and a sea of black and brown pouring from them.

Rachel walked around the back of the car, intercepting the woman everyone called Bugs as she met Alex on the other side.

"I need to help with..." She gestured toward the long black hearse. "I'll catch up with you at the site," Alex said. She turned and hurried down the row with Murray.

Bugs and Rachel walked together down the gentle slope toward the large green tent that covered a freshly dug hole. "I fucking hate funerals," Bugs muttered.

Rachel looked at her for a moment, trying to determine if it was an attempt at conversation or just a general observation. After a moment, she said, "Yeah, they're awful."

"I'm Heather Riley, by the way."

"Rachel Tom."

"Tom. That's an interesting name."

Rachel smiled. "So is Bugs."

The other woman smiled and then looked over her shoulder. Her smile faded quickly. Rachel turned and saw the pallbearers taking the casket down a gravel walkway rather than trying to carry it downhill. They processed past the mourners, who were now seated, and carefully placed it on the mechanism that would lower it into the ground. Rachel's gaze focused on the mother and fiancée, who were clinging to one another in the front row. When Alex took a seat by her side, Rachel wrapped an arm around her and put her head down on one sturdy shoulder. She felt Alex's soft glove in her hair and closed her eyes.

The priest spoke again and Jones's sister stood. This time, she sang "Dream a Little Dream of Me". Alex lowered her head and her lips were against Rachel's ear. "You don't have a shift tonight, right?"

Rachel shook her head, the intimacy of Alex's whisper threatening to destroy her composure. She felt Alex's fingers tighten on her shoulder, just a slight gesture, there and gone, but

Rachel smiled and pressed her face against the wool of Alex's jacket. It was so warm. Cozy, even. She wondered what it would be like to curl up naked in this jacket. She wondered if maybe she'd get a chance to find out soon.

The brief graveside service ended and the priest thanked everyone for coming out. He led the group in prayer and then sent them away with a blessing. Jones's mother, a matronly woman with thick eyeglasses, made her way over before the firefighters could escape. "You worked with Alfred?"

"Yes, ma'am, we did," Murray replied.

She took each of their hands in turn, giving each one a shake and then moving to the next one. "Alfred spoke of you all often. You treated him well."

"He was a good man, Mrs. Jones," Leary said.

The corners of Murray's mouth twitched, but he contained himself before the woman saw it. She thanked them all again and then allowed her son's fiancée to lead her up toward the cars.

As soon as they were out of earshot, Alex asked, "What was the smile about, Murray?"

"Me-ee and Missus...Missus Jo-ones," Murray sang, unleashing his smile.

Alex rolled her eyes. "I was better off not knowing."

They walked up the hill and Murray put an arm around Wizell. Together, they half whispered, half sang, "Got a thaaang going on..."

Rachel grinned. The Weasel was back.

Ignoring the men, Alex rested her hand against the small of Rachel's back and said, "I'm going to go to the firehouse and change, then we'll go to your apartment so you can change into something more comfortable."

"Where are we going?"

"Somewhere without a dress code," Alex said. "I'm not specific on all the details yet, but I know that much."

Alex and Bugs changed on one side of the sheet while the guys were changing a few feet away on the opposite side. Murray said, "We shoulda put the ladies next to a window, then we'd get them sexy silhouettes on the sheet. Hindsight and all that."

"I'm sorry, Murray," Bugs said. "Did you say hindsight or harassment?"

Alex had a sweater and jeans in her cubby and changed into them in record time. Carrying her sneakers in her hand, she wrapped the tie from her dress uniform around her eyes and ducked around the barrier between boys' side and girls' side. "Don't worry, guys, no peeking. The blindfold is as much for me as it is for you."

When she'd made it clear of the cubby area, she pulled off the tie and stuffed it into her pocket. Holt was crossing the apparatus bay, puffing on a cigar, and apparently heading for the front of the garage. "Hey, Holt!" she called, waving politely at him. He turned and frowned at her. "Did you go to the funeral?"

"Nuh uh," he said.

"How's the gym?"

"Eh."

"Well, nice talking to you."

He nodded and lifted his cigar in a salute before he turned around again. She went into the kitchen where Rachel was waiting and touched her on the shoulder. "Ready?"

"Mm hmm."

They said goodbye to the other firefighters they passed, Alex promising she'd catch them the next time they headed to the pool hall. When they were seated in the Jeep, Rachel asked, "So, you change with all the guys, huh?"

"Yeah. There's a sheet between us, though. The guys are gentlemen, despite the façade Murray and Wizell put on."

"I'll take your word for it." Rachel smiled. "So, any thoughts on where you're taking me?"

"Somewhere away," Alex said.

"Good." Rachel nodded and settled into her seat. "Away is good."

While Rachel changed clothes, Alex sat on the couch and sorted through the books on the coffee table — a paperback novel called *Sparks of Love*, a hardback Stephen King alongside a thick novel by Amy Tan, and a leather bound copy of *Oliver Twist*. *Eclectic taste*, Alex thought. *Sort of like the kind of woman who reads classic literature and dates a firefighter.* She looked around the apartment, which was bathed in sunlight thanks to the skylight. It was gorgeous, impeccably clean; the sort of place people like Alex Crawford only saw during a fire.

The bedroom door opened and a few seconds later, Rachel appeared. Her hair down, she was wearing a green blouse that wrapped around her torso, and slacks that hid her long legs and fanned out at the bottom. "What do you think?"

"It doesn't show enough leg," Alex said. "Otherwise, it's perfect."

Rachel grinned. "Well, then. Shall we go?"

"We shall."

Alex buckled her seat belt and then looked over at Rachel. "I don't have a grand scheme or anything. I'm just going to drive until something leaps out at me."

"Sounds like an adventure. I'm game."

Alex smiled and pulled the car away from the curb.

Billy Joel serenaded them until Alex just had to change the CD. "Why don't you look through the other CDs and pick out anything that strikes your fancy. If you like Billy Joel," she said, "nothing in my collection should horrify you too badly."

They finally settled on a Leonard Cohen compilation. "Any preferences?" Alex asked, her finger hovering over the "track advance" button.

"I like all of his songs. Except for 'Alexandra Leaving', of course. It's a good song; I just don't like its message." She reached out and brushed Alex's cheek.

Alex blushed and skipped ahead. "'Hallelujah' is safe, right? There are some other versions that are passable, but nothing beats his chorus."

"I couldn't agree more. His chorus gives me goosebumps."

"If we're not careful, we're going to find out we have too much in common. The relationship will be doomed to last forever."

Rachel put a hand on her chest and feigned horror. "I'll have to be very careful, then. Heaven forbid a lasting relationship." Then she smiled, nudged Alex's arm with her elbow, and started humming along with the music as she watched the scenery flow past the window. She didn't care if they ever found some place to stop; she was content just to be in the car with Alex.

After an hour of driving with nothing presenting itself, Rachel suggested, "You know, we could turn back. I've had a great time just riding with you."

"I promised you a night of adventure."

Rachel reached up and rested her hand on the back of Alex's neck, fingers teasing her hair. "Yeah," she said softly. "And I got it. My heart's been pounding all night."

Alex reached up and pretended to brush something away from her eyebrow to hide her blushing cheeks. "If you're sure." She slowed the car to pull onto the shoulder to turn around. As her tires crunched over gravel, a sign up ahead caught her eye and she laughed.

"What is it?" Rachel asked.

Alex pointed at the wooden sign just visible through the underbrush.

Rachel leaned forward and smiled when she read the announcement. "Oh, this is too perfect," she said. "A winter carnival. There's an honest-to-God winter carnival about a mile up the road." She smiled. "I haven't been to a carnival in ages."

"Looks like Fate is still screwing around in my life. I don't know if I would have noticed it if we hadn't pulled over." Alex reached over the console to take Rachel's hand. "I think we've found out where we're going for our...um...what the hell are we up to, five dates?"

"It's the third, actually."

"Are you sure? Only three? Still, we're well on our way to a real relationship."

The carnival was set up on a boardwalk, just off the beach. The fence between the boardwalk and the sand was lined with Christmas lights, making the entire area look like the world's most cluttered landing strip. According to the flyers, the stands along the boardwalk were set to close at nine. Alex and Rachel wandered hand-in-hand through the displays, the barkers offering them end-of-the-night specials and promising they wouldn't leave without a stuffed bear as big as their heads.

Alex declined all of the games of chance. "No sense pouring money down the drain," she said. "I'm saving my money for something worthwhile — snacks." About halfway down the midway, Alex chuckled and pointed at a storefront. "This is what I was saving my cash for. Feel like a funnel cake?"

"I don't think I've ever heard of one."

Alex feigned dismay. "Okay, we're getting you a funnel cake. You obviously led a very sheltered life and, as your girlfriend, I'm obliged to broaden your horizons."

They stood in line and when they reached the window, Alex ordered a plate. She turned to Rachel and presented the paper plate covered by a mish-mash of thin, deep-fried ribbons made of dough. The entire thing was covered over with a mountain of powdered sugar.

They left the boardwalk and found a nicely secluded spot on the sand to sit and enjoy their treat. As Alex settled the plate on her thighs, Rachel sat beside her. "You called me your girlfriend," she said casually.

"Did I?" Alex honestly hadn't noticed when she'd said it, but she wasn't surprised it slipped out.

Rachel nodded. "Am I?"

Alex leaned in and kissed Rachel's lips gently. "Yes. Now, prepare yourself for a taste delight, a carnival mainstay, a staple of the midway walker's diet. I present to you a funnel cake." She pinched one of the ribbons off and held it between two fingers. "Open wide."

Rachel did as directed, poking her tongue out a bit to accept the offering. Alex laid the sugary morsel on her outstretched tongue. She chewed it carefully, swallowed, and took a swig of her drink.

"Well?" Alex asked.

Instead of answering, Rachel moved onto her knees and leaned forward. She cupped Alex's cheeks and leaned in to kiss her. Alex moved the plate to one side and Rachel settled on Alex's lap, running her fingers through Alex's short hair. She bent down and claimed her lips again. After a few seconds, hoots and whistles began to rise from the boardwalk and the women parted, blushing.

Very aware of the audience they had attracted, Alex stood, drawing Rachel up with her. She picked up the plate and guided Rachel back to the boardwalk. "I haven't had this much fun at a carnival since I was a kid," Alex said with a laugh. "And I haven't been kissed at a carnival since I was sixteen."

"So the carnival where you got a kiss wasn't fun?"

"The carnival was okay, and the kiss was fine," Alex said, "but what happened after the carnival was even more fun."

Rachel laughed and pressed against Alex's side. As they strolled down the boardwalk, Alex spotted a stand selling balloons. It was about to close for the night, so she hurried over. "One green balloon?" she requested.

The man peeled a green one away and handed her the string. "On the house. My last customer of the night."

She took it and stuffed three dollars into the tip jar he still had set up. "My last purchase of the evening."

He laughed and tipped his hat to her — he actually tipped his hat, like some gentleman caller in a black and white movie, and she could barely contain her laughter — and Alex walked back to Rachel's side. She stood close, reaching around and gathering the black hair in one hand while holding the balloon with the other.

Trying to look above her head, Rachel asked, "What are you—"

"Shh," Alex admonished as she cinched Rachel's hair into a ponytail using the string.

Rachel pressed her face against Alex's sweater and smiled, wrapping both arms around her waist. "What if I float away?"

"I'll just have to hold onto you extra tight," Alex whispered to the top of Rachel's head.

"Okay."

They held each other for a few moments before the flow of the crowd forced them to move on. The street lights remained on, but one by one the midway lights went dark. Booths stood empty, abandoned for the night with curtains pulled down over their fronts. Signs proclaimed bargains that were no longer available and knick-knacks that were no longer on the market.

When they got back to the Jeep, Rachel ducked her head and used her hand to guide the balloon into the car so she wouldn't accidentally pop it or get it caught in the door. They sat in the darkness for a while, watching as sweepers moved out and started to clean up the detritus of the day. "Erasing the day," Rachel said softly.

"Yeah."

Rachel looked over at Alex in the darkness of the car. "What was the name of the fireman who saved you when you were six?"

"Michael Graham."

"Do you still feel Fate is trying to get you?"

"Mm hmm."

Rachel reached over and took Alex's hand. "Then do you mind if I hold on real tight, too?"

Alex smiled. "I think it would make all the difference."

Rachel's apartment building almost seemed closed for the night, too. From the outside, a few windows were alight, but only a dim glow issued from the lobby. Rachel opened her eyes long enough to key in her code at the front door, getting them past the security system. Alex escorted Rachel up to her apartment, practically carrying her exhausted date into the elevator. During the trip home, Rachel had grown progressively quieter and her head had dipped toward her chest a few times. Now she was just barely awake, her eyes shut, her weight resting against Alex like a drunk being escorted from a bar.

At Rachel's door, Alex smiled and kissed her cheek. "Hey," she whispered. "You're home. I need your key."

Rachel's eyelids fluttered and she glanced toward the door. She groaned and pushed herself into an upright position. "Right." She fumbled around in her pockets for a moment and finally produced the key. As she stumbled inside, she stepped out of her sneakers and flipped on a light switch. Three lamps in the living room immediately came on. "Do you want something to drink?"

she asked, heading into the kitchen. "I have wine, grape juice, some apple juice."

"It's kind of late. I should probably get going."

"Are you sure?" Rachel's tired eyes focused intently on Alex. "I know we've been joking about what number date we're on, but this is our third date."

They looked at each other for a moment and then Alex reluctantly nodded. "Still, I probably should go."

"Well, okay."

Alex kicked herself. Rachel sounded so damn rejected. She walked around the island and into the kitchen. "I had a really great time today. I never would have imagined it waking up this morning, but you really made today not suck." She tucked a strand of hair behind Rachel's ear. "I was wrong for taking your hair down this afternoon. You look good with your hair up."

Rachel pressed her forehead against Alex's shoulder and whispered, "I really wish you'd stay."

"I know." The two words were half whispered, half sighed.

"So stay. I won't regret it in the morning."

"I-I don't think we should."

"Are you scared of me?"

Alex closed her eyes and kissed Rachel's temple. "Yes."

"I'm just a woman," Rachel said.

"No, you're not. You're not just anything. No matter how much I enjoyed tonight, I don't want to associate my being with you with the funeral this morning."

Understanding dawned in Rachel's eyes. "Oh. Of course. Alex, I'm so—"

"Don't be," Alex said. She smiled. "It's good to know you're willing."

"I am. I want to hold you. I want to be with you." She kissed Alex's neck just below her ear and felt the taller woman tremble. "But I'll wait for you."

Alex stepped back and kissed Rachel's lips, moving her hand from the small of Rachel's back to the curve of her ass, cupping it. Lips parted and the kiss deepened. Alex moaned helplessly as her tongue moved into the warmth of Rachel's mouth. Speaking through the kiss, Alex said, "I should go."

"Then go soon," Rachel said.

Alex broke the kiss and touched Rachel's hair again, taking a moment to release the balloon string. She handed the balloon to Rachel. "Goodnight."

"Goodnight. Don't forget, I want to cook for you."

"I'm off tomorrow night."

Rachel nodded. "Then tomorrow it is. Goodnight, Alex."

Alex wanted to go back to Rachel, kiss her again, just for good measure, but she resisted. She held herself back, knowing that if she touched Rachel again she wouldn't be able to stop touching her. She opened the door and stepped into the hallway, shutting the door before she did something she would regret.

Alone in the apartment, Rachel smiled and whispered, "Suddenly, the night has grown colder." She sighed and tied the balloon string around the back of a chair. She ran her finger down the length of string, making the balloon rise and fall like a fishing bob. Her body electrified from the parting kiss, she went down the hall to take a long soak in a bubble bath.

They hadn't spotted him after the funeral, nor had there been any sign they realized they were being tailed during their insanely long road trip. He couldn't decide if they had a specific destination in mind or if they were just driving aimlessly. When they stopped at the carnival, he climbed out and wandered the midway a few paces behind them, always close but almost never within earshot. They bought a funnel cake and sat on the sand, feeding each other.

He turned away during their nauseating display of affection, waiting until he saw them stand and move down the boardwalk, to resume his surveillance.

Tracking them back to Shepherd wasn't hard. By that time, they were practically the only other car on the road. They stopped outside of an old apartment building and Crawford practically carried the smaller woman inside. He groaned, expecting to not see them again until morning. The neighborhood was quiet, the cars on the street bespeaking the level of money secured behind these walls. It was high dollar, which meant security systems.

He waited a few minutes, watching the front of the building until he saw a window light up on the top floor. He planned to stay until the light went out and then go home, or somewhere he could stop thinking about what they were doing.

To his surprise, Crawford came out of the building a few minutes later. He trailed her at a safe distance until she parked in front of a brownstone in a seedy part of town. It was apples and oranges compared to the neighborhood they'd just left. He parked in an alley and sat in silence, paying attention to the door Crawford entered.

A few minutes later, a light came on in the window over a hairdresser's shop. He drummed his fingers on the steering wheel until the light went out again. He gave her some time, just in case she planned on leaving again, but after half an hour he slipped out of his car. This neighborhood wouldn't bat an eye at the sight of someone getting into a car he didn't have the keys to.

He hurried across the street and worked the lock. He'd picked up the skill at a "camp" that was supposed to repress his criminal activities. Even before his teens, he'd been a holy terror. He snickered at the thought, knowing that the camp had been the training ground for his more horrendous acts. It was there he learned how to set a good fire, there that he'd learned how easy it was to pick someone's pocket.

The lock was pathetic. He was in the car before anyone happened by and spotted him. He went through the glove compartment, looked at her CDs — resisting the urge to break the Billy Joel disc in half — and searched for something good. The bad part about the neighborhood was that Crawford was smart enough not to leave anything expensive in the Jeep overnight.

Then, he found it. A cell phone.

He picked it up and flipped open the front. The screen saver was a St. Florian's cross. He fiddled with the keys until he found the phone book. A smile spread across his face as he read the names and numbers of people near and dear to Alex Crawford's heart. He closed the phone book and went to "recently received calls".

"Tom, Rachel" was at the top of the list. He closed the phone and tucked it into his shirt pocket as he got out of the car. A kid in low-riding jeans and a skullcap sidled by on the sidewalk, eyeing the Jeep. They locked eyes and he slammed the door. "Keep walking, kid."

The boy held up his hands in acquiescence and kept walking.

He patted the side of the Jeep before returning to his own car. The kid had his pick of people to rip off; Crawford was his designated victim. He climbed into the car and sat in darkness for a while, trying to decide what his next step would be.

His neighbor's Sawzall was in the trunk. He checked his watch, drummed his fingers on the steering wheel, and decided there was no time like the present to start orchestrating his next masterpiece.

Alex woke the next morning unsure of what time she'd finally fallen asleep. She had mentally kicked herself the entire way home and, as she stared up at her ceiling, tried to recall her reasons for leaving that had been so clear back at Rachel's apartment. She kicked aside her blankets and slipped out of bed, automatically reaching for her cell phone. When she realized the corner of the dresser was bare, she bent down and searched the pockets of her jeans. Nothing. She sighed and dropped the pants. She'd track down her phone later.

In the shower, she shampooed her hair and, fearing the wrath of Moon Ki-hyun, used the conditioner she'd bought the day before. She was about to step out of the shower but at the last minute, decided to shave her legs. The date with Rachel was at the back of her mind. She'd had reasons for leaving the night before, but damned if she could remember them in the light of a new day. If the opportunity arose tonight, she didn't want her unshaven legs to be the deciding factor in whether she stayed.

Once she was out of the shower and dressed, Alex went downstairs to search her front seat for the errant cell phone. She was annoyed to find the remote for her car alarm had apparently malfunctioned and the Jeep had spent the entire night unprotected. But it still sat in the same space and everything seemed in order, so she wasn't too concerned.

The bad news was that the cell phone was nowhere to be found, not even when she knelt on the passenger side and peered upside-down beneath the driver's seat. She sat down and stared at the floor in frustration. She reached over and fiddled with her CDs, frowning when she saw how cock-eyed they looked. "I thought Rachel put these back a little neater," she muttered, straightening the cases.

With a sigh, she got out of the car and slammed the door. She set the alarm, making sure this time that the alarm chirped, and went back upstairs. As she was unlocking her apartment door, it hit her.

The beach. The phone must've fallen out of her pocket when she and Rachel were sitting on the beach with the funnel cake. She kicked herself again — she was finding a lot of reasons to do that, it seemed — and went to the house phone. She dialed her own cell number and leaned against the counter, chewing her bottom lip as the ring tone sounded in her ear.

After a minute with no answer, she sighed and hung up. She didn't fancy another drive all the way out to that boardwalk, but she couldn't think of any other options. If she did make the trip, she would have to do it soon in order to get back in time for her date. She dialed again, this time Rachel's number.

"Hello?" said a sleepy voice.

"I'm sorry, I can call back—"

"No. I'm up, I'm here." Bedclothes shifted and Rachel cleared her throat. "Alex. Hi. I'm up."

Alex couldn't help smiling. "Hi. How are you?"

"Sleepy," she said. "What's up?"

"I just wanted to let you know I have to drive out to the beach again. I lost my cell phone, so I want to see if I dropped it when we had our funnel cake."

"Oh, okay."

"I just didn't want you to worry if I was incommunicado today. I promise I will be back for dinner. What time should I be at your place?"

"I was thinking seven. We could eat and then maybe watch a DVD, listen to some music, whatever."

The possibilities in "whatever" made the hair on Alex's arms stand up and she smiled. "Sounds good."

"I was thinking of making an Alaska salmon bake. Is there anything you're allergic to? Lactose intolerant, vegetarian, anything I should know before buying ingredients?"

"Well, you should know I'm not a vegetarian since you watched me destroy a steak at Vollie's. And I don't have an issue with allergies. The salmon thing sounds wonderful."

"Okay, so I'll see you at seven."

"Okay."

They hung up and Alex grabbed her leather backpack. She left the apartment, hoping she could track down the right part of the beach.

Rachel hopped out of bed and checked her watch as she dressed. She couldn't believe she'd overslept, but she'd spent a long time last night staring at the ceiling and wondering how she could have convinced Alex to stay. She had a few errands to run, ingredients for the salmon bake to pick up. She attempted to set the world record for showering, then dressed quickly and gathered her hair into a ponytail.

As she was collecting her purse and things, her cell phone rang. She pulled the door shut with her free hand as she flipped the phone open. "Dr. Rachel Tom," she said. "Who is this?"

When there was no reply, she took the phone away from her ear and looked at the display screen. Information Not Available. She grimaced. "Hello?" she repeated. When no one answered, she disconnected and shoved the phone into her purse. She headed downstairs and had just stepped onto the sidewalk when the phone rang again. She sighed and paused, checking the readout. Information Not Available. She silenced the ringer and decided to ignore the phone for the rest of the morning. There was really no reason to keep the phone on. She wasn't on call, and Alex had just said she would be out of touch all day.

He blinked when he saw the woman on the street pause and look down at her cell phone. Surely it was just a coincidence. He couldn't be so lucky.

He smiled as the woman stuck the phone into her purse without answering. She looked different than she had last night, but this must be the same woman he'd seen with Crawford. He put the cell phone down and slipped out of his car to follow her on foot.

Alex stepped out of the bakery and planted both hands on her hips. She scanned the boardwalk and tried to remember where they'd gone the night before. Three businesses were open, but none of them reported anyone turning in a lost cell phone. She spotted a clump of bushes that looked familiar and shifted the sand with the toe of one shoe. She'd borrowed a cell phone from someone in the bakery, so she dialed her number and searched the sand again, hoping to hear the familiar ringing coming from one of the small dunes. Nothing.

She returned the phone to the man in the bakery and reluctantly headed back to her Jeep, casting a look over her shoulder at the sand. If the phone wasn't there, where could it possibly have gotten lost?

He followed Dr. Tom through an assortment of stores and restaurants, pausing outside a fish market and waiting for her to come out rather than following her in. Alex's stolen phone vibrated in his pocket again and he ignored it. He took a moment to see what Rachel bought and tried to get a picture of what she was planning. So far, she'd picked up a small bag of lemons, some parsley, and a bag of pecans. He was stymied. The fish market probably held the undiscovered key ingredient, but it was little more than a long glass counter and a small waiting area, nowhere to hide, so he dared not go inside while she was still there.

From across the street, he peered through the front window and wished the market was on the other side of the street. The sun was wreaking havoc with his spying.

She exited a few minutes later with a large bag, the shape of a box within giving him absolutely no clues. He waited until she got ahead of him before he began to track her again. She seemed happy, practically gliding down the sidewalk as she completed her chores. She stopped at an outdoor ATM and he got into line two people behind her. He ducked his head, pretending to go through his wallet when she turned and walked past him.

After a few minutes of wandering, he struck upon a brilliant idea. He almost jogged back the way they'd come, going back to the apartment house he'd spent all night in front of. He found countless ways to look busy without seeming as if he was loitering — smiling politely to passers-by, tying his shoe, or leaning against the wall and speaking into the cell phone he'd pilfered from Alex Crawford's car.

Finally, after only twenty minutes of waiting, opportunity struck. He had Alex's phone pressed to his ear when he saw the elevator inside the lobby open. This was his chance. He hesitated just long enough for the elevator passenger to get to the front door. Then, he moved onto the front steps just as the tenant was pushing the door open.

"I don't care if that's what he said," he sighed, faking a conversation. He grasped the door and pulled it open, giving the tenant a courteous smile. "Just here to help," the smile said. "Yeah, I'm right outside your building now, Rachel. I'll be up in a minute."

The tenant walked on, seemingly not hearing or not caring about the conversation.

He smiled and went inside. He was damn good at improvising.

Rachel used her code on the intercom and a chirp from the door signaled that it had been accepted. She pulled the door open and made a beeline for the elevator, hoping to get the fish into the freezer before they started to thaw. She'd lost a lot of time getting the idiot connoisseur at the wine shop to admit he wasn't sure of the best accompaniment for her meal and then call someone else to help. She stepped into the elevator and pressed the button for her floor just as someone in the lobby called out, "Hey! Hold the elevator, please."

She did as he asked, sticking her leg out and letting the doors bounce off her calf. The man stepped inside the car and exhaled, leaning against the wall. "Almost didn't make it," he said with a bright smile. "Thanks for holding it."

"Ten years of squat thrusts finally pay off," she said. *Please let the fish be all right,* she whispered in her mind, watching the numbers. "Which floor?"

"The, the fourth."

Rachel frowned. "I'm the only tenant on the fourth floor. Unless...well, the landlord keeps some supplies up there."

"Oh, I'm sorry. I must have my numbers mixed up." He reached over and pressed the button for the lobby.

She glanced at him, suddenly wary. He was dressed casually, in a sweatshirt and jeans, but he seemed somehow uncomfortable in them. He was wearing a baseball cap with a completely straight visor, meaning it was relatively new. "Who buzzed you into the building?"

"The super. I'm helping him out a little today, you know, taking up some of the slack. He's my uncle."

She nodded, but wasn't particularly convinced. She made a mental note to call the super and make sure this guy was on the up and up. He motioned at her shopping bags. "Had yourself a little spree, did ya?"

"I'm preparing something for dinner tonight."

"Ah. Bought something from Fisherman's Wharf, I see?"

"Yes." The elevator doors opened and she stepped out, making sure not to turn away from the man for too long. "Is there anything you need on this floor?"

"No. I should go see my uncle about what he wanted me to do. It was nice to meet you."

She nodded slowly. "Yeah. You, too."

The elevator doors closed and she immediately went to the stairs, leaning over the railing until she could see the sliver of the lobby below. Listening intently, she heard the ding of the elevator followed by footsteps on the tile floor. Her heart pounded as she waited to hear him on the steps, coming up to catch her unaware. Instead, she heard the front door of the building open and close.

She stepped back. Whoever the guy was, she must have scared him off. He should work on his cover story, though. Now that she thought about it, she was pretty sure the superintendent was an only child. No way was he an uncle.

Putting the bizarre incident out of her head, she unlocked her apartment door and repeated her internal mantra: *Please don't let the salmon be spoiled.*

He kicked himself for giving in to impulse. He had only gotten into the building to see how it was laid out. The woman had surprised him by coming home while he was in the lobby, and the opportunity was too good to pass up. But he never should have gotten into the elevator with her.

He pushed aside his apprehension and decided that all was well that ended well. She'd been suspicious from the very beginning, but he felt that she wasn't overly concerned about him. She'd probably already put him from her mind. He wondered if she would mention the incident to Alex over dinner. It was unlikely, unless her life was so without drama that such a minor interlude was all she had to talk about.

He walked back to his car and slipped behind the wheel. He considered calling again, another hang up, but decided against it. Couldn't have her putting the crank calls together with the weird man in the elevator.

Putting Alex's phone in the glove box, he sank down in his seat and prepared for another long stakeout.

Rachel came out of the bathroom in a robe, still combing her wet hair as she went into the kitchen. She eyed the recipe she had propped against the seasoning bowls and gathered the tools she would need to pull this off. "Okay, mix this and that and set aside. Mix these and... Crap!" She noticed the dish required finely chopped pecans. She cursed herself as she looked at the whole pecans she'd bought. How the hell had she made that mistake?

She put the mustard, honey, and butter into a large bowl, nestling the phone between her ear and shoulder as she mixed. She knew she could just chop up the whole pecans, but that sounded like an awful lot of work. Too much work, when she could get the same result from the delivery boy with a single phone call. "Hello, yes, this is Rachel Tom from the Spring Creek Apartments? Yes, Apartment 4. I have a problem. Do you happen to stock finely chopped pecans? You do? Yes, I'll pay extra for delivery. How much do... Just one bag. ... Okay. ... All right... I'll buzz him in. Thank you so much." She hung up and smiled. "Crisis averted."

That done, she skipped to the next step. She quartered the baby potatoes and dumped them into one of the pots of boiling water. The green beans went into the next pot. With the side dishes going, Rachel turned her attention to the main course, beginning with seasoning the raw salmon filets. She didn't know how spicy Alex liked her food, so she kept it at a happy medium. She used a basting brush to apply the honey mustard mixture and glanced at the clock just as the downstairs buzzer sounded. "Right on time," she said with a smile.

She buzzed the delivery man up and was waiting at the door when the elevator doors opened. The same kid who always delivered her groceries smiled at her. "Are you ordering nuts just so you can see me, Dr. Tom?"

"That must be it, Daniel," she said, taking the small bag and handing him a ten. "Keep the change. Get yourself a haircut."

He rolled his eyes and stepped back into the elevator before the doors even had a chance to close. She waved goodbye and went back into the kitchen. "I'm on a roll," she whispered as she mixed the pecans with bread crumbs. She added a small amount of parsley and smiled at the way it all looked on the fish. "Marvelous. It is a good thing."

She turned the knob on the stove to "pre-heat" and then reached for the dial that set the temperature. Her fingers tensed as she gripped it. She took a breath and whispered, "Stop it." As if she'd uttered the magic words, her fingers turned the dial to four hundred degrees.

While the oven heated up, Rachel withdrew the small ruler her mother had ordered her to always keep on hand and stood it next to the thickest filet. "Three inches thick, ten minutes per inch, thirty minutes."

She set the tray into the oven with a, "See you in a half an hour, fellas," and turned the knob to bake.

With nothing left to do, she checked her watch. The food was cooking, the table was set, and the waiting game had begun. She removed a bucket from beneath her sink and filled it with ice. The bottle of wine — pinot noir — was placed in the bucket and wouldn't be opened until just before dinner. With everything cooking, or chilling, there was nothing left for her to do at the moment. She tugged off her apron and went down the hall to get dressed and put on her make-up.

Alex was home in time to change, put on the bare minimum of make-up, and check her messages. No one had called to tell her they'd found the errant cell phone. She sighed and dialed the number once more, hoping for a miracle. Still nothing. Okay, so it was official — her cell phone was missing. Not great, but not the most earth shattering thing in the world. She would call the company and see about tracking it, if it had some kind of GPS transmitter, or just shutting the darn thing down. But not today. She had too much stress already to add dealing with a phone company to the mix.

"Please," she whispered as she headed back out, "let this be the one bad thing that happens today."

Hair blow-dried, make-up applied, dress half on, Rachel returned to the kitchen and checked the progress of her meal through the glass front of the oven. Everything looked good and the kitchen had a wonderful aroma, as well. Shrugging into the shoulder straps of her dress, she used a hanger to zip herself up and then straightened the bodice. Perfect.

She sliced two lemons and laid them on the edges of her finest china plates. They were just average black china — no one to pick a pattern with, sadly — but they were the nicest dishes she owned. She found her wine glasses, holding them up to the light and wiping away the water spots she could see. Rachel set one down on either side of the table and went to the kitchen to dig through her groceries. She found two decent sized sprigs of parsley to garnish the plates and placed them next to the lemon halves.

Her oven timer dinged and she removed the fish from the oven. She pulled on oven mitts and felt her heart skitter against her ribcage as she pulled the door open and a wave of heat washed out over her. She pulled the tray out as quickly as possible, very careful to keep her arms away from the hot surfaces inside the oven. The fish smelled divine, but Rachel used a fork to flick the corner of one filet to make sure it was flaky enough. "Perfect," she said with a pleased smile.

She turned off the oven, looking all the way down the row of dials that lined the front edge of the stove top. She fiddled with them, turning them all a half turn to the right before turning them off again. They were all off, the little red light was dark, the oven was off. She bent down and peered through the glass, making sure the red hot coils were fading back to black. Rachel had never been able to relax around stoves, but her anxiety of making the evening perfect for Alex was driving her to obsessive-compulsive levels.

Finally convinced the stove was actually off, she placed the tray on top of the stove. She was going to wait until the last possible moment to transfer the fish to the plates so they would stay as warm as possible. Her stomach growled its impatience and she smiled as she looked at the clock. Seven minutes until seven. Could she time it or what?

Sneaking a green bean to hush her stomach, Rachel looked around the kitchen for something else to do. Table was set; food, ready; wine, chilled; she was showered and made-up. All she could think about was what Alex would think of her meal. She snuck another green bean and turned her thoughts to the final touch of the evening. She went down the hall and looked at her bed. She didn't have dirty clothes lying around, and the bedroom looked presentable enough, but she wanted it to be perfect if Alex did end up seeing it at the end of the evening. She went in and began tidying.

He watched Alex pace outside the apartment building. She walked into the alcove of the front door a few times before retreating. After a few aborted attempts, she finally stepped up to the intercom and stared at the call button. He wanted to pound on his horn and yell at her to just get it over with, but he didn't want her to know she was being watched. Finally, after an excruciating wait, she pressed the intercom button and, after a brief conversation through the speaker, opened the door and disappeared inside.

"About time," he muttered, sliding down in his seat and watching the highest window. He'd had to cut his preparations short the night before; he hadn't been able to concentrate with thoughts of Crawford and that — woman — filling his brain. So he'd gone home before he was finished.

Now, though, there was nothing to keep him away. He'd finish his masterpiece tonight. He started his car and pulled out of the alley.

Hopefully, by this time tomorrow, another firefighter would be dead.

Alex stared at Rachel for a moment and then sputtered, "Wow. You look beautiful." Alex had worn a button down shirt and black slacks, going with what had worked for her on the first date, but Rachel was in a low cut black velvet dress that ended just above her knees. Her hair was up but loose, a few strands framing her face. "I'm sorry if I'm early," Alex added when she could pull her eyes away from Rachel.

"You're right on time, actually," Rachel said, ignoring the compliment and trying not to blush under Alex's scrutiny.

Alex held up the small bunch of assorted flowers. "I-I didn't know if I was supposed to bring anything. This was all they had down at the shop on the corner."

"They're lovely." Rachel took them and bent to sniff one petal. "I'll just go find a vase, okay? Would you like something to drink?"

"Yes, please. Whatever you have is fine."

While Rachel was in the kitchen, Alex took the opportunity to wander through the apartment. She edged toward the dining room table and admired the beautiful setting: two candles, two water glasses. All that was missing were the flowers, which she had actually remembered to bring. Hiding a triumphant smile at the thought of doing something right, she said, "It smells amazing in here."

"Momma was a chef," Rachel said as she returned from the kitchen with the flowers in a bell shaped vase. In her other hand, she held two wineglasses by their stems. "Would you..." Alex took the glasses and Rachel placed the flowers between the candles. "She taught me how to make a delicious feast in under an hour. It's a helpful trick when you spend half the day in bed before a big date."

Alex laughed and said, "I'm sure it will be marvelous. You look marvelous. Did I say that?"

"You did." Rachel laughed. "You can say it again, if you like, but three times is your limit."

"Well, then," Alex said, "I'll save the last one for later."

Rachel blushed pink and pulled one of the chairs out. "Have a seat. I'll go get our dinner." She got halfway into the kitchen before she said, "Would you please light the candles? There's a lighter right on the edge of the table."

"Sure." The lighter had a long neck with a trigger below. There was a child safety roller that Alex had to push with her thumb before she could activate the flame. It took her two tries before she realized that the trigger was locked in place. She released it and lit both candles as Rachel returned. "Have a lot of kids around?" she joked, waggling the lighter.

Rachel tensed. "Don't play with that."

"Okay." Alex put the lighter down on the table. "Sorry."

Rachel smiled self-consciously and set the plates down. "No, I'm sorry. I'm Ms. Worry Wart about stuff like lighters and leaving the oven on and all that."

"Ah, a firefighter's dream woman."

Rachel grinned and waved toward a chair. "Have a seat."

Alex sat as instructed and allowed Rachel to push her seat in. When she was settled, Rachel bent down and nuzzled the back of her neck. "I'm really glad you came tonight," she whispered.

Alex shuddered.

Rachel stroked Alex's arms before retreating to the other side of the table to pick up the plates. "Dinner is served," she said, placing one in front of Alex and one in front of her chair. She vanished again and returned with a bottle of wine in an ice bucket. "And here's the wine, in case you need a refill."

"Wow," Alex said admiringly. "I thought we weren't going to a restaurant tonight."

Rachel smiled self-consciously. "Well, I couldn't exactly defrost a couple of TV dinners and plop them down in front of you, right?"

"Even a TV dinner would be wonderful as long as I was eating it with you."

Rachel ducked her head to hide her blush. "You keep making me blush," she said shyly.

"Should I stop?"

"Stop and I'll hurt you," Rachel warned.

Alex took the wine from the ice and popped the topper off the bottle. She poured a little more into both glasses. When they were ready, she lifted her glass and toasted, "To Alfred Jones."

"To Alfred Jones," Rachel echoed. Their glasses clinked against each other and they each took a sip. "Now, let's dig in. I skipped lunch and I'm famished."

As they ate, the silence in the apartment was only broken by sounds of silverware on china. Halfway through the meal, Alex picked up her wine glass and took a sip.

"So. The comment I made the other night about feeling like I'm sleepwalking," Rachel said without preamble.

Over the rim of her wineglass, Alex raised an eyebrow.

Rachel dabbed her lips with a napkin and cleared her throat. She looked down at her plate and shifted slightly in her seat.

"I feel I should explain that, just so you'll know. I had an older sister, Rebecca. My idol. She was only a few years older than me, but I just adored her. She protected me. From kids at a playground, mean kids, the world at large; I always felt safe when she was around, even if there wasn't any real danger." Rachel's eyes went flat as she drifted back in time and then snapped to Alex. "Anyway, when I lost her..." Even now, the pain overwhelmed her. She licked her lips and took a drink before starting again. "She died when she was ten. When I lost her, it was like my arms had fallen off. I was adrift. When I was sixteen, Rebecca had been gone for ten years, but I was still adrift. So I started hanging out with women that were stronger than me, women who could protect me like Rebecca had.

"The girl I was seeing when I was seventeen, the girl I lost my virginity to, got 'protect me' and 'prove she's stronger than me' confused. She started to hit me. Once she broke my little finger just to prove she could."

"Rachel," Alex whispered.

She shook her head. "It's fine. I got out of the relationship before graduating high school. She vanished; I got help. It was my first and last abusive relationship. After that, I gave up trying to find women who could protect me and just dated women I was attracted to. Quite a concept, huh? I got past my neediness; I just have a hard time trusting people."

"So, why did you trust me? I mean, not that I'm not thankful..."

Rachel smiled. "That day at the hospital, I stepped out of the elevator and saw you sitting on that bed, and they told me you needed help. Something in me..." She shrugged her tanned shoulders and looked down at her wine. "I don't know. It was like it was the last step of putting the past behind me — helping someone stronger."

Alex shook her head. "I'm not stronger than you."

"You are," Rachel said. She reached across the table and touched Alex's arm. "I promise. That's why I'm so surprised at how hard I'm falling for you. Maybe this is the last step — being with someone strong enough to protect me, but also someone I truly have feelings for."

Alex stroked the back of Rachel's hand. "So, am I replacing your sister?"

"In no way," Rachel said vehemently. "I've given up trying to replace her. You're just someone with strong arms that I want to feel wrapped around me."

Alex shuddered — a very good shudder, the kind she hadn't felt in quite a while — and smiled. "Can we finish eating first?" she asked.

Rachel laughed. "Sure. I can wait that long."

Alex resisted the urge to lick her plate, settling instead for stealing half a small potato from Rachel's plate. "That was the most delicious piece of fish I've ever tasted," she said as she leaned back in her seat. "You are a culinary goddess."

"A culinary demigoddess, maybe," Rachel countered as she stood. "My mother holds the title, even though she's long gone. But I accept your compliment."

They gathered the dishes together and carried them into the kitchen, placing the dishes in the sink to be washed later. Alex put an arm around Rachel as they walked into the living room, the plan being to choose a DVD for part two of their date, but halfway there Alex stopped.

"What is it?" Rachel asked.

Alex bent down and kissed Rachel's lips. Her fingers lightly brushed Rachel's cheeks and moved the feather-soft waves of hair out of the way. Their tongues touched, and the tart taste of the wine was shared between them. When they parted, Alex looked down into Rachel's eyes and said, "It's been a while since anyone looked at me the way you have tonight."

Rachel didn't know what to say to that, so she simply pressed her face against Alex's shoulder. As they embraced, she felt the sinewy muscles of Alex's back, her strong shoulders filling out the back of the shirt. "Remember what I said about wrapping your arms around me?"

Alex flattened her palms against Rachel's shoulders, held her tight, breathed the scent of her hair. "Tight enough?" she murmured.

"I feel so safe with you," Rachel whispered, the feel of Alex's arms around her blocking out the rest of the world. Her lips moving against the crisp cotton of Alex's shirt, she asked, "If I asked you to stay tonight—"

"It would save me having to ask you," Alex said. Her hands had found the bare skin between Rachel's shoulder straps. The heat coursing through her fingertips made them throb.

They moved together, Rachel angling Alex back until she was against the wall. "What—" Alex subsided when Rachel shushed her. They kissed again, but only briefly, before Rachel began to kiss her way down Alex's neck.

She worked the buttons of Alex's dress shirt, parting the two halves and kissing each exposed bit of flesh until she reached the arch of the white tank top underneath.

The feel of Rachel's tongue on her skin was almost too much for Alex. She put her hands on Rachel's shoulders, chin against her collar, watching as Rachel moved lower. Kissing through the material of Alex's tank top, Rachel lifted the hem and nuzzled the exposed flesh with lips and tongue.

As her zipper was tugged down, Alex spread her feet apart. Across the room, she could see her reflection in the window — breasts pressing against the taut tank top as she took a deep breath. Her reflection looked like an oil painting, the only movement the rise and fall of her breasts and her fingers leaving Rachel's shoulders to tangle in her hair as she knelt down. Rachel settled back on her haunches and slid her fingers along the waistband of Alex's pants. She looked up, her dark eyes questioning. Alex nodded, her heart pounding.

Rachel snapped the catch on the pants and leaned in. She kissed the tight muscles of Alex's abdomen as she slowly slid the trousers down, pushing the material down to Alex's knees. Switching focus to Alex's briefs, Rachel brushed the cotton with her cheek and then lightly placed a trail of kisses along the stretch of Alex's thigh. She hooked her thumbs in the elastic and leaned back as she tugged the underwear down.

What followed was a miracle of lips, teeth, tongue tip, and points south. Rachel made quiet noises of half spoken words, their meaning unimportant. What was important was the sound of her voice, the vibrations of her lips, and the thrumming of her tongue as she lapped at her dessert.

Alex turned her eyes toward the ceiling and focused on the black vanes of the skylight. She could see the moon, could see everything, and there, in a hazy reflection, herself. Herself, pants around her knees, with a beautiful woman in a beautiful outfit kneeling before her. She arched her back and moved one hand down to thread her fingers through Rachel's perfect hair as she came.

Rachel was in no hurry to rise. She abandoned Alex's thighs and laid a trail of tiny kisses along her stomach. She kissed Alex's breasts, her shoulders, and throat as she rose to stand before her again. Their lips met, wet lips sliding along dry, Alex's hands slipping around Rachel's waist. "Good?" Rachel asked as she nestled her face into the curve of Alex's neck.

"Mmmm." Eyes closed, Alex tightened her fingers on Rachel's hips and pulled her closer.

Rachel reached down and tugged Alex's pants up, then took a step back and casually re-buttoned the slacks.

"What about you?" Alex asked.

Rachel took Alex's hand and walked backward toward the couch. "We have all night. You should probably pace yourself."

Alex allowed herself to be led and then seated on the couch. Rachel curled complacently against her side, resting her head comfortably against Alex's shoulder. *Pace myself,* Alex thought. *Definitely something I can do.* Still trembling, she kissed the top of Rachel's head as the movie started.

The rafters were sagging, but the ceiling around them looked to be all right. The problem would come when the firefighters began moving across it to effect their ventilation. Come to think of it, they probably used a Sawzall for that, too. Poetic justice, he thought, as he replaced his neighbor's "borrowed" tool in its case. He hoped he would be able to get it back in the shed without the idiot next door catching him.

The sabotage completed, the arsonist gathered the rest of his tools. He had a lot of work to do before the building was ready to burn. Doing the job right would take a long time, he was dismayed to admit, but perfection was better than rushing through and ending up with a firefighter getting hurt instead of killed.

He was still berating himself about that first fire. They interviewed the survivor on the news, made him out to be some kind of hero. They had revealed his nickname was "Weasel" and, twice during the interview, the man had made inappropriate advances to the female reporter. All "Weasel" had done was stay alive. Big fucking deal. And what was he doing with that life? Running around playing grab-ass with the nurses, calling himself "Weasel". What the hell kind of name was that for a grown man? Honestly, he regretted that the self-proclaimed Weasel had survived.

All in good time, he figured, kneeling down to set the first trap in this building. Given time, perhaps Weasel would return to work. Then he would have another personal target. That would be fun. It was nice to have an alternative if his current approach got boring.

As he spilled gasoline down the stairs, he looked at the abandoned building around him. "You were magnificent in your prime," he said, feeling a bit sad about ending this building's life. "You've been forgotten, but don't you worry." He watched the gasoline flow down into the darkness. "You're going to go out in a blaze of glory and a phoenix will rise from your ashes."

Chapter Eleven
Did You F-in' See What Just F-in' Happened?

"You're missing the movie," Rachel said. She smiled and let her eyes drift shut as well. Her hands were under the hem of Alex's shirt and her body was pinned on the couch beneath the other woman.

"So are you," Alex said as she nipped the point of Rachel's chin.

"I've seen it before."

They kissed. Alex pushed her hand between Rachel's back and the couch cushion. "Is it really, really good?"

"Mm..."

Alex rephrased her question: "Is it better than this?"

Rachel arched into Alex, moaned loudly, and bit her bottom lip. "Oh, it's only okay..." She reached for the remote to mute the sound. Her fingers went limp and the remote fell to the carpet with a thud. Alex moved her hand from Rachel's bare shoulder to the scooped neck of the dress. Rachel squirmed away and Alex's hand slipped free. "Please, don't put your hand on my back," Rachel said. She took Alex's hand and placed it on her thigh. "There," she said as she spread her legs.

Alex locked eyes with Rachel and acceded to the unusual request, easing her hand north. Rachel gasped quietly, her breath coming in shorter and shorter gasps as Alex explored higher. Her dress rode up, revealing the tops of her stockings and the edge of her slip. She closed her eyes as Alex cupped her mound with a gentle hand.

Rachel whimpered as Alex's fingertips began to stroke her through her panties. Rachel brought her left leg up and hooked it over Alex's hip. "Is this payback...for what I did to you...against the wall?"

"This," Alex said, moving her hand slightly, "is part one of payback."

"What's part two?" Alex moved her hand again and Rachel cried out in pleasure.

Strong fingers slipped under the cotton and made contact with wet flesh. Rachel shivered and draped her arms around Alex's neck. She opened her eyes and looked up at Alex. "Bedroom."

Alex nodded and reluctantly withdrew her hand. She stood and helped Rachel off the couch. Rachel took the lead, walking

Alex down the short corridor to her bedroom. She left the overhead light off and settled Alex on the edge of the bed. Leaning back on her elbows, Alex didn't take her eyes off of Rachel.

Rachel turned on a lamp and turned her back to the bed. She looked over her shoulder and Alex took the hint, reaching up and tugging the zipper of Rachel's dress down. The material sagged and Rachel let it fall to the floor. She turned back to face the bed as she let the slip fall.

Alex stared raptly as Rachel slowly undressed, documented every article of clothing as it was removed and carefully laid to the side. Alex shed her own shirt, feeling silly in her slacks and bra as Rachel walked nude over to the bed. "I hate being the only one naked," Rachel said, drawing her hand down Alex's bare stomach.

Alex took the hint and reached behind her back, finding the catch of her bra and releasing it. Rachel drew a sharp breath and arched an eyebrow as Alex undid her trousers and pushed them down her legs. She kicked them away, and Rachel plucked one cuff and pulled them off the bed.

"There's a good girl," Rachel cooed. She ran her eyes over Alex's muscular legs, wishing she could spend the entire night just exploring the tight, strong flesh. But she had other ways she was anxious to spend her time. She bent down and kissed Alex's lips hungrily.

As they kissed, Rachel knelt on the bed, straddling Alex's waist and sitting on her lap. Alex moved her hands along the outside of Rachel's thighs, holding her up as Rachel scooted closer and intensified their kiss. Alex moved her hands to tenderly cup Rachel's ass. "No higher," Rachel said against Alex's mouth.

"What?"

"Keep your hands where they are," she whispered.

"Will you handcuff me to the headboard if I don't?"

Rachel purred. "We'll see."

Alex kissed her again and squeezed gently to let her know she didn't plan to stray. At least, not until later when they had the appropriate toys. As a reward, Rachel reached down and moved her hand between Alex's thighs.

Almost an hour later, both nude and tangled in the sheets, Alex made a mistake. She was sitting in the center of the bed, Rachel comfortably facing her on her lap. She had her hands on Rachel's hips and casually slipped them to the small of her back to pull her closer. Rachel tensed in her arms and hissed, "Stop," but it was a second too late. Alex frowned as her fingers passed over rough, scarred flesh. She opened her eyes and leaned forward to peer over Rachel's shoulder.

Rachel pressed her face against Alex's neck, warm tears flowing down her cheeks onto Alex's shoulder. She sobbed, "I was going to tell you."

Alex flattened her palm against the burn, horrified to feel that it spread beyond the span of her fingers. It ran from just below Rachel's shoulder blades, fanning out in a triangle until it faded just above the cheeks of her ass. The scoop of her dress had been just high enough to keep the scars out of sight.

"Oh, Rachel."

"Can you not ask?" Rachel whispered. "Please, Alex. Just make love to me right now. Please?"

Alex moved her hand to Rachel's shoulder. Her other hand went traveling and cupped a sensitive area. Rachel cooed and kissed Alex's shoulder.

Finally sated, they curled together under the blankets. Rachel pressed herself against Alex's side and fell asleep, her hair a dark sunburst on the pillow behind her. Alex watched her, the innocent way her lips parted to murmur at dream companions. She couldn't get her mind past the scar tissue — the way it had felt, the way Rachel's demeanor had changed as soon as it was touched. She eased her way out of bed, taking care not to wake Rachel, and located her underwear on the floor.

She put them on, then settled for her blouse when she couldn't find her tank top. She shrugged it on and left it unbuttoned as she sat in the easy chair across the room. She pulled her legs up onto the chair and watched Rachel sleep. It was just past three in the morning. The streetlight and the moon had melted across the window pane and were washing the room in a muted yellow-blue aura. From the armchair, Alex could see Rachel's profile glowing in the combination of lights.

Who hurt you? she wondered, the feel of that scar imprinted on her fingers. *Who hurt you and how can I hurt* them?

After a few minutes, Rachel stirred beneath the sheet and stretched an arm across the now vacant side of the mattress. Her hand hesitated for a moment and, when she realized she should meet resistance, her head came up off the pillow. "Alex?"

The abandonment in her voice broke Alex's heart. "I'm here," she said softly.

When Rachel sat up, the sheet fell away to expose one bare breast. "I...I thought you left."

"No. I couldn't sleep and I didn't want to disturb you."

"Come back to bed," Rachel whispered, lifting one hand in an imploring gesture.

Unable to resist, Alex stood and undressed before climbing back under the blankets. When they embraced, she felt the scar tissue under her hand again. Rachel flinched, but not as much as she had the first time.

"Now you can ask," she said, her face against Alex's collarbone.

"Not if you don't—"

"It's okay. I can talk about it, but not during... I can talk about it now."

Alex kissed Rachel's temple and, although she was already sure of the answer, asked, "It's a burn, right?"

"Yes." She took a shuddering breath. "I was six. Rebecca picked me up and put me in a closet, and I was mad at her. She was babysitting me and I thought she was just being mean. But then she ducked over me, covered me with her arms and she..."

Alex felt warm tears on her chest and stroked Rachel's back.

"The apartment was on fire," she said, her voice barely a whisper. Her breath was captured between her mouth and Alex's breast. "She was on top of me, crying. There were security bars on the windows so we couldn't get out."

Alex closed her eyes. She was familiar those damn bars — mildly efficient at keeping burglars out, wonderfully efficient at keeping firefighters out and families in during house fires. Murray called them "fuck-me bars".

"I don't know how much time went by. It was s-so loud. I dream about it sometimes, but I don't know how much is memory and how much I've just made up to fill the holes. I remember being curled up with my face in the corner. I remember my sister crying and screaming. I don't really remember the pain. I remember the hospital, but only because you don't forget a hell like that. It's funny, I was permanently scarred by the fire, but all I remember was being hurt afterward in the hospital. When I woke up, my sister was dead and my back was..." She swallowed hard. "My sister took the brunt of the flames. It...some of it got past, burned my back. The main thing I remember is Rebecca's voice in my ear saying, 'Don't be afraid, Rachel, I have you, it's not going to get you.' Over and over again."

After a long moment, she continued. "Since then, I've been terrified of fire. The stove, sure, to cook, I can handle that kind of heat. I get very anxious about making sure the burners are off, but

I can handle it. But, matches. And cigarettes. It's why I got so bent out of shape about you playing with that stupid lighter. It's why I asked you to light the candles in the first place. If I even hold a book of matches, I start shaking like a leaf. So when I saw you in the emergency room, I just thought...I thought, 'This woman ran into a fire. This woman faced a fire and won. I have to meet her.' You made my knees weak." She ran her fingers across the bandages on Alex's wrist.

"Can I ask you...the first time I put my hand there, you tensed up. But afterward, you told me you liked it. Is it okay that I keep touching it?"

"It's numb most of the time," Rachel said. "It doesn't hurt or anything. But when you have your hand there, it's like you're protecting it, protecting my vulnerable spot. That's why I like having your hand there. It's...intimate."

Alex embraced Rachel and fanned all ten fingers over the small of her back. Rachel nuzzled Alex's shoulder. "Are you going to stay until morning?"

Her face in a cloud of Rachel's sleep- and sex-mussed hair, Alex said, "At least."

On his way home, he swung past the doctor's apartment again. All the lights in the building were off and Crawford's Jeep was still parked down the street. He checked his watch and decided they were settled in for the night.

He pressed his foot to the accelerator. Crawford would be back on duty the next day, he assumed. It would be the perfect time to spring his trap.

When Alex woke the next morning, she found Rachel watching her. They made love again before they decided they should get up. Alex took the first shower and Rachel hopped into the stall immediately after. Dressed in the same clothes as the night before, Alex sat in the kitchen and ate a bowl of Crunch Berries. When Rachel emerged from the bathroom in a terrycloth robe, they shared a kiss and Alex poured a bowl of cereal for her. "Milk?" she asked.

"Yes, please," Rachel said.

Alex got the carton she'd found in the fridge and brought it to the table while Rachel poured a cup of coffee. Alex presented the bowl of cereal with a flourish, and a smirk. "It's not exactly Alaska salmon bake with pecans, but I think it'll do for breakfast." She kissed Rachel's temple and brushed a stray lock of hair out of her face. "Happy anniversary, by the way," she said.

"What?" Rachel frowned. "Anniversary?"

"One week ago today, that was when we met in the emergency room."

"A week?" Rachel said, thinking back. "My God. Well, happy anniversary. Did you like the present I gave you last night?"

"Mm hmm," Alex said. "In fact, I think I'm going to play with it again the next chance I get."

Rachel blushed and sipped her coffee. "Do you have to go?" she asked. "We could stay in bed a couple of hours..."

"Afraid so; on duty at noon, and I want to get some jogging in. What about you?"

"Shift at 10:30."

Alex frowned. "So why did you invite me to stay?"

"I kind of like your company." Rachel grinned. "I would've called in sick if you were off."

Alex grinned and stirred her cereal.

"So, jogging. Was last night not enough of a workout for you, dear?"

Alex smiled. "That was a different kind of exercise. A lot of different muscles involved, at least."

Rachel swallowed her mouthful of Crunch Berries. "Are we going out again soon?"

"The sooner the better," Alex said, covering Rachel's hand with her own. "I'll have to check my schedule, compare it with yours."

"Yeah." Rachel nodded. "For two people with crazy job schedules, we've been really lucky this week. We're due for a long period of frustrating conflictions."

Alex looked at the time and stood, "I should go." She leaned down and kissed Rachel, tasting Crunch Berries on her breath. "And you really should know better, being a doctor and all. I expected to find oat bran or Kashi or something."

"I have a sophisticated and eclectic palate. And I'll have you know I do have some Kashi. You just stopped looking when you found the junk," Rachel said. "Be safe today, okay?"

"Always am," Alex said. "And now that I have even more of a reason..." They kissed again and Alex pulled away and headed for the door. "Bye. I love you."

Rachel stopped, the spoon frozen halfway to her mouth, and turned in her seat. Alex was smiling at her from the door. "Yeah, I meant it." She waved again and strode out into the hallway.

Alone in her apartment, Rachel looked down at her bowl of soggy cereal. She rested her chin on her hand and laughed, three glorious words echoing in her head: "I meant it."

Murray grabbed Alex's shoulders from behind and started shaking her back and forth. "Ready? Huh? Ready?" Then he gripped her shoulders and squeezed, giving her the roughest massage she'd ever had.

"You're gonna kill me, Murray," she said.

They were standing outside a flaming warehouse, several different streams of water crisscrossing the face of the building. The shift had been long and dull up until this call, giving Alex plenty of time to think about the night before. Rachel. Every thought came up Rachel. When the call came, the sun had just set and they could see the bright orange flames against the dark sky. Murray had whooped and said, "Looks like we're gonna earn that paycheck tonight, ladies and lad."

They had just arrived and were waiting for word that the fire was being held back before they sent someone to the roof to cut ventilation. Leary approached, tugging his ear. "Murray! Let's go, we've got the all clear! Get up on that roof!"

"All right, all right, it's about time! C'mon, Crawford," Murray said, moving to the ladder.

"No, take Bugs," Leary countered. "Crawford, you're with me. Help me get these fans set up."

"Chief," Alex started to complain.

"Bugs has the saw; she's ready to go," Leary said. "Plus, she needs the experience. Let's go!"

Alex reluctantly followed Leary as Bugs climbed onto the truck with Murray. Leary hoisted the big fan and she was right behind him, uncoiling the cord from another fan as they got it off the truck. They carried the fan to the front of the building and set it on the front steps, stepping back to watch Murray and Bugs scamper up the ladder.

Murray leapt onto the building's ledge with the grace of a dancer, Bugs following right behind him as if choreographed. Leary grabbed his radio. "We're ready down here whenever you give us the call, Murray."

"Things are a bit shaky up here, Chief."

Leary rolled his eyes and thumbed his radio, "Cut it out, Murray. I'm sure Bugs got enough practical jokes at her last house. Just cut—"

"No, it's... Goddamn, I'm like a... Holy shit, Chief!"

There was a crash, a collapsing sound echoing from inside the building as the fire roared toward the sky with renewed life. Leary automatically slammed himself into Alex, his momentum carrying her away from the building in case of collapse. They hit the ground and rolled. Alex immediately scrambled to her feet to look back at the carnage of the building. The fire looked like it had doubled in size in just a few seconds. There was only one explanation for its renewed vigor — it had found a new and plentiful source of oxygen. "The roof collapsed," Alex said in disbelief. "Not again. Not another fucking one."

Leary was already gone, shouting orders into his radio to redirect the water streams. The fire was a different animal now, and he needed to change his method of attack. Alex hurried after him, making herself ready for whatever he needed her to do. She was about to suggest going up to the roof to see what kind of damage they were looking at when she heard a groan in her radio. "Fu...k me."

Alex exhaled, recognizing the voice immediately. "God, Chief. Murray!"

Static burst onto their radios, followed by a very loud and very heartfelt, "Fuck me sideways!"

"Murray?" Leary said into his mike. "Murray, copy; are you ambulatory?"

"Chief! Oh, fuck, Chief, fuck me blind... Hold on."

Leary looked at Alex, eyes wide. After a few minutes of silence, Leary was reaching for his radio to call again when the door of the building was kicked open. A firefighter, uniform charred black, burst out. Judging from size alone, there was no doubt it was Murray. He had another, smaller firefighter held against his side as he stumbled into the cool evening air. He made it only a few steps before falling on his face.

Alex and Leary rushed over and pulled the two away from the collapse zone, both of them shouting for medics at the top of their lungs. Murray thrust his head forward and his helmet hit the ground with a solid thud. He yanked off his air mask and looked up at Leary with wide, half crazed eyes. "Did you see! Did you f-in' see what just f-in' happened!"

"Did you fall through a roof?" Alex asked. She knew how stupid the question was but was unable to keep it from coming out.

"Chief never told me not to," Murray said. He turned and said, "Is Heather okay?"

Alex moved to Bugs, who was being tended to by a paramedic. "Bugs, are you okay?" she asked, grasping the other woman's hand. She didn't breathe until she saw Bugs' eyes swim into focus.

Bugs took a deep breath and her body was wracked with coughing. Alex kept a palm against her back until she could speak. "Murray saved my life," Bugs rasped, coughing between words. Blood was streaming from her mop of blond hair; her steely blue eyes moved back and forth without settling on anything. "Murray saved me," she repeated. "He fucking saved me."

"Yeah, he did," Alex affirmed.

She stood and went over to the chief, who was by the ladder truck. Leary looked at her. "So, Murray tells me the roof is ventilated now."

Alex laughed at the comic relief. "Guess we can turn on the fans." They headed for the front door, picking up the fan Murray had knocked over during his miraculous retreat. As they turned on the monstrously noisy blower, she glanced over at Leary and asked, "Are you okay, Chief?"

"Thought I lost both of them," he said softly. He ran his thumb across his bottom lip, shook his head, and walked away. Alex watched him go, looked down to be sure the fan was operating properly, and then returned to Murray.

Both of them!

Both of them? How was that fair? That wasn't fair!

He smacked his fist against his thigh and allowed himself a mini-tantrum inside the safety of his car. Damn. He had put so much thought into that. It should have been perfect. His initial disappointment when Crawford didn't head to the roof was tempered by the fact he would at least get a sacrificial lamb or two. But how could it all go so horribly wrong? He exhaled and let the rage slowly seep away until he was calm again. He threw the binoculars into the passenger seat and started the car.

He'd have another chance. He would just have to be patient. With any luck, his next trap would get the entire damn company.

Appalled, he pulled out of the parking lot with his headlights off to avoid anyone noticing him. As he merged with the flow of traffic, an idea came to him. Perhaps there was a way to salvage some fun from this fire after all. It wouldn't be the same as a death, but what in life was, really?

He pulled Crawford's cell phone out of the glove compartment and dialed as he drove.

Rachel opened her locker and withdrew a Snickers bar from her stash. It was another hour until she got a dinner break, and the candy would help her make it. She was about to slam the door shut when her cell phone began to vibrate against the bottom shelf. She had already forgotten about the crank calls the day before and picked up the phone and hit the "talk" button without checking the ID. "Dr. Tom."

A low, hoarse voice said, "Your girlfriend just died in a fire. My condolences." He hung up without another word.

Rachel stared at the phone in her shaking hand, eyes wide as her brain processed his words. One part of her brain told her that it wasn't true, couldn't be true; it was just the cruelest joke anyone had ever played on her. Another part of her brain whispered, "What if it is true?"

She dropped the candy bar and stumbled away, leaving her locker door open as she rushed out of the dressing area, hurrying down the hall, building speed until she was running. She burst into the waiting room and snatched the remote from a man sleeping in an easy chair.

She flicked from channel to channel until she found live footage of yet another warehouse fire. She saw the medic truck on the scene with its lights flashing, and the firefighters milling around on two sides of the building. A shot from the news helicopter revealed that the entire roof had collapsed, leaving a gaping maw spitting fire at the sky. From another dimension, she heard the reporter say that two firefighters had fallen through the unexpectedly weak roof.

She hit the floor, her knees crying out in protest as they smacked the linoleum. Later, they told her that she'd screamed loud enough to be heard at the nurses' desk, but she didn't remember that at all.

Finally calmed down enough to sit still, Murray sat on his gurney, looking down at Bugs as he breathed through the SCBA. The fire had been knocked down and all that remained was clearing the wreckage. Leary approached the medic truck, climbing onto the bumper and glancing at Bugs before he said, "All right, Murray, what the hell happened up there?"

Murray pulled his mask off and shook his head. "We...we made it onto the roof, but something was hinky up there, Chief."

"Kinky?" Leary asked.

"No, hinky. Not quite kosher."

"How?"

Murray seemed at a loss for a moment. After he'd had a bit of time to think, he shook his head. "All I remember clearly is falling. I thought I was dead meat for sure." He cleared his throat. "The roof was way too unstable. Shaky. It got really bad after Bugs started cutting, like we were standing on a surfboard made out of plywood. The roof started to buckle, so I jumped and grabbed Bugs. Figured I'd..." He exhaled. "I don't know. I guess I figured she could use me to break her fall or something, I don't know. I wasn't thinking."

"And you just walked away?" Leary sounded as if he wouldn't have believed it if he hadn't seen it with his own two eyes. "That was a three story drop in there, Murray."

"Bugs hurt her knee and hip. Not bad, but I had to help her walk outta there."

"Where did you land?"

"There were no fucking floors, Chief, just air, all the way down to the ground level. We hit this big pile of crap; I don't even know what it was. I was on fire, but Bugs pounded me out and we got outta there like the hounds of Satan were on our heels." He shrugged and muttered, "Probably ain't too far from the truth."

Bugs said something into her mask, so Leary moved to her side and removed it.

"The rafters," she said. "I saw them when we landed, just barely. They were all screwed up."

"It's an old building," Leary said.

"No. They looked like clean cuts, like someone sawed through them."

Leary looked over his shoulder and spotted Crawford amid the overhaul crew. "Apparently the theory that the arsonist is targeting firefighters might hold water after all." He clapped Bugs on the shoulder. "I hope you're a fast healer, Riley. They only give us so many replacements during a calendar year."

"I'll be back ASAP, Chief, promise."

Leary climbed out of the truck and grabbed the doors, seeing Bugs take Murray's hand before he shut the door on them. He turned and stalked back toward the building. If someone was setting traps, like Crawford suggested, if they were trying to kill his firefighters, this was going to be the last damn time the bastard even came close.

"It was like something out of the movies," Alex said, "the way Murray came strutting out of that building with Bugs. Oh, man, me without my camcorder."

Wizell slapped Murray on the leg. This time Murray was the patient and Wizell was a visitor. He and Alex were still in their turnout pants, but the rest of their uniforms had been left down in Leary's truck. "I thought I told you to leave the heroics to me, eh?" Wizell said. "Or at least time them so I'm around to see it. Man, I can't believe I missed Mr. Hero here. Three damn floors, man."

"Excuse me," a nurse said from beyond the edge of the curtain.

"Sorry you missed the big show, Weasel. But did Superman time his heroics so the spectators could watch? Did Batman?"

"You calling me Lois Lane?" Wizell asked.

Alex nodded at the other bed. The nurses hadn't been keen on putting a man and a woman in a room together, but Chief Leary convinced them to make an exception in this case, hospital policy notwithstanding. "If anyone's Lois Lane, it's Bugs here. How's that IV drip working out for you, Riley?"

Bugs gave a thumbs up. "I'm thinking of coming here after shifts from now on."

"Excuse me," the nurse said again.

Wizell finally heard her and stepped out of her way. "Sorry, sweetheart," he said as she entered.

"Murray," Alex said, "you do realize we're never going to let you live this down, right? The teasing begins now. Okay, so, how many probies does it take to completely screw up a ventilation cut? None, if you got Wayne Murray on the job."

The nurse put a hand on Alex's arm. "Excuse me."

Alex looked at her and anticipated the coming objections from the nurse. "He needs his rest; we really shouldn't be in here." The nurses just didn't understand that having fellow firemen around helped the injured. She sighed. "Can whatever you need to do to him wait? We're talking to our friend here." She had a whole list of jokes she couldn't wait to unleash on Murray.

The nurse tried to smile, but it didn't work very well. "I'm sorry to interrupt, but do you know Dr. Rachel Tom?"

Alex frowned at the unexpected change of subject. "Yes."

"I'm afraid there's been an incident."

The blood drained from Alex's face.

Nurse Mary Evanov looked up at the smell of smoke, automatically prepared to chew out whoever had lit a cigarette. Instead, she saw a frightened looking woman with a soot blackened face charging toward the desk. "Rachel collapsed?" She put her dirty hands on the counter and left two starfish-shaped smudges. She was wearing her turnout pants, wide suspenders holding them up over her once white department t-shirt. Her black hair was standing up in spikes, her blue eyes wide and searching. "Is there someone here who knows—"

"You mean Dr. Tom?" Mary asked.

"They said she collapsed." Alex's eyes snapped forward, locking on to the voice of someone who might be able to help her. "Where is she, is she all right?"

"She's fine," Mary said. "She's right this way." Moving around the edge of the desk, she led Alex down the corridor and knocked on the door frame as she stepped inside. "Dr. Tom? There's a—"

Alex shoved past her and made a beeline for the bed. "Rachel, what happened? Are you all right?"

"Alex!" Rachel gasped. She held her arms out for a hug as Alex dropped to one knee next to the bed. The nurse who'd been sitting with Dr. Tom rose from the easy chair and both nurses left the room. Rachel called out, "Thank you, Mary," just as the door closed, then turned her attention to Alex.

Alex sat on the edge of the bed and cradled Rachel in her arms. Rachel motioned for the apple juice sitting on the table and Alex handed it to her. She took a sip and stared down at her sneakers. She was lying on top of the covers, fully dressed, and still wearing her lab jacket. "I feel like such a fool," she said. "Everyone's making such a fuss over me."

"What the hell happened?" Alex asked softly. She brought her hand up to brush at Rachel's hair but remembered the grime on her hands. She returned her hand to her lap but Rachel grabbed it anyway, the soot marring her tan flesh.

"Someone called my cell," she said, keeping her voice low. "He said, 'Your girlfriend just died in a fire.'"

"What!"

"Honey," Rachel said quietly, touching Alex's blackened hand, "of course, I figured it was just a crank call. I got a couple of those yesterday. But I turned on the news and there was this huge fire and they were talking about firefighters falling through the roof..."

"That was Murray and Bugs."

Rachel gasped. "Not that sweet man I met at the funeral? Oh, God, and the blonde—"

"No, they're fine. They're a little banged up; they're downstairs getting the royal treatment, actually, but they're fine." She squeezed Rachel's hand. "And I'm fine."

Rachel sighed and closed her eyes. "I need to get over this. I can't panic and flail and fall down every time you leave for work in the morning. You could die in a fire, but I could get pricked with an infected needle. It's a crap shoot. We can't spend all our time worrying about what might happen."

"Given what happened with your sister... I mean, it's understandable you'd be a little anxious."

"Still, I need to handle myself better. We're going to have to get through a lot of future fires. Might as well start bracing myself now."

Alex rubbed her shoulder. "Maybe you're just...maybe last night..."

With a grin, Rachel pressed her face against Alex's shoulder. "What, you think now that we've slept together, I'm going to turn into an obsessive loony?"

Alex smiled. "You're the one getting all melodramatic in the waiting room."

"I'll be fine." Rachel sat up. "I just have to call my cell company about these damn crank calls."

"Have they all been this bad?"

"No, the ones yesterday were just hang-ups, more annoying than anything else. This is the first time the guy spoke to me."

Alex shuddered. "It's a little frightening, though, right? That someone knows you at least well enough to know about me."

"I'm choosing to ignore that at the moment. The last thing I need is a stalker."

Alex hugged Rachel and kissed the top of her head. "Yeah, I got here first."

Rachel laughed and pulled away, sliding off the bed. "I have to get back to work before they declare me legally insane. Thank you for coming to make sure I was okay."

"What? You thought you could just have a nurse tell me you'd collapsed and I wouldn't come running?" They kissed at the door and went their separate ways.

As Alex reached for the elevator call button, the doors parted and Leary stepped out. He scanned the corridor, seeing her as he glanced to his left. "Chief, what are you doing here?" she asked.

"Been looking for you. They said you were up here. How is...uh..."

"Rachel. She's fine. Just had a fright."

"Glad to hear it." He took her by the elbow and dragged her into the elevator car. "Based on something Murray told me, I called the arson investigator and had him take a quick look at the latest fire. Turns out the rafters were cut through by some sort of power tool. It was deliberate, and it looks like it was done recently."

"How can he tell that?" Alex asked. Her mind was racing. The arsonist was targeting them. *God, what a twisted fuck.*

"Something to do with weather and exposure... He said that the damage, if it had come from wear and tear, the breaks would have been uneven or something." Leary waved dismissively. "I don't know the details. The important part is that I'm sorry for not listening to you before. These fires were definitely set. And the only reason to weaken the rafters is to make the roof unstable. And the only people who would be on the roof of a burning building..."

"Firefighters."

He nodded. "You were right. The bastard is trying to hurt us."

Alex shook her head in disbelief. *How could someone be so twisted?* "Okay, playing devil's advocate, how do we know this fire is related to the other ones?"

"It's just like the other two. This warehouse was also designed and developed from the ground up by Lancaster Building & Development. Project headed by Arthur Lancaster."

Alex groaned and slumped against the wall of the elevator. "So who's the target — us or Lancaster?"

"Von Elm is on his way over to talk with Lancaster now. I figured with your history..."

"Aw, Chief..."

He held up his hands. "Hear me out. Your history, plus, if you walk in looking the way you do now, he may feel sympathetic. We might learn something useful."

"So I'm there to be pitied?"

"No. I was referring to the look in your eye when you thought Murray and Bugs were dead. I'm talking about how Murray said you looked half insane when you heard Rachel might be hurt. I want you to scare that little jackass into cooperating."

Alex smiled. "That, I think I'm capable of."

He watched the news coverage, smiling the entire time, despite his failure to kill anyone. Three fires, one casualty. He was so far behind schedule it was barely tolerable, but this mass panic was wonderful. Every major news station in town was playing footage of the fire, one of them combining their coverage with shots of all the fires in the past week. "Must be a month for fires," one reporter intoned with a raised eyebrow.

"Oh, yes," he responded to the screen. "Oh, yes, indeed."

Helicopters had circled the latest building like maverick honeybees, each making sure their network got its fair share of tragic entertainment.

It was magnificent. He only wished the fire had burned longer. The firemen were far too efficient in knocking the blaze down.

He turned back to his desk and opened the file. Sorting through the paperwork, he tried to decide which would be his next project. Seven buildings, all abandoned and none scheduled for demolition. All skeletons of their former glory, homes to rats of both the vermin and human varieties. They gathered garbage, blocked sunlight; they were called eyesores and wore embarrassing "No Trespassing" signs over their shamed faces. He could get them legally demolished easily enough, but the thought of big machines pushing them over would make him nothing more than a bully. No, with fires, their lives were ended with dignity and notice, at the very least.

No more would they be ignored, forgotten, he vowed. They would not only be given a proper burial, they would go out in a literal blaze of glory. Their final moments would be seen by all, and feared by anyone who had the misfortune to be nearby.

Back when he was first bitten by the arson bug, he had read everything he could find about great fires in history. Seattle, New York, London, Washington, D.C., they had all burned. Each time unsafe buildings were destroyed, vermin were eliminated and newer, stronger buildings were put up in place of the ones that had been destroyed. In the end, these horrific tragedies had led to new jobs and economic booms, giving rise to the thriving metropolises that were known and loved today.

The city would be better for this. The lives of the firefighters were to be the price paid for progress.

He admitted he needed the little waterbugs. By taking a life, the building would never be forgotten. A building that killed a "brother" gained a permanent place in the hearts of at least a handful of firefighters. The death was a sacrifice to the gods.

He had a few things he wanted to try — new accelerants, new traps. He was still furious that his rafter snare had come up empty. He'd worked a long time on that. Ah well, he would just have to up the ante next time.

He pulled Crawford's cell phone from his desk drawer and stared at it for a long time. Was it too soon to put in another call to Rachel Tom? His finger was poised over the button when an intercom on his desk buzzed. He sighed and answered, "I asked not to be disturbed during the news."

"Yes, sir, I'm sorry. But there are some people here to see you."

Frowning, he stuck the cell phone back into his desk drawer and glanced at the door. Who would be here to see him? He had no appointments scheduled. "Yes, certainly, send them in," he said.

The door opened and his secretary escorted the unannounced visitors into his office. He couldn't help smiling. "Ah, Alex. How nice to see you, and Marshal Von Elm. This must be important."

"You could say that," the portly man said. "We need to have a talk about the recent fires, Mr. Lancaster."

Martin Lancaster had to fight to keep his smile. Things had just taken a definite turn for the worse.

Lancaster's smile seemed to waver slightly, but it came back at full wattage a heartbeat later. "Of course," he said, regaining his composure. He straightened his tie and ushered them into the office. "Please, come in." He looked past them at the secretary. "Thank you, Sandra, that will be all, un-unless our guests would like something to drink. Coffee? Tea or lemonade?"

"No, we're fine."

"Okay, thank you, Sandra."

The elderly secretary nodded and stepped out of the room. Lancaster closed the door behind her and indicated the seats in front of his desk. "Alexandra, Marshal Von Elm, or do I remember that you prefer Mr. Von Elm, which—"

"Marshal is fine," Von Elm muttered, sinking into the leather seat Lancaster had indicated.

Alex remained standing, gesturing at her filthy turnout pants as an excuse. She was wearing the same thing she'd worn to the hospital, per Leary's instructions, and had felt incredibly conspicuous waiting for an elevator in the pristine lobby of Lancaster Designs, Inc. "While we're on the subject of names, I would prefer Ms. Crawford. I believe I've mentioned that before." *A couple thousand times.*

Lancaster looked at her for a moment and then held his hands out in a placating gesture. "Very well. I suppose I can't argue with that." He walked around his desk and carefully lowered himself into his own seat. "Now, Ms. Crawford, Marshal Von Elm, to what do I owe this unexpected visit?"

By pre-arrangement, it was Von Elm who spoke. "I was assigned to look over the recent fires in Lancaster buildings. During the course of our investigation, we discovered some disturbing evidence that supports your earlier concern that the fires were the products of arson. We think the same firebug is responsible for all the fires."

"Oh, my goodness." Lancaster's face paled. "I kept hoping I was wrong, and, you know, that it was merely paranoia. But someone like that, running around in a town like this? Do you have any idea who it might be?"

"No," Von Elm said. "At the moment, we're not even sure what the true target is. Every fire seems to be aimed at eliminating the firefighters that respond, but we also have to consider the fact that all the buildings are projects of your corporation."

"Heavens... If you have enough evidence to make a good case..." He leaned forward. "Oh, dear. Oh, my goodness. If somehow my company's buildings a-are more attractive to an arsonist, I offer my most sincere apologies. I could increase security at night, or install security lights."

Alex shook her head. "No, it's not your buildings. I inspected a lot of them myself and they seem sound. We also have to consider that it's just a coincidence. Your company does very well, so the majority of buildings in town are Lancaster properties. The fact that the arsonist keeps torching buildings your company designed might just be because they are so plentiful. Luck of the draw."

"The one time I get the luck of the draw." He smiled weakly and sat back in his chair.

Von Elm frowned. "Look, Mr. Lancaster, basically we just want to know whether you have any enemies; clients who have a beef with you, perhaps?"

"Financial troubles aren't an issue; all these buildings are insured by their owners, I'm sure." He glanced at Alex. "Which I hope you won't take as a motive. It's a smart business practice to—"

"We understand, Mr. Lancaster," Alex cut in. "But try to think. Is there anyone you know that might be trying to get even with you or hurt you?"

He ran a finger along his top lip and stared at the window for a moment. "I'm afraid I can't think of anyone off the top of my head." He sighed and shrugged apologetically. "My enemies, what few there are, tend to aim for my pocketbook. And we're not talking about subtle snipers here. I've had court dates five out of the past eight weeks. If anyone was going to try and hurt me, they'd do it there, in the courtroom, with the legal system behind them."

"I had no idea you were in such legal straits, Mr. Lancaster."

"It sounds worse than it is, really," he said. "Land rights, property lines in dispute, people suing because my new development blocks their view of the mountains or some such nonsense. These things are usually settled out of court."

"Anyone take umbrage at their settlement? Maybe think they weren't getting what they deserved, decided to take a pound of flesh along with their money?"

Lancaster grinned. "As Ms. Crawford could probably attest, Marshal, I'm a very charming man. Usually, when the case is over, the plaintiffs thank me and apologize for taking my time."

Rolling her eyes at the comment, Alex noticed that Lancaster seemed relaxed, almost at ease with the world around him. She frowned. He'd been antsy when they'd arrived, but now that he was hearing their questions it was almost as if he had not a care in the world. "May I ask you a question, Mr. Lancaster?"

"Of course, Ms. Crawford."

"How do you feel about firefighters?"

He blinked and tilted his head. "Well, I don't know. How do you mean?"

"Just in general. If you see a fire engine on the street, what's your first thought?"

Lancaster glanced at Von Elm and shrugged. "I don't know. I hope no one is hurt. Lately I've been hoping it's not my building they're heading for." He smiled. "I must confess I don't spend a lot of my time thinking about them. It's a shame, too, considering the invaluable service they provide."

Hard to believe, she thought, *considering the number of times you've called the firehouse, all the times you've dropped off snacks, all the pestering you've done.* She bit back the cutting remarks lined up on her tongue and said, "Do you know what a flashover is, Mr. Lancaster?"

"Yes." He sighed, scratching his temple. "That's a kind of food, isn't it? No, wait, I'm thinking of turnovers." He glanced at Von Elm, as if expecting a laugh or a rim shot, and then shook his head. "I'm afraid the answer is no, Ms. Crawford, I don't know what a flashover is. What is it?"

"It's not important," Alex said.

"Any other questions?" Von Elm asked. When Alex shook her head, the marshal stood, smoothing his shirt over his belly. "All right, then. Thank you for your time, Mr. Lancaster. We just wanted to confirm that this guy seems to be focusing on your buildings and to ask if you might be able to point us in the right direction."

"I'm sorry I couldn't be of more help." He shook hands with the marshal, then turned and extended his hand to Alex. "It was nice to see you again, Alex."

She looked at him for a moment before she reached out to clasp his hand. She pinched off a smile and nodded her head once. "Back at ya, Marty."

He suddenly tightened his grip on her hand, his eyes blazing for a moment before returning to normal. Calmly, he said, "Martin, if you please."

"Right. Sorry."

He relaxed his grip and Alex squeezed. Martin's foot stuttered forward and he muttered a quick, "Ah," before he could stop himself. Alex smiled and released his hand. He cupped the hand, massaging the knuckles and eyeing the smudges of soot she'd transferred to his palm.

Alex shrugged. "Sorry. Don't know my own strength."

He escorted them to the door of his office and thanked them for letting him know of the potential problem with his buildings. When they were alone in the hall, Von Elm stepped close to Alex and said, "What the hell was all that in there? Flashover, the whole hand deal. Is Lancaster a suspect?"

"Lancaster is a prick," she said, shaking her head. "Leary shouldn't have sent me. I hate this guy."

"Really?" Von Elm said sarcastically, leading the way down the hall. "If only there was some way to decipher your complex system of communication."

She lifted her right hand, showing him her middle finger.

"Now what is that supposed to mean?"

Fuming, Martin walked back to his desk. How much did they know? If they were going to arrest him, or even interrogate him, there was no way they would have just left like that. But Alex — pardon, Ms. Crawford — had been glaring at him throughout the interview, almost as if she knew he was responsible. The marshal seemed as blindsided by her questions as he himself was, so it obviously wasn't a good cop, bad cop performance. Alex had to have seen something that made her suspect him. Maybe he'd let his crush on her blind him to how dangerous an impediment she could be. It didn't matter now anyway.

He sat behind his desk and stared at the closed file of potential targets. Crawford. It all came back to her. She'd been a nice distraction — hypnotic eyes, strong arms — but she was becoming a nuisance. And from what he'd seen of her dates with the doctor, he didn't have a chance with her anyway. Shame, such beauty wasted on another woman.

He leaned back in his chair, wishing there was a way to ensure that Alexandra Crawford would be the sacrifice in the next fire. There was no way to do that unless he was privy to Leary's command decisions. There was by the book, and then there was the experience factor. He wasn't sure he could trust the chief to do the anticipated thing.

He closed his eyes and tried to think of a way to remove Leary from the equation. The only way he could think of to accomplish his goals would be if there was a situation Alex absolutely, positively had to be in. His eyes opened as a plan started to form. There was one way to assure where Alexandra Crawford would be during a fire. It would mean deviating from his original plan, of course, but it would be worth it to get that suspicious bitch out of his way. It would cost him dearly, but he knew it had been leading up to the ultimate sacrifice. He was willing to sacrifice himself for the greater good of the city.

The next morning, Alex left the bunks and headed for the kitchen. She froze when she spotted the cluster of bodies within the changing area, talking in hushed voices. "Whoa. Someone having a panty raid and forget to call me?"

Wizell, instantly identifiable due to the bandages on his neck and his oddly shaped head, turned and flashed his trademark grin. "Hey, Crawford. Come on down; give us a hand."

Chief Leary and Captain Franklin were standing next to him, a sign that whatever they were up to was at least approved by the bosses. William Sawyer, Flannigan's opposite number on the ladder, smiled as he handed her a roll of crepe paper. "Time to get in touch with your artistic side, Crawfish."

It was a tradition in the firehouse to decorate someone's cubby after a big event like a wedding, divorce, birthday, and the like. She looked at the cubby and saw that Murray was the intended recipient this time. Stickers with "Fireproof!" branded on them covered the front of the cubby wall.

Alex smiled as she took a roll of crinkled paper. "What's all this about?"

"Murray's been cleared for duty," Wizell said. "One day after falling through a freaking roof, he and Bugs are both coming back."

"Wow!" Alex's eyebrows rose. "I thought Bugs hurt her leg or her hip or something."

"She was banged up, but she called in this morning and the doc seems to think it was just a bruise," Leary said. "She's going to get an x-ray this morning and then be with us in time for lunch."

"Excellent." Alex, unreeling her crepe paper, innocently added, "But, well, if we're decorating, shouldn't we give Wizell's cubby a sign that says 'Quit milking it, you pussy'?"

Wizell nailed her in the face with a roll of Scotch tape.

Alex was in the den playing a video boxing game with Wizell. Alex's character, Ray "Boom Boom" Mancini, was pummeling Wizell's incarnation of Ali. As Ali got pounded, Wizell griped, "That fire must've affected my reflexes. I swear, I can't move this thumb near as well as I used to."

"There goes your social life," Alex quipped. On the screen, the digital Mancini delivered an uppercut to The Greatest, dropping him to the mat.

She threw her arms up in victory and Wizell cursed at the game. He pointed an accusing finger at her. "It's a good thing you're a firefighter. If you were really Mancini, you would've tainted boxing forever with that dirty fighting."

"TKO, baby. Whine to your momma."

She glanced at the door and saw Bugs watching, a slight smile on her lips. "Hey, Bugsy. Come on; let's show Wizell how dangerous a girl fight can really be."

"I'll take a rain check on that. But could I pull you away for a minute or two? There's something I need to talk to you about."

"I'm all ears," Wizell said, resetting the game for him to box against the computer.

Bugs thumped him on the back of the head and motioned to Alex. "Do you mind?"

"No, it's all right." She patted Wizell on the back. "Next time, I'll be Mancini and you can be Duk Koo Kim."

"No way, man, I know how that fight ended."

Alex was laughing as she followed Bugs into the apparatus bay. They went outside, crossing the grass to a quiet spot next to the kitchen window. Bugs leaned against the wall, withdrawing a cigarette and offering one to Alex.

"No, thanks. What did you need to talk about?"

Bugs inhaled a lungful of smoke and blew it out slowly through her nose and mouth. Alex stood upwind, away from the exhaled flow, and stuck her hands into her back pockets as she waited. Without preamble, Bugs blurted, "I slept with Murray."

Alex blinked, whipping her head around to look at Bugs' face, certain she'd heard wrong. "You, you...what?"

"You heard me." She glanced over her shoulder to make sure they were still alone.

"In the hospital?"

Bugs shrugged.

"Jesus," Alex muttered. Trying to lighten the mood, she said, "'*Dear Penthouse*'..."

"I know how stupid it was; I know I should've walked away, should have known better. I told all that crap to myself this morning when I woke up and realized what I'd done, so we can skip that part of the lecture part of the conversation."

"Are we also skipping the part about your fiancé?" Bugs shrugged. "Shit, Heather. What were you thinking?"

"I was thinking that I'd just fallen through a flaming building with this guy who held my hand on the way to the hospital. I remember feeling more scared than ever before, and him being there for me. I wasn't thinking. When we landed in that building, before he pulled me up, I told myself I was a goner. I didn't think there was a way out. I was lying there, stunned, thinking I was probably paralyzed. I was prepared to die. But then Murray hoisted me up and practically carried me out of that building. If I'd gone up on that roof alone, if he hadn't fallen with me, I'd be dead. How do you think I should handle it with Murray now, short of asking for a transfer?"

Alex leaned against the wall, watching the traffic go by. "Don't try to soft pedal it, or ignore it," she said. "Come right out and let Murray know it was what it was — a one-night stand." She looked over searchingly. "That is what it was, right?"

Bugs nodded emphatically. "Yeah, of course." She took a drag on her cigarette and examined the ash before she flicked it into the grass. "It's just..."

"Uh oh," Alex said, anticipating that even worse news was on its way.

"You never go into a fire without the proper tools. You'll for sure get into trouble if you do. But sometimes, when you're caught off guard, you might find yourself in a flaming inferno without your halligan or your PASS device. We didn't, ah...Murray and I weren't...fully equipped."

Alex frowned. "I saw you on the truck."

"After the fire." Bugs raised an eyebrow and gestured with her cigarette. "After. When we..."

"Oh, shit," Alex muttered. "You didn't use any protection?"

"Murray graduated from high school a long time ago, Alex. Guys don't exactly carry condoms around in their wallets these days. I didn't plan on it."

"You and your fiancé..."

"Paul."

"Paul, then. You don't have birth control pills? A diaphragm?"

Bugs averted her gaze to look intently at the grocery store across the street. "We decided we wanted kids right away. So we...we've been trying."

"I hope Paul has really dark skin," Alex said.

"There's a chance that we...that nothing really happened."

Alex rolled her eyes. "Either what you guys did can lead to a baby or it can't. There's not a whole lot of middle ground on procreation. Which is it?"

"We...uh..." She stopped and exhaled. Finally, she shook her head and rubbed her temple with two fingers. "We did a lot of stuff. But I don't know, I can't remember where we drew the line. If anywhere."

"High school biology time..."

Bugs sighed. "We did what you do to have a baby; I just don't know if Murray...you know...when he was inside."

"Oh, God, please, take these mental images away from me," Alex groaned. She turned and leaned against the wall next to Bugs. "Okay, where do I come in with that? What do you want me to do?"

"I don't know. I just kind of had to tell someone. I thought you'd be the least judgmental, but I guess I was wrong."

Alex laughed. "Oh, no, you were right on the money. You do not want Chief Leary or Franklin or, hell, even Holt finding out about what you just told me. You slept with another firefighter. The chief is highly intolerant of that kind of thing." She tapped her finger against her lips as she thought about the options. "Okay. I assume you know about the morning after pill? Is that an option?"

"My regular doctor is friends with my family. He went to college with Paul, so even with the confidentiality..."

Alex nodded. "The fact that someone close to you would know is a little..."

"Gross. And I'd think about it every time we ran into each other or I had an appointment with him. And who knows, he might spill the beans."

"Does doctor/patient privilege not mean anything to this guy?"

Bugs shrugged. "There's privacy policies and then there's friends for life. There's a chance he'd bring up prescribing the pills the next time he and Paul are out on a good ol' boy drinking binge. I can't risk it."

Alex sighed. "Jesus, Bugs, you're really in it." She scratched her cheek and shook her head. "All right, I know a doctor who can help us. She'll check you out and get you a morning after pill. And from now on, if you're going to make mistakes like this, get your hands on some birth control, all right?"

Bugs sighed. "It was just that it seemed like Murray was the only real thing, you know? After the fire?" She took a drag off her cigarette and shrugged. "I phoned Paul and he was scared. And he was compassionate and loving. But there was a voice in the back of my mind that kept saying, 'He doesn't get it.' He doesn't get how scary it was, or how I thought I was going to die or how I prepared myself to die. And he'll never get it. And then, there was Murray. Who not only went through it with me, but saved my life. And it wasn't just about sex, Alex. It was about him being there. And me being there. And just...being there right then. You know?"

"Yeah," Alex said. She chewed her bottom lip and sagged against the wall again. "Look, we'll have my doctor friend look you over; make sure Murray didn't give you any STDs. She'll make sure everything's good. With any luck, your fiancé will be none the wiser and you go on living with this secret. Can you do that?"

Bugs nodded. "Thanks, Alex."

"No problem." She patted Bugs on the shoulder. "I'll get those tests set up this afternoon, after shift, okay?"

"Sure. I owe you one."

"We're good," Alex assured her. "Just, for the love of God, never pull me aside to tell me you slept with Wizell."

Bugs laughed. "Believe me, that happens and you'll read about it in my suicide note."

They went back inside, spotting Murray in the den playing a video game with Wizell. She put a hand on Bugs' shoulder and said, "Go across the bay."

"And do what?"

"I don't care, just mill about smartly," she said, indicating Bugs should just wander around and look busy. Bugs moved toward the equipment locker and Alex went into the den. She rounded the chair and straddled Murray's legs, blocking the TV. He cleared his throat and looked up at her, his eyebrows raised. "Not that I'm complaining about the view, but I'm kind of in the middle of something here."

"Go talk," Alex said.

"I'm just—"

"Go," she said, nodding into the bay. "Talk."

Murray looked over his shoulder and followed her gaze to where Bugs was standing by the equipment. He sighed and handed her the controller, pulled his legs back and stood up. "You know?"

"A little. Go on, have a nice chat."

He nodded and slipped out of the room. Wizell watched Murray go then turned to Alex, who had taken Murray's seat. "Who does he have to talk to?"

"He knows."

"About what?"

"Again, he knows."

Wizell sighed and shook his head, hitting his controller to resume the game. "Ya stop watching a soap opera for one week and suddenly you don't know any of the characters."

Alex laughed and patted his shoulder. "It's all right. You'll be back in the swing of things before you know it. Now," she said, picking up her controller, "prepare your ass for a royal reaming."

Alex unlocked her apartment door, tossed her bag inside, and went back down the corridor. She picked up the package resting on top of her neighbor's welcome mat and rapped her knuckles against the door frame. She heard a chair hit the wall — a steady series of bangs — and then the shuffling of a walker being pushed across the hardwood floor. When the door opened, the security chain was still in place and a moon-shaped face peered out at her.

"Hello, Mr. Round," she said, exhibiting the package. "You have a delivery."

"Ooh!" His high pitched voice quavered. He closed the door and moved the chain out of the way. When the door opened again, his entire body was revealed. Alex always thought he looked like one of those "It's a Boy!" balloons with arms and legs made of ribbon. He was wearing a green sweater and a white shirt with a bowtie, his entire wardrobe apparently bought from Stock Grandpas R Us. His glasses perched on the end of his button nose, he smiled up at her. "Who's it from?"

Reading the return address before she handed it over, Alex said, "Your son." Both the addressee and sender names ended with Round, so Alex was forced to accept the fact that this man had actually expanded to fit his name. He took the package with a smile. "Looks like another bottle of Scotch," she said.

"Oh, yes, yes, he's too good to me."

"Enjoy it, Mr. Round."

"Oh, I will, I will. And you'll have to bring your boyfriend around and share some with me."

Alex sighed. "I've told you, Mr. Round..."

"Yes, the girls, I remember. But I thought that if you liked that man well enough to let him drive your car, then..."

Alex didn't hear the rest of Mr. Round's reasoning. "Wait a minute," she interrupted, putting a hand on his wrist. "What do you mean 'drive my car'? Who did you see in my car? When?"

He shrugged, more interested in opening his package than her mystery. "I don't know. It was a few nights ago, pretty late. I just assumed he had driven it back from somewhere and was parking it out front."

"Start from the beginning," she said, heart pounding. "A few days ago, you saw a man in my car? What time was it?"

"Well, I was looking out my window at the stars, as I always do, you know. It must have been past eleven. You know, the view from up here is so much better when you get above all the street lights and headlights and—"

"Please, Mr. Round."

He hugged his package to his chest and cleared his throat. "Well, I happened to look down and I saw your Jeep. I saw someone in it and, at first I naturally assumed it was you. Then, the door opened and a man got out. He walked across the alley and got into another car and drove away. I thought you and he had driven someplace in your car and he had brought you home."

"Can you describe the man?"

"He was just a shadow to me. I'm sorry. Did I do something wrong?"

"No, Mr. Round. I'm sorry for asking so many questions. Thank you for telling me."

She bade him farewell and practically ran into her apartment. Her cell phone had been in her car. Whoever had broken into the Jeep had to have stolen it. She grabbed her house phone and dialed her cell, anger growing as she waited for whoever had it to answer. After seven rings, it went to voice mail. She cursed and hung up. She walked across the apartment and leaned against the wall to stare down at the street.

She watched a limping dog, probably the same one from a few nights ago, inching down the sidewalk, and tried to organize the thoughts in her racing mind. Someone broke into her Jeep, left no sign they'd been there, and stole only her cell phone. The coins in her ashtray hadn't even been touched. And in this neighborhood, all cars were just collections of pieces waiting to be dismantled and sold. If the thief had actually destroyed something, her insurance probably wouldn't even have paid for it because of the reputation of the neighborhood. Too many break-ins, too little police presence. The thought of insurance cast her mind back to the fires, and the arsonist.

The buildings were all insured. Maybe Lancaster had hired someone to torch them to get the money. Maybe the lawsuits he'd mentioned were bleeding him dry, sending him spiraling deeper and deeper toward bankruptcy. He found a firebug who liked to watch flames dance, gave him a couple of addresses, and the guy got his rocks off torching a few old abandoned buildings. The firebug is satisfied and Lancaster gets to sit back and wait for the insurance company to call. He gets an instant payday.

But if he was going into debt, he certainly wasn't showing any signs of it. She was still regularly getting called out to building inspections. If the company was losing money, how on earth could Lancaster afford to continue developing all the new buildings? She sighed and sat down on the couch, putting her feet up and closing her eyes.

It was pointless to play detective, especially when there was no actual evidence Lancaster had done anything. She reached for the house phone again and dialed another number. This time, she got a reply on the second ring. "Dr. Tom," a sleepy voice said. "Who, may I ask, is calling?

"The love of your life."

"Okay, Rhonda, but we'll have to make it fast. I'm expecting a call from Alex Crawford soon."

Even though she was sure Rachel was kidding, Alex was surprised to feel her heart skip a beat. "Hey, Rachel, please don't joke like that."

"I'm sorry," Rachel said quickly. "Is something wrong?"

"Long day," Alex said. She covered her eyes with her hand and was surprised to find wetness on her cheeks. "God." She sniffled and swiped at her eyes.

"Murray and Bugs?"

Rachel's voice was calm and soothing, a balm even through the phone line.

"Yeah," she said.

"The fire, or the other thing?" Rachel asked.

Alex had spoken earlier with Rachel about Bugs needing the morning after pill and had explained the whole mess over the phone. Rachel set the appointment for the next day, explaining that the morning after reference was a misnomer and the pill would still be effective if taken within seventy-two hours of intercourse.

She put thoughts of Bugs out of her mind and focused on the real issue, the real thing that had been eating at her since the night before. "The fire. Murray wanted me on the roof with him. The chief overruled him, sent Bugs up instead. If it had been me, Murray wouldn't have been watching as closely. I may have—"

"Hey, what did we just talk about yesterday? No second guessing, no 'what if' or 'if only' talk. You're here. Bugs and Murray are both alive, too. Really alive judging by the tests I'm supposed to do tomorrow." Alex couldn't help smiling at that. "It just wasn't your time. It wasn't theirs, either."

Alex stared at the ceiling. "Time. That doesn't matter."

"What do you mean?"

"Someone is setting these fires. They're trying to kill firefighters. The fire yesterday, the rafters on the roof where Bugs was trying to ventilate had been sawed through. The roof was too weak to hold their weight and it collapsed. Someone is trying to kill us, Rachel."

There was silence on the other end of the line. After a moment, she said, "My God, Alex. Who would, who could be that depraved?"

"Some psycho." *What with your stalker, it seems like a good season for psychos.* Something snapped together in Alex's mind like puzzle pieces. She blinked and said, "Maybe someone warped enough to call and tell you that I had died in the fire."

"You think the arson and my prank calls are connected?"

"They have to be." She sat up. "My neighbor told me he saw someone in my car a few nights ago. I figure that guy stole my cell phone, but I didn't put it together with your crank calls until right now. Shit," she said. "This guy has all my numbers. He has all my contacts. He's the one who's been calling you."

"This is scary, Alex."

Alex blanched as the final puzzle piece slid into place. "He may not be targeting firefighters anymore. He may be targeting me."

Chapter Thirteen
Slowly, Sadly, Lonely

Martin Lancaster had a perfect view of the town of Shepherd outside his office window. Night had fallen and most of his employees had gone home. Some of them had families; others might even have night jobs. The majority of them were married, either to a person or to some vice. He wasn't sure what they did outside these walls and he didn't pretend to care. His secretary had stopped by to see if he needed anything else before she left, and he had sent her away. He knew she was widowed and had two grown kids; he'd seen their pictures on her desk and knew them only as Ugly Boy and Slutty Girl. Their real names were of no importance to him.

He was taking the night off, a well deserved rest from the exhausting work of setting fires. As much as he hated to admit it, he was becoming disillusioned. What good was the grand plan if the fires didn't do what they were supposed to? The firefighters were pretty much in the same position they'd been before he'd burned the derelict buildings, minus one stinking probie. For all he knew, that kid was meant to die in a fire anyway. He couldn't claim that one with any sense of pride. It was like bragging about stepping on a spider — no thrill, no skill, no guts.

The city was quiet. He wondered if there would be any accidental fires about town. Perhaps another arsonist would come to his aid. It wasn't like he held the monopoly on setting blazes. If someone else joined in the fun, well, it would be all the more fun, wouldn't it? It would turn that damn investigator on his ass trying to catch two birds with one net, or something like that.

He sipped his vodka and grimaced. It had been his father's drink and he'd never seen the appeal. But his image of a CEO, the mental picture of the man behind this desk, always included a tumbler of alcohol, almost always vodka. So he kept up the tradition.

The vodka was a salute to his grandfather, a Russian immigrant who had come to this country and promptly been beaten and robbed in an alley. He'd survived, but only just barely. When he was up and about once more, he sold most of the family's meager possessions and used the money to buy the building flanking the alley where he'd been robbed of his dignity. Anatoly Laenko became Anthony Lancaster. Everyone in the family had a traditional Russian name to go with their American name. Behind closed doors, they called the bland American monikers their code names. Maksim Laenko, the only son of Anatoly's only son Artur, was Martin Lancaster to the world at large.

Anatoly had taken the one building and transformed it into two. He refurbished the buildings, made them sparkle, and then sold them both for a profit. He sent Artur to college to become an architect, all the while building the family fortune in anticipation of the day Artur would take over for him.

When Anatoly was fifty, his son came to him with a diploma and a plan. He turned his father's business into Lancaster Designs. Martin had been in the office, buried in the fluffy cushions of his grandfather's couch, watching as Artur put an arm around his own father and motioned at the windows. "America tried to take you away, Father. Together, we shall take this single, small town and we will make it ours."

Artur took over the company when Anatoly retired, demonstrating a keen eye for the business side of things as well as for the design aspect. When Anatoly died, the company transferred to Artur, who immediately began to prepare Martin to take his place. By that point, Martin was fresh from a series of troubled youth camps and had gotten good at pretending to be normal. Artur was sure he would be a great successor to the family empire.

With Artur in charge, the company's profits tripled, his name graced the front page of local papers, and his face appeared in all of the business magazines. But as his fame grew, so did his depression. Arthur Lancaster was the bright boy of business, the millionaire that everyone was scrambling to hire. Artur Laenko was a secreted man, a cipher hidden in the shadows.

Maksim, known as Martin to his schoolmates, was dragged to the company office and forced to sit through hours of board meetings and business lunches when he should have been out on his own, being a boy. As much as he hated his father for stealing his childhood, he started to become a carbon copy of the man. All outside influence was overwritten by his father's lessons.

One night, looking over a blueprint and well into his bottle of vodka, his father gestured at the building on the paper. "She is waiting to be born, Maksim. Buildings, they breathe, and when they are left, forgotten, they die. They die slowly, sadly, lonely."

Martin had never been able to get the image out of his mind. His first fire had been an accident, an expedition into one of his father's unoccupied designs to look at the empty offices. He'd kicked over his lantern by accident and watched in horror as the gas spread in a wide pool. He'd run away, hiding and watching when the firefighters showed up. That night, the building had been on the news and a reporter had come by the apartment to speak with his father.

When they left, Artur sadly clapped his son on the back and said, "The building may have fallen, but its death makes way for something new, and that will breathe new life into this city. What more could an entity hope for, Maksim?"

He had only nodded, dazed at what he had inadvertently accomplished.

Although it was the most amazing excitement he'd ever felt, Maksim never attempted to repeat the act, even after his father's descent into dementia and his own subsequent takeover of the company. Burning a building was exhilarating, but it was also dangerous. But when he met Alexandra Crawford, something clicked in his mind. Firefighters rushed into burning buildings and put their lives on the line. If their lives were given in sacrifice, the building would live on in the minds of others.

His first intention had been to approach Crawford as a partner. After all, if anyone knew about burning a building and getting away with it... But she'd proven to be far too noble for that. He continued to request her for his inspections, deeply in lust with her by that time. Of course, even that was nothing more than an empty dream. He would never bed her. More's the pity.

He pinched his lips around a mouthful of vodka. That doctor... It was unnatural, what they were doing. He was furious with himself for wasting so much time with Alex. He'd been wasting time with everything lately, it seemed. He was irritated with how long it had taken him to realize that. Planning one building at a time, trying to eliminate random firefighters, the trick would be to target specific sacrifices. Alex Crawford would be the first and, alas, the final sacrifice he would take in this manner.

The fire marshal's office was adjacent to the police station, basically a lean-to wedged between the garage and the main building. It was dwarfed by the buildings on either side, hunkering in their shadows as if trying to go unnoticed. Alex parked her Jeep in the visitor's lot and walked around the side of the building to avoid meeting any officers. She had no problem with the police; they performed an invaluable service, just like the fire department. But she did get irritated at how crime ridden her neighborhood was, and how the police seemed to have just given up on it. Not to mention that on slow days, the rivalry between departments became the sole source of entertainment for some people.

She restrained a groan when she saw two uniforms heading her way across the lawn, grinning when they recognized her. "Hey, Sparky," one called. It was the police department's name for every firefighter in town.

"Hiya, Officer Fife," she replied. Fife was the fire department nickname for any and all cops. Another popular nickname was "Officer Keystone". She was glad there'd never been a slapstick comedy about firefighters.

The cop was unfazed by the Don Knotts reference. "Are you playing in the softball tournament this year? Always interested in adding some eye candy to the line up."

She rolled her eyes as they crossed paths. "Mm, not this year, Barney."

"Come on, Sparky. It's for sick kids."

She smiled and shrugged her shoulders, continuing on to Von Elm's office. She knocked on the outside door and slid into the cluttered one room extension. With cardboard boxes and mountains of paper on every horizontal surface, it seemed more like a paper storage room than an actual office. Von Elm was in the center of it all. He looked up as she rapped on the doorframe and waved her into the office.

"Nice housekeeping," she said. "If you want to see Leary so bad, just drop by the station now and then, don't make him come to you."

"Huh?"

Alex gestured at the fire hazard surrounding her.

"Oh. Well, what can I say? Do as I say, not as I do," Von Elm said. "Have a seat. You didn't come through the building?"

"I went around back because I wanted to avoid as many cops as possible, no offense."

He laughed and shook his head. "Ah, none taken. When you straddle the line between policeman and fireman, you find it difficult to side with one or the other. Unless one of them happens to be in the room with you."

Alex smiled. "A cop with the cops and a firefighter with us. What are you when you're at home with your wife?"

"Casanova," he said. He winked and stood up, gesturing at the coffee maker. "Anything to drink?"

"No, I'm fine."

He poured a cup for himself and sipped at it before he resumed his seat. "I got my reports on those fires you and Leary were asking about. Without a doubt, all three were arson. Guy wasn't even trying to cover his tracks."

Alex leaned forward and took three of the files from the top stack on his desk. "So you're thinking it was the same guy all three times?"

"Pretty sure. Had a lot of the same characteristics. He liked to build little bonfires, pour gas all over them. Didn't worry too much about leaving a trail of accelerant, neither." He motioned for the file she was looking at and she handed it back. "Have you seen the building Wayne Murray and Heather Riley were in yet?"

"No."

"This is killer." He leaned forward and framed a square with his hands. "The guy, this arsonist, cuts the rafters to weaken the roof, right? If Murray and Riley had fallen here, here, or here," he pointed to different portions of the roof on the schematic, "they would have hit the top floor. Cement, reinforced, they'd be dead or paralyzed. And if they had been paralyzed..."

"They would've burned to death."

"Precisely. But since they fell where they did..." He showed her another series of photographs. "The building originally had an open air lobby. All three floors looked out over it, so it was a wide open space. When they fell, they landed on a huge pile of cardboard boxes. The pile broke their fall enough that they weren't hurt nearly as badly as they could've been."

Alex frowned. "Why did a warehouse have a lobby?"

"It wasn't a warehouse," he said. "More like a factory. As far as I can tell, they made boxes."

"Okay, why did a factory have a lobby?"

"Hey, I didn't design the place. What do I know about the whys?"

Alex leaned back in her chair. "So it's not just abandoned warehouses anymore, it's pretty much any building designed by Lancaster."

"Or his father," Von Elm pointed out. "Did some reading up on that family. Weird stuff. Did you know they all have two names?"

"What do you mean?"

"Russian and English both. It was mentioned in some tabloid by a former housekeeper of theirs. Our friend Martin is known as Maksim Laenko when he's at home. Martin is his public name. Lady I spoke to said he got bent outta shape if you called him Marty."

She nodded. "Yeah, we saw that when we were at his office."

"Oh, yeah, the handshake thing," Von Elm said. "He did get a little perturbed, didn't he?"

"He was pissed," Alex said. "Maybe something you ought to keep in mind if you have to interrogate him about something."

Von Elm smirked. "I like the way you think. Keep 'im on edge, make him angry."

"Getting back to the buildings, did you find any traps in the latest building besides the cut rafters?"

"You mean more flashover rooms like the ones that burned Jones and Wizell? No, none of the rooms in the third building showed signs of that. I looked over the room that killed Jones, by the way. It was hugely bad. Was anyone in there with him, like a partner or something? You guys do that two in, two out arrangement, right?"

Alex felt her back tense. "Yes, there was someone in with him," she said flatly. "Why? Are they responsible for what happened?"

Von Elm shrugged. "Maybe. I mean, the signs of flashover are obvious. But you can get distracted in a fire and you miss what was obvious in training. I was asking more because this report said another firefighter went in behind Jones. I was wondering how the hell that person managed to survive. Seems impossible to me."

"Me, too," Alex said softly. She tapped the files against her thigh and then held them up. "Do you mind if I take these?"

"No, they're copies. I have a couple more in the cabinet over there." He nodded at the opposite end of the room and then looked down at his desk. "Or, here. Aw, they're somewhere."

"Okay. Thanks, Bill."

"No problem, Alex. And by the way?" She turned back to him. "You Sparkys have more class than a roomful of Barneys."

Alex grinned and saluted him before she left.

Heather Riley sat on the exam table, waiting as Rachel updated her chart. "Okay. That should take care of you for the time being. You can come back in for a checkup in a month or so, just to make sure everything is still going well. You may experience headaches, stomachache, breast tenderness, vaginal spotting, and dizziness, and your period might not show up on the right date." She closed the file. "I'd really feel more comfortable sending this over to your regular physician."

"I really appreciate you helping me out, Rachel. I guess Alex told you why I don't want this in my medical file."

"She did. Don't worry. The doctor/patient confidentiality prevents me from saying anything, though I do think that for medical reasons, your doctor should have a complete file on you. Unless something further comes out of this, I guess there isn't any reason for it to be an issue." Rachel rose from her stool and walked across the exam room. "I understand your need for privacy in this situation."

Bugs smiled ruefully. "Well, let's be honest, Doctor. You can't exactly know what I'm going through here."

Rachel frowned and leaned against the counter. "How so?"

"Well, you know, you and Crawford don't exactly... I mean, the problem of contraception isn't really high on your list of things to worry about."

Rachel felt unduly irritated by the woman's attitude, and since Bugs had turned the discussion to a personal level, she set aside her own professional manner. "I understand you made a mistake. I respect you're doing the right thing by having a doctor check you out. But if I may be frank?" Bugs shrugged. "I feel sorry for your fiancé. I can't even begin to imagine what that man is going through. Or what he would be going through, if he found out about this."

"You're forgetting that he can't imagine what I went through. Murray held me as we went through hell. I may have taken a ring from someone else, but Wayne Murray understands me in a way someone outside the department never could." She glanced out the window and hesitated, debating whether or not to say the next bit. Finally, she said, "And I'm sorry, but unless you and Alex are fooling yourselves, you should admit you're in the same boat."

"I understand Alex," Rachel said. She kicked herself as soon as she said it. It sounded defensive, even to her ears.

Bugs shook her head. "Not the way another firefighter could. It's like we're soldiers. When we come home, everyone pretends to know what it was like on the battlefield, but no one does. Not unless they were there with their life on the line."

Rachel didn't want to admit that Bugs had a point. Irritated by the excellent argument the woman was making, she decided to terminate their exchange. Checking her watch, she said, "I have another patient, so if you're done theorizing..."

Bugs gathered her jacket and slipped off the table. "I'm not saying you don't love each other. I love Paul. I'm just saying that you need to either accept that you'll never entirely understand one another or end it now before anyone gets hurt."

Rachel held the door open, silently inviting Bugs to leave. She followed her into the corridor and watched as she waited for the elevator. Her mind flashed back, reminding her of the moment etched in her memory; the way they'd hunkered down in a closet, the way her sister's face hovered over her like a ghost in the darkness. She remembered the insane heat, the almost unbearable heat as her back blistered and scarred.

She remembered the process of debridement, a fancy word for the torture she'd undergone. She had wept, lying face down on the table while nurses peeled away layers of dead skin. The long soaks in the tub, the unbelievable pain... She had always thought pain ended when the fire was out, had never dreamt it persisted for so long afterward.

The nurse who had held her hand during the procedure was named Nancy. She had dark hair and lips so red. When Rachel was discharged from the hospital, it was Nancy who pushed her wheelchair out to the parking lot. Sitting on the curb with the nurse, her back numb and foreign under her sweater, she'd hugged Nancy and thanked her. They both cried, Nancy saying she was sorry about Rachel's sister. Years later, Rachel would pinpoint that as the moment she decided to become a doctor.

As Bugs stepped into the elevator, Rachel snapped out of her reverie and said, "Alex and I understand each other, better than you'll ever know, Ms. Riley." She glanced at her watch again and hurried back to see her next patient.

Alex sat in the den and read Von Elm's files on the arsons. Gasoline used in all of the blazes, used to ignite piles and piles of junk. All of the buildings were abandoned, which, in that section of town, was hardly surprising. Wizell and Sawyer walked in, talking about some game. Sawyer carried with him a constant cloud of cigar smoke, a trait that never failed to remind Alex of her father. "Hey, guys."

"Are you watching the Seahawk game?" Sawyer asked.

Alex looked at the dark television set, looked back at Sawyer. "Take a wild guess, Will."

"Mind if I..."

"Go right ahead." She went back to her reading.

Sawyer grabbed the remote and dropped onto the couch next to Murray. He lifted his boot and rested it on the edge of the table. He found the game he was looking for, watched a play, and looked over at Alex. "What're you reading?"

"Some of the fire marshal's reports on these arsons."

"You thinking about going over to the dark side?" Sawyer asked.

"Just checking it out," Alex said.

"Does he think they're related?" Murray asked.

When Alex nodded, Sawyer exclaimed, "Hot damn. Fire bug, right here in our own damn town. What we oughta do with these arsonists is tie up their hands and legs and just toss them into the next big fire we have. Give 'em a taste of what they want." He sipped his soda and turned back to the game. The scoreboard revealed that the Seattle Seahawks were leading. "Aw, kick ass. Come on, Hasselbeck," he said, scooting forward and leaning toward the TV.

Murray cleared his throat, trying to get Alex's attention without alerting Sawyer. He cleared his throat and leaned forward. "So, everything is, you know, taken care of?"

"Yeah, it's all good, last I heard."

Murray exhaled in relief. "Look, you know that I didn't—"

"It's all good," Alex said. She jerked her head toward Sawyer, even though he was still engrossed in the football game.

Murray smirked and said loudly, "Hey, I slept with Bugs last night. It was a mistake, so Crawford's doctor girlfriend helped smooth things over for me."

Sawyer took a sip of his drink.

Turning back to Alex, Murray said, "He's like Rain Man with Judge Wapner when it comes to the Seahawks, man. Turn on a game and he turns into, like, a brain damaged monkey."

Sawyer slapped Murray on the back of the head. "It just went back to commercial, numb nuts. And if you had five hundred bucks riding on this game, you'd be a little hypnotized, too."

Alex grinned and turned her attention back to the files on her lap. There had to be something to connect Lancaster to the fires other than the fact that his father's company designed the buildings. It was circumstantial at best and any defense attorney would destroy that line of attack before they got within spitting distance of a courtroom. The fact that Lancaster brought the information to them himself made it look even more ridiculous.

She yawned and rearranged herself on the cushions. It was going to be a long night and she planned to stay awake long enough to find any hint that they were on the right trail.

Martin walked into his dark apartment to the music of a ringing phone. Dumping his briefcase and coat, he grabbed the phone and said, "Lancaster."

His secretary began speaking rapidly, out of breath and whispering. "Mr. Lancaster, that fire marshal is here again. He wants to talk to you about—"

"I know what he wants to talk about, Sandra. It's why I'm not there. Just tell him I'm out for the day, hell, for the rest of the week. I don't wish to be disturbed until next Monday. Tell him that. I'm sure he'll understand."

"But, Mr. Lancaster, he's like the police."

"I know that, dear. But at the moment, I'm merely someone who interests Mr. Von Elm. He can't drag me in without accusing me of a crime. So, for the moment, I'm incommunicado. Whatever he wishes to speak with me about will keep until Monday."

"Yes, Mr. Lancaster."

He hung up on her, loosening his tie with a weary groan. The name Martin Lancaster grated on him. The ups and downs of the business world, the posturing and the grandstanding, all that unsightly carrying on; he didn't know how his father did it. He walked through the apartment, shedding his Oxford shirt and tie and standing bare-chested in front of the picture window in his living room.

Shepherd was a small town, but it was all his. The Lancaster name stood proudly on dozens of buildings in the small burg that surrounded him. But none of them bore the name Laenko. He felt a deep regret that his grandfather's name would soon be forgotten, a footnote in the town annals. Toward the end, he remembered his father responding more and more to the name Arthur, his correspondence arriving addressed to Arthur Lancaster rather than his traditional name.

The old man had grown weak in his later years. It still saddened Maksim to remember his father's steady decline into dementia. It was hard to watch a family member succumb to such a nasty disease. But his father's decline had freed Maksim to use the company for his own purposes, to begin planning his mission to revitalize the city. Had Artur been in his right mind, he would have immediately seen what was going on and put a stop to it.

With the lights still off, he walked across the room and looked at the city map he had pinned to the work table. Tonight, he was going to go off his routine. Tonight, he would not only burn a building that was still thriving, his target would be of another's design. He hated that; it would be the same as setting fire to someone else's child. Sacrifice was one thing, but what he was planning was something completely different. Maksim Laenko was many things, but a murderer?

Yes, after tonight, he would be. Without a doubt.

He dressed slowly, picking his clothing carefully. He would need the maximum protection from the heat he would be experiencing. He had an old air pack and SCBA that he'd found in a surplus store, along with a hood and gloves. It was another departure for him; he would be remaining in this fire. It was his pièce de résistance, the biggest and most important element of his little puzzle.

He put everything he needed to carry into a duffel bag and slung it over his shoulder, then stepped into the corridor wearing a ratty sweatshirt and jeans. Martin Lancaster was still in the apartment. Tonight, Maksim Laenko was being released from his prison, an unfair incarceration that had lasted his entire life but ended tonight. He could almost feel his tongue adapting, wrapping around its natural accent.

Yes, tonight would be different. Tonight was the final piece.

Let Von Elm come and ask his questions whenever he wanted. After tonight, Martin Lancaster, Rachel Tom, and Alexandra Crawford would all be dead.

Just before midnight, the alarms started. Alex tossed Von Elm's reports on the table, pulled on her turnout pants, and followed Sawyer and Flannigan to the trucks. The Seahawks game was immediately forgotten as Sawyer jumped over the back of the couch and raced for the apparatus bay. "Hope you don't choke on my fumes when I leave you in the dust, Flanny."

"In your dreams, cowboy," Flanny called back.

Wizell slid into his seat and reached back to slap Murray on the knee. "Back in the saddle again, Hoss. Feels good, don't it?"

"You have no idea. I'm never leaving this place again."

Alex was strapping her helmet in place as the radio blurted out the fire location. She spun in her seat and stared wide-eyed at the radio. She had to have heard wrong. "What did they just say?" she asked, shouting to be heard over the engines and Murray's whooping.

"Spring Creek Apartments," Wizell told her. "Shee-it, I've been there. The alleys are narrow as hell on either side, cars on either side of the street. This is gonna be a goddamn nightmare."

Alex didn't need Wizell's description of the streets around Spring Creek Apartments to visualize the scene. She remembered it very clearly from a few nights before. It was Rachel's building.

Chapter Fourteen
To Live and Die in a Blaze of Glory

Rachel walked across her silent living room and pushed open the window. She closed her eyes as a wave of cool air blew past the curtains and washed over her. Her hair was still wet from the shower, but the night was just warm enough that she didn't shiver. She leaned on the sill and put her face against the screen to peer down toward the street. Cars lined both sides of the block, restricting late night travelers to a single lane. A few halos of light stretched from the lobbies of the other buildings on her block, street lights standing proudly in their own orbits of pale yellow.

A man in a green jumpsuit was meandering along the sidewalk in front of her building, using a back-mounted sprayer to wash the leaves from the building's stoop. From open windows, she could hear her neighbors James and Teresa singing along with their record player. Classical opera. James, rotund and proud, was the neighborhood Pavarotti. From the floor directly below her, a cat mewled for food from her owner.

Rachel smiled and stepped away from the window, remembering the old Sesame Street tune: "Who are the people in your neighborhood?"

She padded barefoot into the kitchen, humming the children's song, and turned on the light over the stove to check the levels of her cereal boxes. She spotted the candles that had burnt during her date with Alex and smiled at the memory. It had been a long time since she'd had a night like that. She could barely remember the last one. The way Alex held her during the movie, the way they'd just seemed to fit together in one corner of the couch, the way they'd fit together later.

She sighed and grabbed a Snapple from the fridge, twisting off the cap as she returned to the living room. She wanted to call Alex, to see what was happening. She knew the firehouse could be boring some nights; maybe she'd appreciate a call. Of course, they did sleep at the firehouse. If they had already gone to bed, she would hate to wake Alex.

As she checked her watch to see if it was too late to call, the sound of breaking glass echoed up from the street. She nearly dumped her drink as she stood up and rushed back to the window. She looked down at the street in search of the vandal responsible. The sidewalk washer was nowhere in sight, but neither was anyone else. She scanned up and down both sides of the street twice and saw nothing that looked like a car thief or opportunistic teen.

She was about to call the building manager when someone in the hall downstairs started yelling, "Fire! Fire, get out now! The building's on fire!"

She tied her robe around her waist, kicking herself for wearing only her pajama bottoms and a tank top, and hurried for the door. Outside in the hall, she headed immediately for the stairs. Her bare feet slapped on the steps and her robe swirled around her legs as she hurriedly descended. She peered over the banister and saw her neighbors doing the same, the opera music still blaring from James and Teresa's apartment. She could see fire flickering on the ground floor, dancing back and forth across the walls. "Oh, hell, there really is a fire," she said.

When she reached the second floor landing, she was surprised to see someone heading up toward her. He wore a green jumpsuit and black gloves, and his face was covered with an antique SCBA. She was confused until she saw the big semi-transparent tank on his back, the liquid inside sloshing back and forth in time with his ascent. *The sidewalk washer. What the hell?* "Did you see what happened?" she asked.

"Building is on fire," the man said. Something about his voice, almost familiar. He had a vaguely Russian accent, but she couldn't think of anyone she knew of that nationality.

"Why are you going up? Is someone trapped up there?"

"No," the man said, looking at her through the glass of his mask. "But there will be in a moment."

Before she could process his cryptic remark, his gloved fist slammed into her stomach just below her rib cage and knocked the air from her lungs. As Rachel collapsed, the man ducked down, pressing his shoulder against her soft belly. Hoisting her onto one shoulder like a bag of laundry, Maksim carried her back the way she'd come. In the lobby below, the little bonfire he'd started was beginning to spread. He heard the familiar buzzing of a fire alarm and smiled. Phases one and two were complete. Time to start phase three.

Alex's heart was pounding as they sped through familiar streets toward Rachel's apartment. *That's where I bought her flowers*, she thought, turning to watch the florist shop fly by.

"Hey," Bugs said softly. Alex turned to look at her, surprised to see tears in the other woman's eyes. "I'm sure she's okay. Someone probably just left their stupid space heater unattended."

"I'll throttle the bastard if I got all dolled up for a fucking space heater," Murray griped from the front seat.

"Take a number." Alex smiled; glad for a bit of relief from the pain lodged in the center of her chest. *Rachel will be fine*, she chanted. *Rachel will be fine. The odds of her being hurt are astronomical.*

A more pessimistic voice reminded her of the arsonist running around.

An arsonist who has only torched empty warehouses. An arsonist who, if we're right, is only torching buildings designed by his own company.

So far, anyway...

This building is from the forties, she returned. *No possible connection to Lancaster or Laenko or whatever the hell his name is.*

The truck screeched to a halt between two rows of cars parked bumper to bumper. "Ain't these people heard of parking garages? Pain in my ass..." Murray said, easing the massive truck down the narrow lane. Miraculously, he avoided hitting any cars in the process and stopped in front of the Spring Creek Apartments. Classical music boomed from an open window somewhere, providing an ironic soundtrack to their arrival. Alex climbed out of the truck and scanned the people milling about on the opposite sidewalk watching their building in flames. She didn't see Rachel and her knees threatened to buckle as she moved along the side of the truck.

Swinging the door open, Murray stood on the runner and shook his head. "Oh, mama. No one can tell me this isn't arson. Smell that? Whoo, smells like a gas truck took a piss down this street."

Wizell stood at the front of the truck, radio to his lips, talking to the chief. He looked across the street at the evacuees standing in their bare feet and bathrobes. "We're at the site now. Visible fire in the lobby of Spring Creek. Residents have been evacuated and are outside the perimeter. Preparing an entrance to extinguish. Advise, over."

Murray quirked his lips as he walked all the way around one of the cars at the curb and onto the sidewalk. "Have to walk through a freakin' maze just to get to the back of the truck." His boots splashed on the concrete and he looked down, frowning. "Holy hell, man. Yo, Lieutenant, did someone already try to put water on this thing?"

Wizell was half turned, radio still to his lips, when it happened.

A bag landed on the sidewalk a few feet away from Murray, exploding on impact. The bag was on fire and, once it landed, so was the pool in which Murray was standing almost ankle deep.

"Holy shit. Incendiaries," Wizell breathed. "Murray! That's gas on the sidewalk!"

By the time the warning was given, it was too late. Murray's boots and turnout pants were aflame. He screamed and backpedaled toward the street as the fire surrounded his lower body. Alex came around from the back of the truck, her progress stymied by the cars' proximity to the side of the truck. The rearview mirrors kept getting in her way, so she decided to take a more direct action. She unhooked her axe from her belt and used it to chop the mirrors off the sides of the cars. They fell to her feet, shattering on impact, and she stepped over them.

As she reached the equipment rack, she yanked a fire extinguisher from its bed and jumped onto the hood of the nearest car. She fell to her ass, sliding down the hood until her boots hit concrete. Wizell had pulled Murray to safety and was using his own coat to beat at the flames spreading on Murray's legs. Bugs was watching everything from the side rails of the truck, watching Murray with a horror-stricken expression. Her whispered, "Oh, fuck," summed up everyone's thoughts.

Alex aimed the nozzle of the extinguisher and screamed Wizell's name as a warning. The lieutenant stepped back, allowing her to coat Murray's charred legs with the foam. When the flames had died and she was sure that the fire truck itself was far enough from the pool on the sidewalk so it wouldn't be caught up, she tossed the extinguisher to Wizell and turned to look over the building. Nothing but empty, dark windows. The lobby seemed abandoned, but that didn't mean a damn thing. "Bugs, did you see anyone?" she demanded. When Bugs didn't answer, still staring at the screaming Murray, Alex grabbed her collar and yanked her forward. "Did you see who dropped that bag," she asked again.

"There are no residents visible in the windows of the building," Wizell said as he approached, coughing into his glove. The operatic aria ended and the street was briefly thrown into a momentary, overwhelming silence. When the next song started, Wizell said, "We're staying put until the chief can get here."

"Firemen!" a voice from across the street called. "Firemen!"

Alex and Bugs raced over, zeroing in on a rotund man in a button down shirt and boxer shorts.

"This fire...oh, hell, how the hell did the street get on fire? Is that fireman okay?"

"Is there anyone still in the building?" Alex asked, ignoring the man's questions. She was still scanning the crowd for Rachel's face, praying she was just somewhere in the back, out of sight.

"I haven't seen the woman from the top floor. She's a doctor, I think."

Alex felt something seize up inside of her as she spun around, eyes drawn to the top apartment. She started across the street but Bugs grabbed her.

"We can't get in there until this sidewalk fire is out. And Wizell says we're not making a move until the chief and the ladder can get here."

"What the hell is keeping them?" Alex demanded.

Bugs hesitated. "He's not sure." Alex pulled away and stormed to the end of the truck, Bugs trailing. "Alex, we have to fall back. We have to be with Wizell when—"

"You can sit with Wizell and Murray," Alex said as she unhooked the collapsible ladder from the side panel. It could be extended up to fifteen feet, but was now only about five feet long, easily managed by one person. "I have to go." Alex hoisted the ladder onto her shoulder and moved toward the neighboring building. "I have to do this. Listen, Wizell should've told you to do this and if anyone asks, he did tell you, all right? Get the A-Triple-F down on this sidewalk, get this fucking sidewalk extinguished and flushed." Bugs was staring at the sidewalk, so Alex spanked the side of her helmet with the flat of her hand. "Heather! Do you hear me?"

"Yeah, what? You have to do what?" Bugs asked, following Alex. They were walking away from the Spring Creek Apartments. "What the hell are you going to do with a fifteen foot ladder? The fire is back that way."

Ignoring her, Alex silently gave thanks for the endless drills where she'd been forced to lug a thirty footer the equivalent of nine flights of stairs. The metal clanged noisily next to her head, banging on her helmet, but it was barely even noticeable. As she approached the neighboring apartment house, she saw that the pool of gasoline ended well before the front door of this building. No doubt about the target here, making her all the more certain as to the culprit.

Lancaster would pay.

The wind was knocked out of Rachel's lungs again as she was tossed onto the bed. She rebounded off the mattress and fell to the floor in a heap. An instant later, the intruder was on top of her, dragging her across the carpet until her head impacted the wall. "Please," she gasped, trembling as he hooked his hands under her armpits and dragged her into a sitting position. "Please, whatever you're going to do, please..."

"Shut up," he said.

He grabbed her wrists and fastened a pair of handcuffs around them. "Stay right there and I'll not have to hurt you." He moved back to the bedroom door and left her alone.

She struggled against the handcuffs, tugging on them to test the chain while casting anxious glances at the door. Rachel rushed to the hamper and retrieved the towel she'd used after her shower earlier that night and wrapped the moist cloth around the lower half of her face. It wouldn't help much, but it was better than nothing.

Who the hell was this man? Her mind raced, trying to place him. He seemed vaguely familiar. The man she'd stood next to in the laundry room, the man on the corner who always seemed to buy his newspaper at the same time she did, the man...

The man next to her in the elevator!

She crawled over her bed, searching the nightstand for her cell phone. She had just found it when the intruder returned. He looked at the spot where he'd left her and slowly tilted his head to the right until he spotted her. She held her hands up in front of her face. "Please, no..."

He shoved her back roughly and grabbed the phone when it tumbled onto the mattress. He checked the display screen to make sure she hadn't made a call, and then hurled the phone at the closet door. She hit the floor and crawled into the corner where he'd originally put her, hoping he wouldn't punish her. He sighed and said, "Where's your lighter?"

"What?"

"Your lighter," he repeated harshly. "My damn lighter is out of fluid."

"T-the kitchen, one of the drawers in the kitchen."

He grabbed her by the handcuff chain and pulled her toward him. She was half dragged and half crawling behind him and gasped when she realized his destination. The bedroom closet. She began to fight him, pulling with both hands to hold herself back. "No!"

"I can't trust you; you're a troublemaker. Get in there."

Her sister's face flashed in front of her — the smoke, the heat, her back aflame..."No! I can't go in there!"

He looked down at her, shook his head, and then shoved her backwards. Her back slammed against the wall and she whimpered in pain. "Have it your way." He jabbed a finger in her face. "Sit. Do not move."

She squeezed her eyes closed and shook her head frantically. "Just don't make me go in there." Humiliated by her reaction, Rachel covered her face.

He watched her for a moment to make sure she stayed put, then squared his shoulders and strode from the room. Rachel crawled into the corner and covered her face with trembling hands.

Alex carried the ladder into the lobby of the neighboring building. As she ran up the stairs with it bouncing on her shoulder, her mind flooded with images of Rachel. Rachel in her arms, Rachel underneath her and pressing against her thigh... She shook her head to clear the distractions, focusing on what she had to do. The floors were all deserted, the residents most likely scrambling down to the street for safety.

As she passed the third floor, a bare-chested man in sweatpants nearly ran her down on the landing. "What's with all the damn sirens?"

"Your building is on fire," she lied. "Get out. Now."

"Aww, shit, man, my dope!"

She grabbed his shoulder and shoved him toward the stairs. The pothead stumbled, but started his descent.

At the top landing, she shouldered her way through the emergency fire door and set off an ear-ringing alarm. Ignoring it, she grabbed the ladder with both hands and carried it like a lance as she ran across the roof. The alley between the two buildings was way too narrow for a ground ascent. But it was also narrow enough for a ladder to bridge the gap.

"Crawford!" The chief's voice made her jump, coming from the radio nestled between her turnout coat and her shirt. "What in the hell... What..."

She grabbed her radio and said, "I'm sorry, Chief. I couldn't not try." With that, she silenced her radio and continued her mission.

She rested the ladder on the lip of her building and extended the sections until the far end rested against the edge of the Spring Creek building. She was panting, her arms and legs trembling as she crawled from one side to the other. Once on the roof of

Rachel's building, Alex pulled off her helmet and yanked the hoodie up over her head, leaving only her face exposed. Her SCBA covered that, protecting her from the heat. She prayed Rachel had something protecting her. Equipment in place, she grabbed her ladder and trotted across the roof until she found what she was looking for.

Rachel's skylight.

She grabbed the ladder with both hands and used it to stab at the sloped glass. The ladder sank into the dark room like a knife into a wound. She felt it hit something and peered down through the thick black-gray smoke. Alex angled the ladder until she felt it wedge against what she assumed was the couch, then stepped back and used her axe to open a bigger hole in the skylight.

She mounted the ladder and slowly lowered herself into the apartment. Once on the ground, the entertainment center caught her eye. The same TV where they'd watched that sweet movie about the dwarf who liked trains. Well, most of the movie, Rachel had almost fallen asleep in her arms right here, right here.

Save the reminiscences for later, she chided herself. She turned and scanned the living room. Smoke trickled across the ceiling of the entry hall, hesitantly spreading toward the living room and kitchen. The front door stood wide open, the hallway outside a vivid tableau of Hell. Fire was on the stairs, quickly rising to engulf the topmost resident. The smoke was already covering the ceiling, darkening every bright surface and leaving a thick cloud above her head.

Dropping into a crouch, she navigated the living room and felt along the floor. She banged her arms against the legs of chairs, against corners of a desk, into the wall. She couldn't find anything, could barely see. The smoke was getting thicker. She found the hallway door, knowing it led to the bedroom. It branched off from the entry hall, mere inches from the open door.

She reached up as she passed and pulled the front door shut. She knew it was only forestalling the inevitable. With the skylight open, she knew it wouldn't be long before the fire sniffed out a new source of oxygen and ate its fill. "Rachel?" she called, one hand on the wall next to her to guide her way. "Rachel! Can you hear me?"

Her voice, filtered through her breathing mask, didn't carry very far. She passed the bathroom, kicking herself for not bringing the thermal imager. The smoke around her was a wool blanket now, the air almost certainly not breathable. If Rachel were still here, if she were still conscious...

She put that thought out of her mind and moved forward. "Rachel!" she called again. Still no reply.

The bedroom door was closed and she had an image of Rachel, asleep in bed, slowly enveloped in smoke and gases until...

She did a quick scan of the doorframe and saw no signs of a flashover, put the back of her hand against the wood and felt no evidence of heat beyond. She turned the knob and pushed the door open, entering the bedroom on her knees. Rachel's bed was empty, the covers pulled taut over the mattress indicating she hadn't been to bed yet.

Could she have been in the living room? Had she somehow missed her?

There! A muffled sound, like a voice. She moved across the room and crawled around the bed. There on the floor, between the nightstand and the bed frame, Rachel looked up at her with terrified eyes. Alex was relieved to see the lower half of her face was covered by a towel. A rag was nowhere near the best protection against smoke and carbon monoxide, but definitely better than nothing.

Alex knelt by Rachel, touching her soot covered face, brushing her hair away from her eyes. "We're going to get you out of here, okay?"

Rachel lifted both hands — they were restrained by handcuffs — and pawed at her mouth.

"No, honey, we need to keep that on for now. It's keeping you from breathing in smoke." She helped Rachel out of the corner. "Stay low, hands and knees. Just stay with me and I'll get you out of here." She looked around and whispered, "Is Lancaster still here?"

Rachel nodded, tears in her eyes.

"Okay, we'll get out of here before he even knows I've got you. Okay? Now come on, I'll lead the way."

They got onto their hands and knees and quick-crawled out of the bedroom. The front door of the apartment was now a rectangle of firelight. If Alex hadn't closed the door, the hall would likely have been in flames by now, cutting them off from the living room and their only point of egress.

As she crawled past the open bathroom door, she heard Rachel cry out behind her. She misinterpreted the sound and turned to look back, missing the silhouette that stepped out from the dark square of the bathroom door beside her like the specter of some dark nightmare.

Lancaster reared his foot back and buried his boot in Alex's stomach. She rose a few inches with the impact and rolled to one side with a cough. Lancaster delivered several more kicks to her torso before he stepped forward and slammed his foot down on her face. The mask cracked, but didn't shatter.

"Your irons!" Lancaster shouted through his own mask. He held up a gun so that she could see it, even in the dying light, and repeated, "Remove your irons!"

At the madman's mercy, Alex unhooked her axe and halligan tool and tossed them both toward the bedroom door. "How in the hell are you planning to get out of here, Marty?" Alex asked.

"The name is Maksim," he replied, his voice now heavily accented. Both of their voices were muffled by their masks. "You will show me proper respect, woman!"

"You're a moron, Marty," Alex said. "We're all going to die right here. Was that your plan?"

"Yes," Rachel gasped, the wet cloth now hanging around her neck. Martin or Maksim or whoever he was stood between the women. Rachel was sobbing openly, her hands between her knees. "He's sacrificing himself to kill you, Alex."

Alex couldn't believe her ears. "Why?"

"To live and die in a blaze of glory, to have the flames carry me from this life. It is the death you have been seeking, Alex. The memorial for which you will always be remembered. This building will serve as our tombstone, Alex. You, a fallen firefighter, braving this inferno to save the one you love. You'll go down in history, Alex. Perhaps they'll write a song about you one day." He raised the gun and shrugged. "Or, perhaps not."

"No!" Rachel shouted.

Lancaster hesitated, raising the gun slightly before he turned to look at Rachel. "You are an innocent. Perhaps I will allow you to escape. I have no issue with you once Alexandra is dead and gone."

"The ladder is in the living room," Alex said to Rachel, not moving her eyes from Lancaster's mask. "Pull it up after you and use it to crawl to the building next door."

"No! I'm not leaving you!"

"Such loyalty. Perhaps if Alexandra is not physically able to go," Lancaster said, "perhaps you would leave her if that was the case?"

They didn't have time to consider what he was asking. Lancaster altered the angle of his pistol and pulled the trigger. Alex howled in anguish and grabbed her left thigh with both hands.

"Go, Dr. Rachel," Lancaster said. "Go or it will be as if you fired the weapon yourself." He fired again and Alex's body jerked. He had hit the same leg, a little closer to the knee this time. Alex cried out again, her body tensed and bowed.

Lancaster looked at Rachel and shrugged. "Well, Alexandra, it would appear as though your girlfriend is as stubborn as you are." He turned the gun back to Rachel. "I will do you a favor and release you from your misery, save you from a fiery death with one small bullet."

"Don't do it," Alex said hoarsely. "Just, let her go. Rachel, go."

"Such loyalty," Lancaster mocked.

"Please, Rachel," Alex all but sobbed. "Please."

Lancaster sighed. "If you're going to beg..." He cocked the hammer and said, "Goodbye, Alexandra."

Alex closed her eyes and waited for the bullet. Instead of the gun firing again, she heard Lancaster's howl of pain. Opening her eyes, she saw Rachel pull the bloody halligan away from Lancaster's arm. The claw-hammer end was dripping with blood.

Rachel adjusted her grip and swung the three-pronged tool again, this time burying the blade in the soft flesh of Lancaster's stomach. The blow knocked him back and something cracked as he slammed against the bathroom door. He slumped, his hands trembling as they wrapped around the tool imbedded in his gut.

Rachel knelt over the man's crumpled body and unhooked his mask, then she picked up the gun and shoved it into the pocket of her pajama pants. She fit the mask over her own face before turning to Alex. "How badly are you hurt? Can you..."

"I can't move my leg." Alex's voice cracked and she squeezed her eyes shut. "Oh, fuck, Rachel..."

Rachel looked down. The left leg of Alex's turnout pants was dark red and the spatter on the wallboard behind her indicated that the bullet had gone out the other side of her thigh.

"It hurts so much."

Rachel straightened and, after a few tugs on the seam, tore the sleeve off her robe. She bent over the wound and wrapped the cloth around Alex's upper leg. "Is that too tight?"

"No."

She tugged again, making it tighter, and then made a double knot so it wouldn't slip free. It was a piss poor excuse for first aid, but it would have to do for now. "I won't leave you," Rachel said. "Come on."

She knelt and got Alex's arm around her shoulder and pulled her up. They moved in a crouch toward the living room. The flow of sweat on Rachel's face started up again as if someone had turned on a faucet. Alex was like dead weight, her boots scraping behind her like weights.

"Y'can't...lee me...here," Lancaster gasped from the hallway behind them. They turned to look at him, at the blood dribbling from his mouth like drool. His eyes were wide and glassy, his face white where the SCBA had protected him. He pushed himself away from the wall, stumbled, and fell to his knees. One hand clutched his stomach where Rachel had hit him with the axe and his hand was red with blood.

"To live and die in fire," Alex managed to say. "It's time for the dying part, you sick fucker."

They turned, leaving Lancaster alone in the hall. "There's a ladder coming out of my skylight," Rachel said as they inched toward the couch.

"Yeah," Alex said. "I like to make an entrance on the third date."

"Fifth date," Rachel said. Her laugh turned into a cough behind her mask. They stopped at the foot of the ladder and stared up at the night sky through the jagged hole in the skylight. "Alex, are you going to be able to do this?"

"Yes," Alex said. "Definitely." She put a hand on Rachel's ass and pushed her forward. "You go. I'll follow you."

Rachel hesitated, cupping Alex's face with both hands. Through the hood, the helmet, her mask, and everything between them, they looked at each other. "You come up after me," Rachel whispered, her breath fogging the mask. "I will not leave this building until you are with me, do you understand? I wi— I can't leave without you."

Alex clutched Rachel's neck and bumped their facepieces together. "Go. I'm stubborn, but I'm not suicidal. Go. I promise I'll be right behind you. I just don't want to fall on you if it takes me more than one try."

"Okay." Rachel turned and ascended the ladder, taking the rungs much faster than Alex would have thought she could. When she reached the roof, she turned and gripped the top rung with both hands to steady it. "Okay, Alex. Hurry!"

She grabbed the highest rung she could reach, then lifted her right leg and placed it on the lowest. The heel of her boot caught the rung and held her foot in place. *Good. Good. Excellent.* She exhaled and looked up; the ladder was suddenly a mile long, stretching up toward Mars or Saturn or God. She couldn't do it; she wouldn't make it, there was no way with one leg...

It's okay. We didn't expect a woman to do as good as the guys, anyway.

The voice was loud and clear, echoing in her helmet as if it had been broadcast over the radio. Captain Al Shannon. He hadn't wanted a female in the academy, thought she would pull down the curve. If they lowered their standards to let women in, then it stood to reason that the same standards would let a lot of sub-par male candidates into the department as well. *Hell in a hand basket* had been his phrase of choice. Using both arms and neither leg, Alex pulled herself up.

Need some help, sweetheart?

She reached up, arm trembling, gritting her teeth as she reached for another rung. The heat was unbearable. Her uniform hung on her like an anchor, the air pack on her back weighing on her shoulders as if it was trying to pull her back into the apartment. The night sky surrounding Rachel's face looked so inviting.

I'll just give your tush a little push, how's that, darlin'?

With a determined cry, she drew herself up another rung. She lifted her right foot, her left leg banging uselessly against the metal ladder.

"Please, Alex!" Rachel cried from above.

Another wave of heat slammed into her like a physical blow, knocking her against the metal skeleton of the ladder. The fire had gotten into the apartment; somehow the door had opened. She didn't look back, couldn't afford to be distracted from her mission.

One hand up, hold tight. Don't fall. Pull. Hold tight, next hand up. Lift leg, drag leg...

Oh, God, her shoulders burned. Her back was on fire, wasn't it? She couldn't breathe, couldn't see, her lungs were on fire. Something was pulling on her. Oh, God, someone had grabbed her jacket with both hands! Lancaster was alive and he was pulling her... Up?

"Please!" Rachel sobbed. Her hands were balled into fists around Alex's jacket, pulling on her like she was a rag doll. Alex pushed up with her one good leg and finally breached the skylight. She fell on top of Rachel, pinning her to the tar of the roof. They clung to each other, both of them rasping, staring at each other through the fogged glass of their masks. "You're out!" Rachel said, her voice high pitched, frantic.

"Get the ladder," Alex said, forcing herself up onto her one good leg. Rachel struggled with the ladder and eventually pulled it up rung by rung, as if it was climbing her. The ladder stretched fifteen feet above her head and fell backwards, hitting the roof with a loud clatter.

Alex pointed to the edge of the building and Rachel got to her feet, dragging the ladder to where it needed to be. Alex hopped along after, her left leg completely useless, and met Rachel at the edge.

"Oh, God," Rachel whispered, looking down.

The neighborhood was now completely awash in yellow, white, and red lights flickering and flashing and dancing on the brick walls all around them. Alex was panting, weak in every sense of the word, looking at the ladder that was their last obstacle before freedom. She pulled off her helmet, yanked her SCBA off and dropped it onto the roof.

"Rachel," Alex said, her voice hoarse. Rachel looked at her, saw the mask was off, and removed her own. Her hair was wild, her face dark with soot. "Where did your handcuffs go?"

Rachel lifted both hands, revealing the cuffs were still intact and locked, only they both hung from her right wrist. The thumb on her left hand looked like a slab of rubber someone had tacked on with crazy glue. She had dislocated her own thumb to get out of the restraints. "We don't have much time," she said. "Do you go first?"

"You go first," Alex said.

"Because you don't want me to see if you fall to your death?" Rachel asked, eyes gleaming with tears.

Alex touched Rachel's face, smearing soot from the palm of her gloves. "I love you."

"You proved that tonight." Rachel gripped Alex's forearm. "And you said it before, but I've never said it to you. I love you, Alex."

Alex brushed her thumb over Rachel's cheek, leaving behind another smutty mark. Rachel's hands suddenly went to Alex's gear. She unhooked the air pack hanging from Alex's back and dropped it onto the ground before going after the buttons of her turnout coat.

"Sweetheart, now isn't the best time," Alex said, smiling weakly.

"You wish. Still have your sense of humor, I see," Rachel said with a smile. When the coat was removed, Rachel asked, "Your uniform. How much does it weigh?"

"Fifty pounds, give or take..."

"Good Lord," Rachel said. Leaving the pants but emptying the pockets, Rachel said, "Okay. Get on the ladder. Hands and knees."

Alex did as instructed, her left leg sticking out as she couldn't bend the knee, and peered down at the filthy alley below. Water was running through it like a river, meaning that her colleagues were hard at work below. Rachel bent down behind her, hands on the ladder on either side of Alex's feet. "Push with your right foot. Climb with your hands like you're climbing a regular ladder."

Sweat dripped from Alex's face as she did as Rachel directed. Push, grip with one hand, and then the other. It was slow going, but Rachel was right behind her, whispering encouragement. "Good, just a little more, good, good, we're getting there, baby."

When Alex fell onto the neighboring roof, a sense of euphoria washed over her. She rolled onto her back, opening her arms as Rachel came off the ladder behind her. "You did it!" Rachel said.

Alex rose onto her elbows and kissed Rachel, long and hard, before rolling onto her side. "We still have four flights of stairs to get down. Help me up?"

She put an arm around Rachel and limped to the stairwell door. Adrenaline faded as they descended, and the pain in Alex's leg slowly became unbearable. Her pants leg was dark red, streaked with blood; her foot left a wet and bloody trail in its wake. With every step, Alex felt the blood pooling in her boot. The pain was immeasurable, but it hurt even more to think about what this injury meant to her life, her career. She pushed that thought away as she tightened her arm around Rachel.

One floor at a time, Alex focused on Rachel's support against her side. She tightened her hand on Rachel's hip and closed her eyes. She saw Rachel on her stomach, arms wrapped around a pillow as Alex stretched out over her. Hugging Rachel from behind, their legs intertwined under the sheets. Dragging her fingernails along Rachel's flank, from the curve of her breast to the curve of her hip.

The cold night air hit her and her eyes snapped open. They had made it to the street. She realized that Rachel's hand was on her stomach and she was supporting most of Alex's weight. Alex planted her right foot and took all the weight she could bear. "Sorry," she whispered.

"Shhh." Rachel scanned the street as she yelled, "Help! We need help over here!"

Paramedics descended on them. The entire middle lane of the street was now filled with fire trucks, dozens of faceless firemen weaving in and out between their vehicles. The street looked like a plate of spaghetti, with hose lines lying on top of each other, piled on top of each other, almost sinking in a sea of water.

The paramedics helped Rachel and Alex to the corner, loading them into the waiting ambulance where they were each stretched out onto a gurney. Another oxygen mask was fitted over Rachel's face, her eyes weakly moving to focus on Alex lying next to her. Two of the EMTs had cut away the leg of Alex's pants and were working on the bullet wounds.

Alex turned her head slowly, eyelids hanging heavy. Her eyes were the brightest part of her entire body, almost painfully blue against her soot- and smoke-smeared face. She smiled lazily behind her mask and reached out, opening and closing her gloved fingers in a grabbing gesture.

Rachel reached out and took it, squeezing as tight as she could. She heard someone say, "We have to get her to a hospital," and then the slamming of the doors of the ambulance. The same someone said, "We're losing her!"

They were halfway to Shepherd Memorial when Alex's grip weakened and her hand dropped away from Rachel's.

When Rachel next opened her eyes, her gurney was being pushed down a familiar corridor. She recognized the orderly over her head, the doctor walking alongside her, and the paramedic at her side. "Alex," she gasped, weakly pawing at the rail and trying to roll onto her side.

"Take it easy, Dr. Tom," the doctor said. "Just lie still."

"Where's Alex?" She saw the doctor's quick glance at the paramedic, but Rachel moved too slowly to see the response.

"Don't worry about her right now. Okay?" the doctor soothed. "Just close your eyes and try to relax."

"Is she dead? Is Alex dead?"

"We don't know much at the moment," the doctor said.

Why couldn't she think of the man's name? Malcolm something. Or was it Dr. Malcolm? "I w-want..." Her words dissolved into coughs, her entire body shaking with the effort. Her throat felt raw, her lungs tightening in a vice. She breathed deeply, pushing her head back into the pillow and squeezing her eyes shut.

"Dr. Tom, don't try to talk," Dr. Malcolm said.

It was a pointless admonition; she was already unconscious again.

Bugs and Wizell pushed their way through the charred black door, shining their flashlights across the remnants of the living room. "Fire didn't spread too far in here," Bugs said, kicking the edge of the sofa. It seemed to have been smoked and charred, but not completely burnt.

"It didn't need to go looking for oxygen... Got a broken skylight here. Fire came in, took a deep breath of outside air, and had a seat right where it was," Wizell said. He walked toward the center of the living room, lifting his boot when something cracked beneath it. "Broken glass on the ground. Fire didn't blow this out."

"Lieutenant," Bugs called from the back hall. "Got a body."

Wizell backtracked, joining her outside the bathroom. "Jesus," he whispered, kneeling down next to the coal black mummy.

He surveyed the scene, professionally determining what must have happened. Whoever it had been had tried to open the apartment door and had gotten a flashover for his trouble. He had stayed alive just long enough to crawl down the hall in an attempt to escape the flames. His arms and legs had pulled in toward his chest, the remnants of his face twisted in a shriek of horror or pain. Probably both. Wizell looked away from the gory sight and spotted something against the wall. "Is that a halligan over there?" he asked.

"Looks like it," Bugs replied. She knelt down and picked it up. "There's...could this be blood all over it?"

"Fire investigators will want to see that." Wizell stood. "Let's get the rest of this junk cleared so we can get the hell out of here."

"This is where Crawford was heading."

"Yeah," Wizell said.

"Do you think she's the one who killed this guy?"

Wizell shrugged. "Dunno. If not, I hope she got some licks in, at least."

Bugs put the halligan back where she'd found it and followed Wizell back into the living room to begin the overhaul.

The hyperbaric chamber was horrendous; a tight, glass tube that made her feel as if she were on display. Doctors milled around outside, speaking to each other in quiet voices about her. Many of them, she knew, were kick starting the rumor mill. Huge fire, one of our own is a victim, firefighter heroically saved her. She would be a reluctant celebrity for the next few days, until the next big thing hit.

Every now and then during treatment, pressure built up in her ears and she plugged her nose, exhaling as hard as she could. She wiggled her jaw and stared at the ceiling through her glass tomb. Eventually, she closed her eyes, moving only to pop her ears and ignoring everything else around her. All she wanted was Alex, but she knew that she would never hold her ever again.

Another fire, another loved one lost. She closed her eyes, unsure whether crying was allowed in the hyperbaric chamber.

Back on her gurney, on her way back to her room, she kept her eyes closed. They thought she was sleeping, thought she couldn't hear them.

She only heard two words of their gossip exchange: dead firefighter.

When she was feeling up to it, Rachel sat in the wheelchair they insisted she use and wheeled herself over to the window. Her thumb had been popped back into place, her burns treated, and she'd seen enough of that damn hyperbaric chamber to last a lifetime, though she still found herself short of breath even after a trip to the bathroom. Dr. Malcolm had reassured her that the symptoms would fade but, if they persisted, to let him know and they'd take care of it.

"About the firefighter who saved you. Alex Crawfo—"

"Don't," Rachel said. *Don't tell me she's dead; don't tell me she sacrificed her life for mine.* She didn't want to face that. She didn't want the guilt or the pain.

She didn't talk except to give other doctors information about her condition. A newspaper reporter called, but she hung up on him. She accepted no visitors. Murray and Leary both asked to see her. She had been touched, but still she turned them both away. The people checking in on her were ghosts, memories of faces that faded in and out of the room without her paying much attention.

"A very lucky woman," they all said. Lucky to be alive, lucky to have escaped without any serious injuries, very, very lucky.

Days weren't important. Nights hurt. She stared out the window, watching the blue sky and clouds and wondering why, today of all days, it wasn't raining. Her mood demanded dark rain clouds, torrential downpours, lightning filling the sky. Abandoning the stupid wheelchair, she got up and walked to the chair by the window. She curled up in a ball and rested her cheek on her knee, staring at the blasphemous sunshine outside and feeling her tears start up again. She hugged her knees to her chest, eyes flat, heart aching.

"Didn't you want to see me?" Alex asked.

"I couldn't bear it," Rachel said to the auditory apparition, closing her eyes and fighting her tears. "I'm sorry, I just couldn't."

"Do you want me to go?"

Rachel frowned and slowly looked over her shoulder. Alex was sitting in the doorway, sagging in a wheelchair. She was wearing a hospital gown, her left leg sticking out in front of her, sheathed in plaster. Her face was tortured, a bandage peeking out from under her bangs. There were heavy bags under her bloodshot eyes.

Heart pounding, Rachel leaned forward in her chair. "You're alive!"

Alex wheeled into the room, looking confused. "Yes, of course. Didn't anyone tell you? They said—"

Rachel hurried over and dropped to her knees in front of the wheelchair. She reached out and flattened her palm against Alex's chest, sobbing when she felt the steady throb of her heartbeat. "They didn't, well, I didn't let them. I heard there was a dead firefighter and then, then whenever someone brought up your name, I made them stop. I didn't want to make it true."

"Looks like it paid off," Alex said with a weak smile. "I've been in and out of consciousness, but they told me you were doing well. They said you didn't even want to hear my name. I thought maybe, maybe you blamed me for everything that happened."

"No," Rachel whispered, still tracing Alex's features with her fingertips. She still didn't quite believe it was true. "I couldn't bear to hear them say the words. Say you were dead."

Alex kissed Rachel's lips. "I'm alive. We're both alive."

"Yes, we are. And what about...Lancaster? Laenko, whatever the fuck his name was?"

Alex sniffled and touched Rachel's chin, her neck. She couldn't keep her hands off Rachel's skin. "They found his car a block away from your building. My cell phone was in the glove box. They checked out his place and found gasoline, plus some evidence that he'd practiced the rafter cutting bullshit. There's no doubt in Von Elm's mind that Lancaster was the arsonist."

"He's going to jail?"

"No, he's dead. Do...do you remember what happened?"

The night flashed back to her and she remembered swinging that tool. Rachel lowered her eyes. "Oh." She barely even remembered doing it. All she remembered clearly was Alex's scream, the blood on the wall. "Oh," she said again. "I...I killed him. I wish I could say I felt bad about it, but—"

"He was going to do the same to us. Don't you dare shed a tear or have a moment's regret for saving my life, for saving both our lives."

Rachel nodded and then looked up. "Wait. The dead firefighter. If they weren't talking about you, then who?"

Alex leaned forward, pressing her forehead against Rachel's. "Murray."

"Oh," Rachel sobbed, her voice cracking.

"No, babe, Murray is alive. But it was touch and go for a while. His legs were burnt very badly. He got an infection, everything that could go wrong..." She paused and chewed her bottom lip. "He'll be better, though. Eventually. And with enough physical therapy, he'll even be back on duty."

Embracing Alex, holding her as tightly as possible, Rachel spoke into Alex's shoulder. "I've been dead since I...since I thought..."

"I thought you were mad at me; for bringing that man into your life, for doing this. I spent all this time downstairs, enduring all these surgeries, and all I could think about was how none of it mattered if you were mad at me. And the thing that was killing me was that even I thought it was all my fault. And you, I understood if you didn't want to see me again."

"It wasn't your fault," Rachel said. "And I love you so much."

Alex closed her eyes, tears dripping onto Rachel's hospital gown. "You're leaning on my leg."

"Oh, God, I'm so sorry!" Rachel laughed and released her. Wiping her cheeks, she said, "There's a lounge down the hall. I'm sure they'll let us use it if we want."

"I'll go anywhere with you, love." Alex stroked Rachel's hair and gestured to her lap. "Do you wanna bum a ride?"

Rachel laughed. "I'd love to."

"Well, then, hop on, pilgrim."

Rachel gathered her robe around herself and sat on Alex's lap. She wrapped an arm around Alex's shoulders and looked down at how she was situated. "Is this okay? Is your leg—"

"My leg is fine." She stroked Rachel's back and then shifted in the seat. "Dear Lord, you're heavy."

"Wuss," Rachel said. She leaned down and nuzzled behind Alex's ear.

"Seriously, how can you weigh this much when your ass is so bony?"

Rachel closed her eyes, brushing away a few tears. They rolled down her cheeks as she nipped Alex's ear. "Shut up and drive, woman."

Epilogue
Early the following summer...

Rachel walked into the cabin and set her armload of groceries on the kitchen counter. "I'm back," she called. She pulled off her sunglasses and leaned over the counter to scan the living room. "Alex? Are you here?"

When there was no reply, she proceeded to put away the refrigerated groceries and grabbed two bottles of tea. She carried them with her onto the deck, taking a moment to admire the crystal blue waters before she looked for Alex. She smiled when she saw Alex, stretched out on a chaise lounge wearing denim shorts and a bikini top. Her eyes were hidden by a blue SFD ball cap, but Rachel knew she was asleep.

Taking a moment to admire her lover, she focused on the small black knee brace wrapped around her leg. The cast had been removed months ago, but the brace would be around for a while. One of the bullets had done a significant amount of damage to her quadriceps. Until it was given a chance to heal, she was on desk duty with a regular physical rehab schedule of stretching and light resistance training, with strength training to follow much later.

Rachel put the bottles down on the table, straddled Alex's lap, and carefully lifted the ball cap. Sure enough, she was completely unconscious. Rachel smiled and kissed her lips until Alex began to respond. "Morning, sleepyhead."

"Hi," Alex said drowsily, pushing herself up in her seat. "God, how long have I been sleeping?"

"I don't know," Rachel said as she moved to her own seat. "I just got back from the store. Good sleep?"

"Mm." Alex rubbed her eyes. She blinked and looked out at the bay backing up against Rachel's property. "Easy to fall asleep. It's so beautiful out here." Sailboats were bobbing back and forth, easing toward the open strait from their cozy personal docks. Rachel's own boat waited lazily next to her dock.

"I love it here," Rachel said.

Alex glanced over. "I'm glad. Really. Even if it means I have to drive out here every damn weekend, I'm happy you're in a good place."

After the fire, Rachel couldn't stand to stay in her apartment. She took a leave of absence from the hospital and moved into her family's cabin on Squire's Isle, a small island that was fifty miles and a ferry ride away from Shepherd. She had planned to spend her time relaxing and working through the mental trauma from the fire, but she was unable to stay away from work. With Alex's blessing, Rachel officially quit her job at the Shepherd General and started working at the island's hospital. She quickly discovered that getting back to work was much better therapy than going to a psychiatrist.

Alex stayed in Shepherd for her rehabilitation but took the ferry to the island as often as possible. If she couldn't get away or her leg refused to let her drive, Rachel packed up and went back to Shepherd for a weekend. It wasn't the ideal way to build a relationship, but they were making it work.

"You know, you could still move back to Shepherd. Get your job back, move in with me," Alex said.

Rachel smiled. "We've talked about that before. Your apartment is just a little small for two people. Plus the neighborhood..."

"Right," Alex said. "I admit I'm grasping at straws; I just hate the idea of you living so far away." She looked down at her feet. "Regardless of my attempted bribes, the hospital here is lucky to have you. And I don't blame you at all for wanting to live in a place with this view. You know I support you, whatever you want to do."

Rachel reached over and took Alex's hand. "I'm leaving Shepherd. I am not leaving you. Tell me something? How goes the job back in Shepherd?"

"Subtle change of subject," Alex teased with a rueful smile. "I'm still on the desk. Von Elm offered me a job in arson investigation a while back, but it would just be like showing up late to every party. Everyone else gets to have all the fun and I'm stuck with the cleanup afterwards." She rested her head on the pillow of the chaise.

Rachel watched her carefully. By department standards, Alex's leg was currently too weak to meet the physical demands necessary for being a firefighter. She would be slower, weaker, less able to get herself or a partner out of a dangerous situation. Murray was already back at work, threatening to drop his drawers and show off his new grafts should anyone question how much of a bad-ass he was. Meanwhile, Alex was on the sidelines massaging her thigh and wishing her muscles would accommodate to her needs just a little more quickly.

Alex looked up and found Rachel staring at her. She turned away, self conscious. "Don't worry, honey; I'm not fooling myself. I know I need the time to heal, but I feel so useless. I'll just have to grin and bear it, and keep aimlessly shuffling papers until I'm a hundred percent again."

"Maybe," Rachel said.

Alex looked over. "Unless you're willing to amputate your leg and donate it to me, and even then there's a healing period. Not to mention the serious height consideration."

Rachel smirked. "Nothing as drastic as a transplant, at least not of a leg. I just meant that maybe there's a more productive way for you to shuffle papers. What if you moved out here? The island has one fire department for both of its townships, but even the two towns combined equals an area a whole lot smaller than Shepherd. I'm just thinking..."

Alex tilted her head. "You have that tone."

"What tone?"

"The tone that says you're testing the waters, holding something back to see how I feel."

Rachel smiled. "You know my tones?"

Alex shrugged and smiled proudly. "I don't know, do I?"

"I went to City Hall and asked about the fire department for the island. Now, I just told you there are two townships on the island — December Harbor and Sholeh Village."

Alex scoffed. "I'm looking for a job and she's giving me geography lessons."

"Hush." Rachel slapped Alex's bare thigh. "Both towns are serviced by the same department, the Squire's Isle Fire Department. It's a mostly volunteer organization with a handful of officers in charge. Until recently."

"What happened recently?"

"Over the past couple of years, there have been a lot of job vacancies — retirements, people moved away or changed jobs. The point is, the department hasn't had any officers on its roster since the fire chief retired last year. The sheriff has been pulling double duty and it's starting to wear a little thin."

"Okay," Alex said, still not comprehending. "I'm just a firefighter. Even if I wanted the chief job, they couldn't give it to me for at least, I don't know, three or four years. And that's at the bare minimum."

"You don't need to be a chief," Rachel said, smiling broadly at Alex's interest. "If you take the lieutenant's test and pass it, you'll be an officer. If you're an officer in this department, you're the highest head on the totem pole. You'd be the acting chief."

Alex frowned. "Really?"

"Babe, you're a terrific firefighter. You know your stuff, better than the sheriff ever could. He would be grateful to hand over the reins; he would probably give you a 'get out of jail free' card for coming to his rescue. And, in a couple of years, you take the captain's test, then the chief's, just to make it official."

"So I would be living on the island?"

"Yes."

Alex bit her lip and looked out at the bay. "Wow!"

"You don't have to say yes. I'm just...it was an option that was out there and I took the initiative. If you tell me to butt out, I'll butt out, but—"

"Thank you," Alex said. She reached out and took Rachel's hand. "You...it means so much to me that you would do this."

Rachel smiled and squeezed Alex's fingers. "So you'll think about it?"

"No. It's decided." She smiled and said, "I'll talk to the mayor and the sheriff tomorrow before my ferry leaves."

"You're still leaving tomorrow?"

Alex nodded. "Yeah, babe. I'm still warming the bench back at Shepherd. But don't worry, now I'll be using the time to pack my things and tie up loose ends. Next time I come back here, I'll be looking for a place to stay." She raised her eyebrows and smirked. "Any ideas?"

Rachel gestured toward the door. "I have a foldout couch in the living room."

"Can I use it?"

"You could," Rachel said, "but you won't."

Alex grinned and pulled Rachel to her, moving aside to let her onto the chaise. They slid together, side by side, kissing softly. "I love you," Alex said, fingertips lightly smoothing the feathered hair off Rachel's temple.

"I love you, too." Rachel closed her eyes and rested her head on Alex's chest. Alex stroked her hand up and down Rachel's back, enjoying the warmth beneath her palm.

They'd walked through fire together, braved a madman in a burning apartment, and they had come out of it. Not unscathed, but not broken, either. When Alex exhaled, her breath ruffled Rachel's hair. When Rachel exhaled, Alex could feel the warmth spread across her chest like a wave. She could still hear Heather Riley saying that her fiancé hadn't understood, could never understand, what she went through. Alex knew that no one else on Earth would ever understand her better than Rachel Tom.

She raised her left arm and turned it, eyeing the scars that were now barely visible below her wrist. The result of Martin Lancaster's first fire, the small embers that had seared her skin and brought Rachel Tom into her life. She hated the man, but the greatest gift she'd ever been given, she owed to him. She kissed the top of Rachel's head and whispered again, "I love you."

Rachel was asleep and didn't reply, but her fingertips tightened against Alex's stomach.

In a while, Rachel would wake up and slap Alex's shoulder for letting her sleep so long. They would go inside, Rachel would cook something, and they would retire to the sofa for TV or a movie. A while after that, they would go to bed and eventually sleep. But there was time for that later. For now, the sun was still low in the sky, the sailboats were still tacking to and fro on the horizon, and there was a beautiful woman tucked against her side, sleeping peacefully.

Later, they could deal with later. For right now, Alex had everything she wanted or needed within arm's length. She closed her eyes and put her head back, falling asleep with a smile tugging at the corners of her lips.

She was a very lucky woman.

Geonn Cannon is an Oklahoman native whose characters refuse to come from Oklahoma. He started out thinking he wanted to be an actor, but two years in an acting class led him to realize he much preferred creating fictional worlds to being a small part of it. He lives in Oklahoma with a cat or two, a family member or three and a few dozen characters constantly poking his muse in an effort to get him to write.

Learn more about Geonn by visiting his website: www.geonncannon.com

Other works by Geonn Cannon:

On the Air

ISBN: 978 - 1 - 933720 - 32 - 6 (1-933720-32-8)

Nadine Butler is a popular disc-jockey at KELF, the classic rock station in Squire's Isle, Washington. She's currently in the closet with her girlfriend and she thinks she's happy that way.

And the end of a bad day, Nadine goes to a Town Hall meeting to take sides in a book-banning debate and manages to out herself in front of the town.

Desperate, under pressure and under siege from the startled, family-oriented advertisers and the station's unsupportive owner, Nadine does one last show. With help coming from some unforeseen corners, she decides to make the most of her last time on the air.

Gemini

ISBN: 978 - 1 - 933720 - 56 - 2 (1-933720-56-5)

Molly Page is a successful chef in charge of her own kitchen on Squire's Isle. But despite her success, she still feels incomplete. The feeling is magnified when she learns her estranged twin sister has died in a car accident. Suddenly, Molly finds herself utterly alone. The world slips even further off its axis when a mystery woman arrives on the island and reveals that she was her sister's partner.

Forced to see a side of her sister that she always denied existed, Molly is forced to relive painful memories on her way to slowly discovering who she really is.

Available at your favorite bookstore.

LaVergne, TN USA
27 September 2009
159147LV00003B/139/P